FINDING REDEMPTION RANCH
(*Edenton Bay Romance* Series, Book 2)

Elizabeth Woodrow

Cover design by Vila Design

Published by Van Rye Publishing, LLC
Ann Arbor, MI
www.vanryepublishing.com

ISBN: 978-1-957906-06-5 (paperback)
ISBN: 978-1-957906-07-2 (ebook)
Library of Congress Control Number: 2022948980

Warning

FINDING REDEMPTION RANCH is a work of fiction in which a woman struggles to escape an abusive relationship. As such, this book necessarily contains language and scenarios related to physical and emotional abuse, which might be triggering for some audiences. Reader discretion is advised.

Dedication

For my Quill & Cup sisterhood. This journey truly wouldn't be the same without you!

"For he has rescued us from the dominion of darkness and brought us into the kingdom of the Son he loves, in whom we have redemption, the forgiveness of sins."

—Colossians 1:13-14

Contents

Chapter 1

Emelia Taylor

"**S**hut up, you stupid little brat!" Gary bellowed.

I hurried into the living room. Gary's fist was in the air, aimed at my daughter, Quinn. Horror and shock fought for space within my body, but I couldn't afford to freeze like I usually did when I was the target of his rage. Holding my breath, I placed my body between his fist and Quinn.

Gary squared his shoulders and glared at me. His chest heaved. "Get out of my way! That girl needs to be taught a lesson! When I tell her to hush the first time, she needs to do it!"

The heat of anger raged inside me. It was one thing to make me a personal punching bag but something else entirely to make my daughter one. The fire within me rushed out, my body stiffening in defiance. My chin lifted in the air. "You'll touch her over my dead body!"

"That can be arranged!" Gary shouted as his lips curved up at the edges.

My blood ran cold. Before I could defend myself, the back of Gary's hand collided with my cheek so hard that I lost my footing and fell backward. He yanked me up, twisting my arm behind my back, forcing me to bend forward, away from Quinn. Pain surged up my arm. I bit my lip. If I had cried out, he would've hurt me more. I flailed against his grip but to no avail.

"Mommy!" Quinn cried out. "Stop it! You're hurting her!"

"Quinn, go to your room," I could only get out in a whisper.

Quinn's feet pitter-pattered against the hardwood floor, moving in the direction of her bedroom, and relief found me for a moment. Quinn would be safe, and this pain I felt—this, I was used to.

Gary threw me against the wall, and my breath expelled from my lungs. He wrapped his hands around my neck. He squeezed and squeezed. I couldn't breathe. *Was this the end?* He usually didn't take my words so literally, but maybe he really had been intent on making me a dead body. *Is this the last time I'll see my daughter?*

I clawed at Gary's hands, but his grip never faltered. Spots appeared in my vision, and everything turned bright white. *Is this the light everyone talks about going into when you die?* He released my neck from his stronghold and stomped back to the couch, slamming his body into the cushions.

"Go make me some dinner, woman. Get up off the floor and . . . Oh, come on, ref! What a stupid call!" Gary leaped from the couch into a standing crouch.

By the time I found the energy to move, Gary was, once again, engrossed in the football game. I slowly stood with my hand on the wall to guide me up. I made my way into the bathroom I shared with Gary. I turned on the faucet and splashed cool water on my face. My head snapped to my reflection in the mirror. I stared into my eyes before they moved to the bruise forming on my cheek.

Why am I with him? Gary was a monster in every sense of the word. Did I deserve better, or was he the best I could do? It wasn't as if we were married or that he was Quinn's father. *If I*

2

stay, will he kill me? I grabbed my bottom lip with my teeth. *If I leave, will he do the same?*

I couldn't let Gary do anything to Quinn. I had to get us out of there. *What have I become?* I glared at the bruises on my face and the ring from his hands around my neck. *What kind of mother am I to allow my daughter to be subjected to such violence?* Tears stung my eyes as my chin trembled. I touched my cheek and winced. My fingertips lightly grazed my neck.

As I took the washcloth from the drawer to wipe my face, a medicine bottle caught my eye. I plucked it from its resting place. It was Hydrocodone from the last time I "took a tumble down the basement stairs while doing laundry." That's what Gary told the doctor anyway. *I can put some in his beer.* That would possibly give us time to get away. My chest heaved in a sigh. *Can I really be that kind of person? To drug someone?* Yes, to save Quinn and me. I stared at the bottle. If I put it in his beer, would three be enough? With shaking hands, I slid the pills into my front pocket and sucked in a deep breath before going to check on Quinn.

"Mommy!" Quinn leaped into my arms as soon as I opened the door, her eyes red and swollen from her tears. Her body was still trembling. My heart broke even more.

Yes, it was time to get out. "I'm okay, baby." I set Quinn's feet down on the floor.

"You promise?" Quinn glanced up at me. Was that her sadness and fear or my own reflected in her eyes?

I gently swiped a strand of Quinn's blonde hair behind her ear and lowered my voice to a hushed tone. "We're going on a secret trip tonight, okay? But we have to keep quiet about it. Alright?"

Quinn glanced up at me with her green eyes and simply nodded in response.

3

"I'm going to go fix dinner. You stay here, and I'll come get you when it's time to eat."

Quinn's lip quivered as she nodded.

I closed the door. I leaned against it as if the strength of the door would somehow seep into my back. I couldn't stand to see Quinn like that ever again. I inhaled and exhaled deeply, stood up straight with my chin raised, and tiptoed to the kitchen. I didn't want to agitate Gary any more than we already had. The aroma of fried chicken and mashed potatoes I prepared was nauseating, my senses on overdrive.

After I plated Gary's food, I crushed the pills into a powdery dust. I planted my hands on the counter and leaned into them. My heart raced, and my palms were sweaty. I pushed myself away from the counter and wiped my hands down my pants. *You can do this, Em. You have to. For Quinn. For yourself.* I straightened my back and swept the powder into my palm before funneling it into Gary's fresh beer. *Please let this work.* I inhaled deeply, pausing before I edged into the living room and set Gary's plate on his TV tray. He always ate dinner in front of the television. That night, I had never been more thankful for it.

"Throw this in the trash," Gary ordered, tossing his empty can in my direction. Lucky for me, I caught it before it hit the floor. I closed my eyes and let a sigh pass my lips. He shooed me away with a flick of his wrist.

I closed my eyes once more. *Please let this work.* Fear bubbled in the pit of my stomach. *What if he realizes I did something to his drink? What if it doesn't work?*

I didn't exhale fully until I was back in the kitchen. I set food for Quinn and me on the kitchen table and retrieved Quinn from her room. As we ate in silence, I glanced around the small room. The light overhead bounced off the white cabinets and countertops. It was a pristine kitchen. Everything had its place. I learned that lesson quickly. Gary would take his white glove, literally, and swipe it across everything. Counters. Cabinets. Door frames. If there was a speck of dirt or dust or grime, it wasn't long before that same glove was swiping across my face.

Has he had any of his beer? I peeked around the corner. I couldn't tell. My body shook at the thought of finally getting away.

"Okay. Go get ready for bed, Quinn. When I'm done with the dishes, I'll come tuck you in." I glanced down and nodded at her as I picked up her plate from the table in front of her.

"Yes, Mommy," she responded quietly before scurrying off to brush her teeth.

How would I explain to a four-year-old that her world was about to be flipped upside down—that the only "father" she had ever known wouldn't be there anymore? Would she be sad? Mad? Feel nothing at all?

I dried the dishes and put them in their proper places. As I padded back to Quinn's room, my fingers danced around my neck. I could still feel the heat from his hands.

"Do you want a bedtime story?" I asked as I slipped into Quinn's room and sat down on the edge of her bed.

"Yes, pwease." Quinn rubbed her eyes with the backs of her hands. She picked a book about a princess who got the prince in the end. We had read it a million times. It was her favorite. I laid back on her pillows so she could see the pictures. My mind drifted to thoughts of whether I'd ever be good enough to find a prince. Did I even deserve to? Once the story came to an end, I peeked over at Quinn, who had fallen asleep.

"Sweet dreams, princess." I leaned over and kissed Quinn softly on the forehead before I pulled the covers up over her shoulders. I turned off the light and closed her door.

If I don't leave tonight, I'll be dead soon. Maybe even Quinn, too. We have to get out!

As soon as I strode into the bedroom I shared with Gary, I fell onto my side of the bed. I was beyond exhausted. My throat burned, and my eyes desperately wanted to close to end the nightmare of a day. *Don't fall asleep, Em! You have to stay awake!*

It felt like an eternity before I heard the television shut off. Gary's heavy footsteps coming down the hall echoed in the air, louder as he approached the doorway to the bedroom. My heart pounded inside my chest, and I was sure he was going to hear it. I fisted the sheets. They were stiff and scratchy, as unwelcoming as Gary and the situation I was in. To some relief, he didn't turn on the light. If he had turned on the light, he would have noticed I wasn't sleeping, and he would have forced me to do things I didn't want to do. But I also didn't want him to see that I was fully clothed under the covers. I sucked in a deep breath but didn't exhale.

The bed shifted under Gary's weight as he fell into it. The stench of alcohol permeated the air. Bile rose to my throat. For a while, he didn't make a sound. He would eventually start snoring, but I had to wait until then. Once he did, he would be dead to the world. Hopefully, after the pills in his beer, he would be more so than usual.

When Gary's sawing-a-log snores filled the air, I slid out of bed as gently and as quietly as I possibly could. As my feet hit the floor, my heart raced, and my limbs shook. A bead of sweat trickled down my spine. I glanced back. I squinted against the darkness. The only movement from Gary was his chest rising and falling with each breath. I slightly exhaled. I wouldn't be able to breathe until my daughter and I were safe . . . if we ever would be.

Before leaving the room, I grabbed some clothes that were within arm's reach. Gary's wallet rested on the dresser. I paused long enough to grab what money was inside—$400. What was he doing with . . . *Em, that's not important. Get Quinn and get out!* As I scrambled down the hall, my breath rang in my ears.

I grabbed Quinn's favorite overnight bag and filled it with my things and quickly shoved some of her clothes inside along with Horsey—her favorite stuffed animal—and her favorite blanket. With every haggard breath I took, pain raged inside my throat. I swept a shaky hand across my forehead to get rid of the sweat that had beaded there. I swiped my clammy hands across the back of my pants before gathering Quinn out of bed.

"Come on, sweetheart," I whispered into Quinn's ear. I flung the bag over my shoulder and crept to the front door. Each time the floor creaked under my feet, I stopped, and a lump formed in the middle of my throat, choking me just as Gary's hands had earlier. I glanced back, waiting for Gary to appear to stop me. Once I safely reached the door, I slipped my feet into my shoes, swallowed hard in an attempt to dislodge the lump, and cracked the door just wide enough to slip through.

Hurdle one—get out alive—complete.

Chapter 2

Emelia

"I need two tickets for the next bus out of town," I breathlessly told the clerk behind the window at the Greyhound station. My eyes constantly checked my perimeter for any signs of Gary.

"The next bus leaves in thirty minutes, heading to Edenton, North Carolina." The clerk peered at me with pity in his eyes, his gaze sweeping from my wild eyes to my throat. His warm smile told me he understood my urgency.

"I'll take it. How much?" I rapidly tapped my fingers on the counter and bounced back and forth on my feet gently, as though rocking Quinn as she slept in my arms with her head on my shoulder.

"Do you need return tickets?"

"No."

"That'll be $121.98."

I slid the money through the hole at the bottom of the window. "Come on. Come on," I whispered to myself, willing the man to move faster.

"Have a safe trip." The clerk glided the tickets and my change back to me.

"Thank you." I snatched the tickets, shoving the change into my pocket. I readjusted my sleeping Quinn and hurried to get lost in the small crowd. I had never wanted to be invisible more than at that moment.

I prayed to whatever god might be listening for us to get away safely. I found a place to sit to wait for the departure time. It was in a corner where I had my back to the wall. *Always have your back to the wall, Em.* I had to be able to see everyone coming and going. I rubbed Quinn's back as she slept against my chest.

My mind flooded with memories of what had transpired that evening. In that moment on the floor, I realized I had nothing to lose by trying to leave. There was a chance that if Gary found us, he'd kill me. But I knew if we stayed, my death would've been imminent. *Where would that leave Quinn?* He would either take her, or she would go into foster care. I didn't want either outcome.

The thirty minutes it took for the bus to arrive were grueling. *Oh no! I forgot her booster seat!* I would just have to deal with it. I wasn't going back to get it, that was for sure. I kept my eyes moving in every direction, waiting to see Gary barreling toward us. Once we boarded the long, gray bus and flopped into a seat, careful not to disturb Quinn, I exhaled deeply.

Hurdle two conquered.

I laid Quinn in the seat next to me. I dug her blanket and Horsey out of the bag and gently covered her. My eyes remained glued to the door of the bus. My leg jiggled frantically. "Come on! Come on!" I begged under my breath. My heart pounded in my chest. The driver was taking forever. What if Gary found us?

Finally, the driver boarded. "Good evening. Thank you for choosing to travel with Greyhound. Our first stop will be Philadelphia, Pennsylvania, so sit back, relax, and enjoy the ride."

9

Relax? How can he tell me to relax at a time like this? I wasn't sure I'd ever be able to relax again. Would I always have to look over my shoulder, wondering if that was the time Gary would find us? So many questions. No real answers. Only time would tell. When the bus rolled into motion, my heart began to settle—a little.

Hurdle three—get out of Norristown, Pennsylvania—almost complete.

The driver's voice filled the air just after our departure. "There'll be a forty-minute layover in Philadelphia."

My heart raced again. Stopping so close wasn't safe. My hands became clammy, so I wiped them down the length of my thighs. I willed my heart rate to slow. I inhaled and exhaled deeply as I closed my eyes and rested my head on the back of the seat. I, again, prayed to whatever deity might be listening and cared about us at all. *Please keep us safe.* I opened my eyes, scanning the entire length of the bus on both sides.

As the driver pulled into the station in Philadelphia, he informed us, "We'll get back on the bus in forty minutes."

I glanced at my watch—11:00 p.m. I stepped into the aisle, hoisted our bag over my shoulder, and scooped Quinn out of her seat. Leaning over, I snatched Horsey from the chair. Quinn would never forgive me if I lost him. He was her absolute favorite. It was the only childhood thing Gary allowed her to have. I bought it for her for her third birthday. It was the start of her obsession with horses.

I hoped the trip would be easier once Quinn woke and could walk. As I entered the station, my eyes scanned every direction. My breath hitched in my throat. Gary could've been waiting for us even though I was pretty sure he was still out cold. I found a seat against the wall, facing the door. Quinn was fast asleep. It would take grenades going off to get her to wake up. My eyes remained on the door until it was almost time to get back on the bus.

We should use the restroom before we board again. Definitely don't want to squish into the tiny bathroom at the back of the bus.

"Quinn, honey, can you wake up so you can use the bathroom?" I gently set her on her feet but held on until she was awake enough to stand on her own.

Quinn rubbed her eyes before opening them. "Where are we?" she whispered as she glanced around the stall.

"We're on our trip, remember? I told you about it before dinner." Quinn's little body trembled as I spoke. "It's okay, sweetie. I promise." I squeezed her close before helping her onto the seat.

After we both were done and had washed our hands, I swept Quinn back up into my arms. Once again, I found a seat against the wall, facing the door. I held her a little tighter to my chest as she fell back asleep. I watched people move about the station. A man in tattered clothes was laid out on a bench sleeping. There were more men than women, I noticed. I didn't know if that was really true or if I was just hypersensitive at that moment.

It had only been forty minutes since arriving in Philadelphia, but it felt like forty hours. When it was time to depart, I looked around in all directions as I walked out of the station. There were too many dark corners where Gary could've been lurking, waiting to attack. He did it when he was angry. Other times, he did it for his own amusement, just to terrorize me.

I exhaled deeply as I laid Quinn in a seat by the window at the back of the bus, then slid in next to her.

"Welcome back or welcome aboard," the driver greeted everyone. "We'll be making three short stops on our way to our next layover—in New York City. We will be stopped for four hours before you will board another bus to your final destination. We won't get off the bus until our arrival in New York unless, of course, one of those stops is yours. As always, thank you for choosing Greyhound." The driver hooked the microphone to the receiver and took his seat behind the wheel. I studied him for a moment. His voice was smooth as silk and somehow comforted me.

As the bus jostled down the highway, I stared at my little girl sleeping in the seat next to me. She was tiny in the oversized chair. Her long, blonde curls rested against her cheek. I brushed her hair to the side and smiled briefly. I still couldn't believe we'd escaped. I had thought about leaving so many times before. I wasn't sure what had made me stay. Fear perhaps? Fear that I wouldn't know the first thing about taking care of us? Or fear of what Gary would do if I wasn't successful?

I ran my fingers over my neck. I could still feel Gary's hands there. Squeezing. I stifled a yawn. *Em, you have to stay awake.* I rubbed my eyes and straightened in my chair. It was no use. My eyes refused to stay open. With adrenaline racing through my veins, sleep wouldn't come, but I kept my eyes closed anyway. Just so they could rest.

"Miss, you have to get off the bus," Gary said as his fingers wrapped around my wrist so tight that I could feel my own pulse. My eyes fluttered open. When I looked up, I saw Gary's face. I gasped and nearly jumped out of my chair.

I closed and opened my eyes once more. This time, standing in front of me was the bus driver. "I'm sorry," he said. "I didn't mean to scare you. We've arrived in New York City. You'll be switching buses in about four hours."

"Oh. Okay. Thank you. I'm so sorry." I scrambled to my feet. My legs wobbled from waking to Gary's face. No matter that it was imagined. It unnerved me. Once I felt sturdy on my feet, I snatched our bag and gathered Quinn.

New York City. I'd always wanted to visit but had never gotten the chance. I glanced at my watch. I had no idea what to expect from "the city that never sleeps" at 1:30 a.m. I clutched Quinn closer as I trudged through the station door. *Yuck! What is that smell?* Some sort of mixture of body odor and urine. I gagged as I squished my nose to Quinn's shoulder and did my best to breathe in and out through my mouth. I glanced around. There were more homeless people than travelers. I overheard someone mention something about rain coming. The homeless must have gone there to get out of the impending weather.

What was I going to do for four hours? Have more paranoid thoughts about Gary, I was sure.

I spotted some vending machines. As I strolled over, I fished a couple of dollar bills out of my front pocket. I bought a pop and a pack of cheese crackers. With snacks in hand, I found a seat in a corner, away from everyone—facing the door, of course. Always had to keep my eyes on the exit.

I sat and cradled Quinn in my lap. I opened the can and took a swig. The liquid burned as it slid down my throat. I wasn't sure if it was the bubbles or the aftermath of the choking, but I felt it. It was a reminder I was still alive. I had another chance to give Quinn a life without fear and violence.

"Ma'am, do you have a couple of dollars you could spare?" a man asked, his clothes dirty and tattered. He stood way too close for my comfort.

I glanced up at him. "I'm sorry. I don't."

"Are you sure? You look like you have money to spare." The man inched closer.

Did I really look like I had money to spare? I did what I could to broaden the distance, but there wasn't much room as

13

the arm of the chair dug into my thigh.

"Excuse me. Is this man botherin' ya?" another man inquired with a deep, silky, southern drawl.

The homeless man's eyes grew as big as saucers. "I was only asking her for a couple of dollars, but she is being stingy."

"Well, it *is* her money," my rescuer pointed out while standing with his hands on his hips.

"It's not that . . ." I started to say but thought better of it.

"Here. Take these four dollars and leave her alone." The kind man stretched out his hand toward the homeless one, who snatched the money and scurried away.

"Ma'am, are you okay?" My rescuer leaned down slightly in an attempt to make eye contact.

I studied him from his feet that were adorned with dusty, well-worn cowboy boots, up his denim-covered legs and plaid button-down shirt, to his defined arms where the cloth of his shirt strained against them. And then there was his chiseled face and hazel eyes. His eyes were the perfect blend of brown and green. Covering his dark-brown hair was a nicely broken-in cowboy hat. Nope. Definitely not from New York City. Or at least not what I would expect from The Big Apple.

I opened my mouth, but the words strangled in my throat. "I'm fine. Thank you," I finally managed to utter.

"Okay, then. Have a good trip." The man tipped his hat and strutted away.

Wow! I watched as he departed. He was definitely a man who could get a woman's heart pumping. Under different circumstances, mine would have been one of them. But I didn't trust my instincts. Not when it came to men anyway.

As I continued to monitor the door, I drank my pop and ate a few more crackers while waiting for the bus to arrive. I left a few crackers for Quinn in case she woke up on the bus. I checked my perimeter regularly.

When our bus's arrival was announced over the loudspeaker, I breathed a sigh of relief, stood, grabbed our bag, and readjusted Quinn to a more comfortable position on my hip. We were the first to board, so I went to the very last seat.

As I sat in my seat, a man boarded. My heart leaped almost out of my chest. I recognized him as the man who helped me with the homeless guy. My eyes widened as a trickle of sweat slid down my back. My breath lodged in my throat. *Is he following me? Did Gary send him?*

My leg bounced up and down. I bit my bottom lip. *Calm down, Em. You're just being paranoid.* I did my best to calm my nerves. I didn't want to, but I knew if I didn't close my eyes and slow my breathing, I was going to have an anxiety attack. My eyes drifted closed, and I counted to ten. I wanted to keep my eyes on the man, but my exhaustion overtook me.

My eyes flicked open just as the bus pulled into the station at the next stop. Finally, we were further away from Gary. Almost far enough to breathe.

As I saw the man from New York step off the bus, I inhaled deeply. I closed my eyes and whispered softly out into the universe, "Please keep us safe." I peeked at Quinn. She had awakened at some point during that leg of the trip. I could see she'd found the crackers as she was covered in crumbs.

For the first time since escaping Gary, I chuckled. I held my hand out to Quinn and glanced at my watch—11:40 a.m. "Come on, sweetheart. Looks like we should grab some lunch. We have fifty-five minutes before the next bus." I held Quinn's hands as she jumped from the bottom step of the bus.

"Yay! I'm hungry. Where are we going, Mommy?" Quinn skipped along beside me.

"I told you. We're taking a Mommy and Quinn trip."

"Okay." Quinn grinned up at me.

We grabbed a sandwich, a bag of chips, and water to share from the little café inside the station. As we were eating, I saw the man again. The hairs on the back of my neck stood at attention. I clenched my hands into fists and closed my eyes. *One, two, three, four, five, six, seven, eight, nine, ten.* When I opened my eyes, the man had disappeared. I blew out a breath. I hoped I'd feel better once we got to where we were going.

By the time Quinn and I were done eating, it was time for the final leg of our trip. Once again, the man took a seat on the same bus. *He couldn't do anything to us on the bus, right? If he wanted to, he would have done something already, right?* I kept my eyes on him during the ride, just in case.

At 4:40 p.m., we finally arrived in Edenton, North Carolina. I exhaled deeply as the bus rolled to a stop. I hoped this place was far enough away from Gary.

I stepped down from the bus, turned, and helped Quinn. As the man descended the stairs right after Quinn, my breath refused to leave my body like a defiant toddler. *Is he going to grab us when no one else is around?* I waited by the bus stop, which was just a sign in front of a gas station, until I saw him disappear around the corner.

I exhaled sharply and pulled Quinn in the opposite direction. As we ambled down the main road leading into town, I scanned our surroundings. We passed by extravagant Victorian homes. Dogs barked from backyards. Birds chirped as spring was making room for summer. I wished I'd had more time and energy to admire the quaintness of it all.

I glanced over my shoulder to see an old silver Dodge Charger barreling down the road. *Gary!* It looked just like his car. I whimpered as the car drove past without slowing down. Music and laughter from the car full of girls blasted from the windows. My heart dropped, and my knees almost gave out. I swiped a tear from my face as I darted into a café with Quinn in tow. Even though we had escaped, we would never truly be free from Gary.

Chapter 3

Gary Mason

I opened my eyes and sat up in bed. I grabbed my head as it buzzed from sitting up too fast. I moaned as the room spun around me. *What happened last night?* I hadn't drunk *that* many beers. My head pounded. In an attempt to clear the fog, I squished my palms into my eyes and moved them from side to side.

I rolled out of bed and trudged into the bathroom. A medicine bottle was on the counter. *That's not where it belongs.* I plucked it up, squinting my eyes so I could focus on the label. Hydrocodone. What was it doing on the counter? *I'm going to seriously hurt that woman. When will she learn?* She must have found it after our scuffle the night before.

I ran my hand over my face and studied my disheveled appearance in the mirror. How many beers had I drunk? I glanced back in the mirror and then at the bottle. My eyes grew wide. *No! She wouldn't dare!* My blood began to boil deep inside.

"Emelia! What did you do to me?" I bellowed as I clenched the bottle.

I barged into the living room. No one was there. I glanced in the kitchen. I was alone. I charged down the hall to Quinn's room. It was empty. Her bed hadn't been made. Quinn, unlike her mother, knew how to follow the rules. Rule number one, always make the bed after waking up. I threw the bottle of pills. As it hit the floor, the bottle cap flew off, and pills scattered everywhere. I screamed at the top of my lungs, "She's going to pay for this!"

I went back to the bedroom for my wallet. It was open on the dresser. *It isn't enough that you left me? You had to steal from me, too?* My jaw clenched, and my fist squeezed my wallet as I stuffed it into my back pocket. I punched the top drawer. Sweat rained down my face. I was like a boiling pot, ready to explode. She only had $400; she couldn't have gotten that far. The bus station was down the road. *I'll start there.*

I grabbed my keys off the hook and darted out the door. I couldn't believe she had left me. Stupid wench. I didn't think she'd have the guts to leave. As my anger rose, my foot pushed the gas pedal. *I'll have to make sure I have a better grip on her. If she lives, that is.*

I waited in line at the ticket counter. When I got to the window, I slammed a picture against the glass. The woman behind it jumped. "Have you seen these two people?" I asked as I scowled. She quickly shook her head in response. "Are you sure? Take a closer look." I wanted to grab the woman by the hair and make her look closer at the picture.

"I'm sorry, sir. I haven't seen them. I just came on my shift."

Stupid, useless woman! "UGH!" I hollered out. I pulled at my hair with fisted hands. In my brain, I mulled over what I could do to find Emelia. Then, a name floated into my mind. *Eureka!* I knew just who to call. He would find her for sure.

I plucked my phone from my pocket and dialed. "Wayne, I have a job for you. Can you meet me in an hour?"

"Sure. What do you have for me?"

"I'll tell you when I see you. Meet at our ol' greasy spoon?"

19

"I'll be there."

I hung up the call and shoved my phone back in my pocket before I sped down the road. About thirty minutes after I arrived, the passenger side door opened, and Wayne slid into the seat beside me. "What do you need?" he asked.

"I need you to find someone for me. She drugged me and left me for dead." I knew it was an exaggeration, but I needed to add urgency to the situation. I tossed her picture into Wayne's lap. He plucked it from his leg. "I don't care about the kid, but I need you to find *her*. The faster you find her, the more I'll pay you. The only way she could have gotten out of here is by bus. But check the train stations, too. I'll check car rentals. She doesn't have a car and doesn't have enough money for two plane tickets. But we can't leave any stone unturned."

"Okay. What's her name? What's the kid's name?"

My fists clenched as her name passed my lips. "Emelia Taylor. Kid's name is Quinn."

"I'll find them." Wayne exited the car with not another word.

He had to find them. I slammed my fist against the steering wheel. *Emelia can't leave me and not suffer the consequences!* Thought I had taught her that lesson early on. Guess it wasn't one that was learned properly. *She'll learn this time!*

Chapter 4

Emelia

As I opened the door with *Courageous Café and Bakery* stenciled on it, the jingle bells clacked against the glass. I flinched and squeezed Quinn's hand.

"Ow, Mommy. Too tight," Quinn cried out, trying to pry her tiny hand from my ironclad grip.

"I'm sorry, baby." I loosened my hold on Quinn's hand.

In December, Quinn and I had been putting up decorations just before Christmas. Gary had been watching television, and we were being too loud. He snatched the jingle bells and pummeled me with them over and over again. They made the same sound each time they struck a part of my body. He made sure I never forgot to keep the noise down while he was watching a show.

In the café, I inhaled and exhaled deeply, breathing in the scents of the cookies, cakes, and all the other pastries. I loved baked goods. It was probably how I managed to pack on weight, resulting in my 240-pound frame. Food had somehow become my comfort during the years of abuse. Food was my constant companion that didn't care if the house was pristine or if I was being loud or quiet.

"I'm hungry, Mommy," Quinn spoke up from behind me.

"I know, sweetie. We're going to get you something, but

we have to wait in line and be patient."

"Welcome to Courageous Café and Bakery. What can I get for you?" the girl behind the counter cheerily asked as we finally made it to the front of the line. Her hair was the same blonde as Quinn's.

"Hi. Can I get a coffee, a milk, and a grilled cheese sandwich, please?" I asked.

"Sure. That'll be five dollars and fifty-seven cents." The girl smiled. "Go ahead and have a seat. I'll bring your order out to ya."

"Oh. Okay. Thank you."

We plopped down at a table near the window. I wasn't sure how long we'd be able to stay in the little town of Edenton. It would only be a matter of time before Gary found us. When he wanted something bad enough, he stopped at nothing to get it. No matter what.

I had no idea what lay ahead for us as I had never heard of Edenton until the man at the bus station said it. But I vowed never to leave us vulnerable again. I had done that enough in my daughter's four short years.

"Here you go." The girl, whose name tag read *Caitlyn*, interrupted my thoughts as she set our drinks and Quinn's sandwich on the table. "I gave her a cookie, too. Hope that's okay."

"Thank you. That's very kind of you." I forced my lips into a half-grin. The tightening of my face caused pain to shoot through my cheek. I did my best to hide the wince. I had gotten good at hiding the pain over the years. I had no other choice. If I didn't hide it, I would just get more of the same from Gary.

"Let me know if you need anythin' else."

"Thank you."

Quinn had already snuck a bite of her cookie. When her gaze met mine, her lips formed a sheepish grin. I raised my brow. "Quinn, eat your sandwich first."

Quinn slowly slid the cookie back onto the plate and picked up one of the sandwich triangles. "Thank you for the food, Mommy."

"You're welcome, sweetheart." I ran my fingers through her mussed hair and tucked a strand behind her ear.

After Quinn finished her sandwich and cookie, she stretched her arms over her head, and a loud yawn escaped.

"I guess we'd better find somewhere to sleep tonight," I suggested. We stood from the table as I guzzled the last of my coffee. I set the cup on the table and flung the strap of our bag on my shoulder.

"Excuse me. I'm sorry. I didn't mean to eavesdrop, but did I hear you say you need a place to stay?" a woman behind us asked. She was about the same size as me, give or take, but with fiery red curls for hair.

Heat rushed to my cheeks. "Ye-yes I did."

"I'm sorry. Where are my manners? Living with all men will do that to a girl." The woman wiped her hands on her jeans before extending one in my direction. "My name is Callie Andrews."

Living with all men? What kind of place did she live in? I hesitantly slipped my hand into hers. "I'm Emelia, and this is Quinn." I probably should have given fake names, but I didn't want to confuse Quinn any more than she already was. There was also the fact that whenever I lied, which I was completely horrible at, Gary would pummel me in the face once he learned the truth. That only happened once. I hadn't told a lie since.

"You can come with me out to Redemption Ranch. We have some cabins available. We just added family cabins, so they are empty. If you'd like to, that is."

"I don't have much money. I'm not sure I can afford—"

"Oh, we don't accept money. In order to stay, you'd have to help out with ranch chores."

I giggled softly. My eyes grew wide with doubt. "I know nothing about being on a ranch."

"Don't worry. I didn't either when I arrived here a couple of years ago. The man who runs the ranch, who is now my husband, taught me everything I know. Do you want to go see some horses?" Callie bent over to Quinn.

"Yes!" Quinn screeched in reply. "Can we, Mommy? Pwease?" she begged, grabbing Horsey from her chair.

"I suppose one or two nights wouldn't hurt. Just until I figure something else out or if we are even going to stay here."

"Then, come with me." Callie motioned with her raised hand. "See you later, Caitlyn." She waved behind her.

We followed Callie out the door. I was careful to hold the jingle bells so that they didn't make any noise on the way out. When I was out the door and had it shut behind me, I breathed a sigh of relief. As I turned and faced the road, Callie was standing next to an old, yellow Jeep. My brows raised in question long before my words were asked. "You want us to ride in *that*?"

Callie's cheeks turned rosy. "It's perfectly safe and runs great. My husband insists on it." She rolled her eyes.

"I don't have a booster seat for Quinn," I remembered, peering around as if one would magically appear on the sidewalk.

"We'll get one for her. For now, you both can ride in the back, and I'll drive as carefully as possible." Callie's welcoming smile dissolved my reluctance to go.

"O-okay." I wasn't very comfortable with the idea, but Quinn had been safe enough on the bus. I shrugged before helping Quinn into the back seat. I buckled her in before doing the same for myself.

"So, what brings you to our little town?" Callie asked as she started down the road.

"Just trying to find our way." I stared out the window as the buildings that made up the town disappeared and were replaced by trees.

"I totally understand that."

I exhaled deeply when Callie didn't ask any more questions.

It wasn't long before the paved road became dirt. For the last day of May, the temperature in North Carolina was warmer than in Pennsylvania. The air in Edenton didn't seem to suffocate me, though. I wondered how much of that wasn't because of the weather. A few of the trees along the road appeared as if they were still struggling to push their blooms out. *Me, too, trees. Me, too.* I wanted our lives to be in full bloom. I was hoping being in Edenton, away from the violence, was the start.

"Here we are." Callie turned off the engine.

I peeked out the window to see a row of cabins on either side of the dirt road. They were bigger than I imagined. When Callie mentioned them, my mind immediately went to a family home on one of those old pioneer shows. The cabin before me was a far cry from that. The front had a porch with two rocking chairs and a little table between them. The door was painted a coral pink, which was a nice contrast to the dark wood of the cabin. "Love the color of the door," I said as I climbed out of the Jeep.

"Picked it out myself. My favorite color." Callie giggled as she jutted her chin in pride and held up the keys. "Shall we?"

"Yes." My eyes fell on Quinn, who had fallen asleep at some point during the ride. I unbuckled her seat belt and lifted her out of the seat.

Callie grabbed our bag. "Aww. She looks so sweet. I'll get

the door."

"Thank you, Callie."

Stepping over the cabin's threshold, I briefly peeked around the room. It was a beautiful rustic cabin that I hoped to admire fully after I laid Quinn down. I stopped at the first bedroom and found a twin bed with a nightstand and lamp. I laid her on the bed, hoping she wouldn't stir. I knew she was still exhausted from the long bus ride, even though she had slept for most of it. I readjusted Horsey so that he was in the crook of her arm.

I scanned the room. There was so much I could do to make this a room Quinn would love. *Don't think like that!* I closed my eyes tight and shook the thought from my head. I didn't even know how long we were going to be there. Gary could show up at any time and either drag us back to Pennsylvania or kill me or both. It wouldn't do to dream of things that were never going to happen. I sighed heavily.

"Callie, I can't thank you enough for letting us stay here . . . for however long."

"It's no problem. Maybe we can go into town tomorrow and pick up some things to help Quinn settle in."

"That's sweet of you, but I don't have money for that, and I have no idea how long we'll be staying." My cheeks flushed.

"Oh, we have funds set aside for things like this, so it's no problem." Callie waved her hand at me.

I contemplated as I sucked my bottom lip between my teeth. "Are you sure?"

"Absolutely!"

"I suppose a few things might be okay." I couldn't help but return a shy smile.

"I'll let you get settled. Dinner, or supper as the guys around here call it, is at six at the main house. There's a map of the ranch on the table over there. If Quinn is awake and you both want to join us, come on over. If not, I'll send one of the guys with a couple of containers of food. Okay?"

"Thank you so much. That's very kind of you." I could hardly believe our luck! This kind of stuff never happened to me.

"It's what we do around here." Callie raised her arms out to her side as her shoulders lifted and lowered in a shrug. "There are towels and linens for the beds in the hall closet over there." She strode to the closet door and opened it before turning back. "And Emelia? Welcome to Redemption Ranch." Callie slipped out onto the porch and shut the door behind her.

I exhaled deeply, not realizing I had been holding in a breath. *Wow! I can breathe.* For the first time in four years, I could breathe without the fear of being clobbered. That was going to take some getting used to. I grabbed our bag and traipsed down the hall to the other bedroom. It had a simple queen-sized bed with a light-colored wood frame. The bedside table was made from matching wood. A small chest of drawers rested against the far wall. I wanted so badly to unpack my bag but needed to be ready to flee at a moment's notice.

Gary had told me many times that if I ever left him, he would hunt me down. He would follow through on that threat—of that, I had no doubts. I drank in the air, attempting to maintain my composure. I made the bed with tight corners, just the way Gary liked. I studied the bed for a moment before messing it up. I stuck my tongue out at the bed as if it were Gary sitting there.

A giggle escaped my lips. I could still smell the scent of stale cigarettes and bad body odor from the bus, so I took a shower. My hope was the stench would escape my nostrils and be replaced by the aroma of whatever soap was stashed away in the bathroom.

Before my shower, I grabbed Quinn's blanket and crept into her room to lay it across her body. The only movement was her chest raising and lowering. My heart overflowed with love for her.

Chapter 5

Luke Herring

"So, he looks good?" Colt asked after he prayed over the food.

Everyone sat at the long, wood kitchen table, just like we did most every evenin'. Everyone was engrossed in their own conversations. I had just arrived back at the ranch. Colt Andrews, the owner of Redemption Ranch, had asked me to go to New York to check out a stallion he had received a call about. The stallion wasn't performing the way the owners had hoped, so if the ranch didn't take him, he was going to be put down.

"He looks perfect, Colt. He's a bit wild—at least, what I saw of him. But he's young and strong. I think he's going to be a great addition to the ranch. He should be here tomorrow or Friday." I popped a piece of chicken into my mouth.

"Great. You'll need to come up with a name for your horse, then."

"Wait. What?" My brows furrowed.

"I really appreciate ya goin' up there for me. You're gonna have more responsibility around here, and you're gonna need a horse to do it."

"Wow. I don't know what to say. Thank you, Colt. That means so much to me." A goofy grin spread across my face.

Colt smiled in return before turnin' to his wife. Callie started to buzz about a new arrival at the ranch. The last time we had someone new was when Callie arrived almost two years before. She had been good for the ranch, but she had been even better for Colt. They got married at the previous Harvest Festival. I loved their story and the love they shared. As much as I'd have loved to have someone to share my own love story with, I wasn't sure God had anyone for me that could handle the demons inside my head.

"Did you tell her to make sure the door was tightly shut?" Colt chuckled at Callie.

Callie rolled her eyes. "No, but I'll make sure to say something." Her sarcastic tone said otherwise. She set some containers on the table next to me. "Luke, can you take these to cabin 114, please?" She moved the containers closer to me, pulling me from my reminiscing.

"Sure." I sighed as I scooted the chair out from the table. My keys jangled when I removed them from my pocket. I snatched the containers off the table and strolled out the door. I jumped into my truck and headed to the cabins. If the new arrival had been a man, Callie would have teased Colt about havin' competition or somethin' like that, so I was curious to meet our new arrival. I chuckled and shook the thought from my head.

After stopping outside cabin 114, I slid down from the driver's seat and jogged around to get the containers out of the passenger seat. As I stood at the cabin's front door, I balanced the containers in one hand and raised my other to the door to knock. The squeal of a child's laughter filled the air. My lips curved up slightly at the ends, and my heart skipped a beat. The door opened, and my eyes moved to the person on the other side of it. My legs buckled a little. I hoped she didn't notice.

"It's you!" I blurted out before I could stop myself. She

was the woman from the bus station in New York—the one the homeless man was harassin'. What were the odds?

"Oh, are you okay?" she asked as she reached out to take the containers from my hand.

Yep! She noticed my legs. *Great first impression, Luke.* "Got 'em?" I asked, keeping my hand underneath the bottom container.

"I think so. Thank you so much. It smells delicious."

"Yeah, Richard is a magician in the kitchen." I tried to bounce back from my blunder. I ran my hand over the back of my neck.

She made eye contact with me for the first time. Her eyes grew wide, and what I saw in them was fear, as if she was lookin' into her worst nightmare. What did I do to make her fearful of me? I was completely perplexed. "Wh-what are you doing here?" she asked with tremors in her voice. Her face turned white. Her hand flew to her heart.

"Uh, I live here," I spoke, more forcefully than I had intended. I planted my hands on my hips.

"Oh." She took a thoughtful pause. When she glanced in my direction once again, her eyes reflected regret. "OH." Her shoulders slumped into a more relaxed posture, and her hand fell back to her side.

"Who's here, Mommy?" A little girl peeked around her mom.

"Um . . ." Her shoulders lifted in a shrug as she peered up at me.

"I'm Luke. And who might you be?" I leaned down to the little girl.

"Hi, Wuke. I'm Quinn. Do you wanna come pway with me?" She grabbed my hand.

My heart almost instantly melted. I glanced up at Quinn's

mom. Her eyes were once again as big as saucers. I chuckled. "Ya know what? Ya need to eat ya supper."

Quinn's tiny face scrunched in confusion. "What's supper?"

"It's what they call dinner here," Quinn's mother informed her. "Why don't you go wash your hands before we eat?" She placed her hand on Quinn's shoulder.

"Okay." Quinn threw her hands up in a shrug and scurried off to the bathroom.

"So sorry about that." Emelia's cheeks went pink.

I lifted one shoulder in a shrug. "No big deal. I love kids. When you both are up and ready tomorrow mornin', why don't ya bring Quinn over to the stable? She can help me feed the horses."

"Oh, that's not really necessary."

"Oh, but it is. Everyone has to pitch in around here." My eyebrows raised, and my mouth flashed a half-grin. "So, I'll see ya in the mornin'."

I stepped off the porch, and my heel caught on the small step, causing me to lose my footin'. *Please don't faceplant!* When I regained my composure, I slowly turned around with my eyes closed, and my face raised to the heavens. *Please, Lord, if You love me at all, let the door be closed.* I opened my eyes and scanned to the door to find it wide open with both Quinn and her mom standing there. They both were shaking with giggles. I forced a sheepish grin as my cheeks burned from the heat of my embarrassment.

Way to go, Luke! You're such an idiot. She's just a woman—a woman who doesn't need your kind of trouble. I shook the thoughts from my head as I climbed into my truck. I started the engine and revved it once, just like the woman revved my heart. There hadn't been a woman who had done that for quite some time. I chuckled. She didn't need someone like me in her life. From the marks I saw on her neck and the bruise on her cheek, she had enough troubles of her own. It still didn't take away the curiosity of wantin' to know more. First place to start was her name.

As I stopped in front of my own cabin and shut off the engine, I wondered what it was about her that drew me in. Maybe it was her eyes. They danced between blue and green. It was like watchin' the ocean waves ebb and flow between the two colors. The bruise on her cheek did nothing to detract from them. It did make me wonder what she had been through, though.

"Ugh!" I wiped my hands down my face. "Get yourself together, Luke." I slumped out of the truck and trudged inside.

Chapter 6

Emelia

The next morning, after Quinn and I showered and dressed, I set one of the muffins Callie thoughtfully included in the food Luke delivered on the table. "We're going to go see Luke this morning to feed the horses. Would you like that?" I asked as Quinn climbed up on the chair at the table. Horsey was tucked under her arm as always. I knew she would want to go; she'd never seen a horse in person before.

"Yay!" Quinn exclaimed, raising her fists above her head.

"Eat your muffin, and then we'll walk down to the stable." By the time I slid the last bite of my own muffin into my mouth, Quinn had already finished and was throwing her paper towel and muffin wrapper in the trash can. I didn't remember a single time when Quinn had ever eaten that fast. "Let's go brush our teeth, and we'll go."

After our teeth were clean, we made our way to the stable. I admired the trees and scenery along our walk. The Magnolia trees and wildflowers of all kinds were blooming all around us. The oranges, greens, reds, and yellows painted our surroundings. Most were in full bloom, but there were a few with bulbs waiting to flourish in the sun. Their scents invaded the air. I closed my eyes and breathed in deeply. I relished the peace I felt here. I hoped it would last.

"When we get there, listen to Luke, and do what he tells you, okay?"

"Okay, Mommy." Quinn skipped along ahead of me, barely listening to my voice in her eagerness to reach the stable.

As we neared the entrance to the stable, I glanced around. It was long with cream siding and a red roof. The center jutted out further than the sides.

Quinn ran inside. "Wuke! Wuke, are you here?"

"Quinn, you're going to startle the horses," I scolded her.

"Hey there, Quinn!" Luke greeted as he strode out of a stall. He grinned at me. "Hi. I'm sorry, but you never told me your name."

"Oh. I'm Emelia."

"Nice to meet ya, Emelia." Luke stuck his hand out. I slowly placed my hand in his. Warmth trickled through my hand and up my arm. I quickly removed my hand from his grasp. Luke spun around to Quinn. "So, are ya ready to help me with the horses?"

"Yes!" Quinn squealed before a sheepish grin formed on her lips. "Sorry, Mommy." She turned to Luke. "Mommy said that I would startwe the horses. Whatever that means." Her arms went up into the air before falling back to her sides.

"Well, that is true," Luke confirmed. "Startle just means scare." He touched his finger to Quinn's nose.

"Good morning, Emelia," Callie greeted from behind me.

"Good morning." I turned as a smile formed on my lips.

"How did you sleep?" Callie placed her hand on my shoulder. I flinched, and her hand retreated. "Sorry."

I glanced at Callie, studying her face. Reflected in her eyes was something I never thought I'd see: understanding.

"Would you like to take a walk?" Callie asked. It seemed more like an order than a request.

35

"Oh, um . . ." I motioned toward Quinn.

"That's no problem. Hey, Luke, can you keep an eye on Quinn for just a little bit?"

"Sure. No problem." Luke didn't even glance in our direction as he answered.

"Well, okay then." I followed Callie out of the stable.

Once we were a good distance away, Callie turned to me. "So, it's obvious you are in some kind of trouble." She nodded toward the bruises on my face and neck. "In order to keep you and Quinn safe as well as maintain the sanctity of the ranch, I need to know what's going on." She sat down at a picnic table in the center of a small gazebo.

"Wow, you don't beat around the bush, do you?" I sat down on the opposite side. The wind rustled, causing the scent of hay and horses to waft in the air.

"Not when it comes to the ranch or the family that has been built here."

"Okay." I inhaled deeply. "What do you want to know?"

"Anything you feel is important for me to know."

I stared off into the distance. "Where do I even start?"

"Why don't you start with what brought you here?"

"Okay. Well, my boyfriend, Gary . . . I guess my *ex*-boyfriend now . . . has been abusive for the last few years. Night before last, he went after Quinn for the first time." I glanced down at my twisted hands. "I said he would touch her over my dead body, and as you can see, he tried to make that happen."

I ran my fingers over my neck, then swiped a tear at the corner of my eye. "I don't know what made him stop. But as I laid on the floor, I knew it was time to get out. And Quinn and I left on the next bus out of town." I figured I didn't need to bore Callie with the details that followed.

"Do you think he'll come looking for you?"

"I have no doubt about it that he will. I'm terrified he'll find us and of what he'll do when he does." My voice cracked.

"You're safe here with us. Plenty of men to protect you both. Of *that*, I have no doubts."

"Thank you so much for letting us stay here, Callie. I'm not sure how long we will stay or if we'll move on, but I appreciate your kindness."

"You're welcome to stay as long as you'd like. As I said before, it's what we do here. Would you like to go into town and get the things you need?"

"Oh, that's not necessary. Right now, we have all we need. Besides, I don't have anyone to watch Quinn."

"I have just the person for that. Even if you aren't here for that long, I'd like to help make Quinn's room special and more her own." Callie grinned as she stood from the table and walked away.

"Okay." I sighed. I had a feeling it was no use arguing with her. I fell into step beside her.

"Let me make a phone call." Callie held up her finger as we arrived back at the stable. She stayed outside as I proceeded through the door.

"Mommy! Mommy! I hewped Wuke with the horsies! He said I did a good job, too."

"She really did," Luke agreed as he came out of the stall, wiping his hands on his thighs.

"You did? Did you have fun?" I bent down to Quinn.

"Yes. It was so much fun! But hard," Quinn confessed, wiping her hand across her forehead.

I glanced up at Luke. "Thank you for letting her help."

"No problem. She's a lot of fun. Great little girl." He winked before bending down to Quinn. "Thanks, darlin', for ya

37

help today. Maybe tomorrow ya could help again?"

"Can I, Mommy?" Quinn gaped up at me, hope glistening in her eyes.

How could I refuse those eyes? "I don't see why not."

"Yes!" Quinn squealed.

Luke held up his hand for a high five. Quinn slapped hers to his. I watched their interactions. For both of them, it seemed as if it was effortless—as if they had been around each other her entire life. Yes, that was what the beginning of Quinn's life should have been like. My heart skipped a beat. *Whoa, heart! Get a hold of yourself! This guy is way out of your league.* The last thing I needed in my life was a man—even one who seemed as sweet as Luke. Gary had been sweet, too—until he wasn't. I was going to have to be careful not to let Quinn get too attached to the ranch. Me, too, for that matter.

"Okay, Caitlyn Logan will be here shortly to stay with Quinn," Callie announced, interrupting my internal argument with my heart.

"Mommy, where are you going?" Quinn stared up at me, concern filling those emerald-green eyes.

"Callie and I are going into town to get some things we need for our cabin." I swooped Quinn into my arms. "We won't be long. I promise."

Quinn's lips formed a pout. "I want to go with you." She twirled the tip of my hair around her finger.

"Quinn, Caitlyn will make sure you have lots of fun," Callie reassured her, which, in turn, reassured me.

"Okay." Quinn squirmed out of my arms at the sound of a car pulling up. My heart raced. A girl with blonde hair stood from the driver's seat. *Oh, the girl from the café.* My heart calmed.

"Hi, Caitlyn," Callie greeted her.

"Hey, Aunt Callie. How are ya?" Caitlyn and Callie embraced in a hug.

"Good. I'm good. And you? Are you getting excited about graduation and going off to college?"

"I am. I can't wait. Of course, Mom and Dad are concerned about me going so far away." Caitlyn rolled her eyes. "Because of my diabetes and all."

"I'm sure they are. Well, Caitlyn, this is Emelia. Emelia, this is Caitlyn."

"Nice to officially meet you, Caitlyn." I flashed a shy smile.

"Nice to meet you, too."

"Mommy, who's this?" Quinn asked after running over to us from where she had been standing with Luke. "She's pretty."

"Quinn, this is Caitlyn. Remember her from the café yesterday?"

Quinn scrunched her nose as she tried to remember. Finally, her face lit up like a light bulb. "You gave me a cookie!"

"Yes, she did," I confirmed. "Caitlyn is going to hang out with you while I go into town. Okay?"

"Hi, Quinn." Caitlyn beamed down at her.

"Hi, Caitwyn." Quinn waved.

Caitlyn glanced at me. "Take your time. We'll be fine."

"Thank you." I gave Quinn a quick hug and kiss. "You be good for Caitlyn, alright?"

"I promise, Mommy."

"I'll be back soon." I was reluctant to leave Quinn with a complete stranger, but Callie seemed to trust her, and Callie was someone I was starting to trust—as much as someone could trust after only a day.

"Promise?" Quinn grabbed my hand.

"Pinky promise, sweetheart." I ran my hand down her

39

cheek before lifting my pinky to her.

"Okay." Her bottom lip protruded as she linked her pinky with mine.

I watched as Quinn grabbed Caitlyn's hand and skipped away. It was amazing to see Quinn's demeanor change so much and in such a short amount of time. I could still see her hesitation with her "promise" question, but that was to be expected under the circumstances. Quinn could relax at the ranch, though, and be a child.

"Are you ready?" Callie asked.

"What? Oh. Yes. Let's go."

Once we arrived at Rachel's Discount Mart, which was somewhat like Wal-Mart back home, we perused aisle after aisle. "Oh, what about these?" Callie asked, holding up a set of pink and white sheets with cowgirls and ponies on them.

"Those are adorable. How much are they?" I sucked my bottom lip between my teeth.

"Don't you worry about that." Callie tossed the sheets into the shopping cart.

"Are you sure?"

"Yes. Now, let's see what else we can find." Callie pushed the cart down the aisle. "How about this?" Callie spun around and hopped down the aisle on a stick horse.

Laughter bellowed from my lips. "Oh, we must!"

As we strolled down the aisles, we were able to find a pink comforter with a pony on it, along with some curtains the same shade of pink. We also found a horse nightlight lamp and a few stuffed animals.

A man's voice from a few aisles over caused my feet to freeze to the floor. My eyes grew wide as saucers. My knees buckled. I gripped the shelving next to me to keep from crumpling to the floor.

"Emelia, what is it?" Callie raced to my side.

"Gary," I whispered.

"What? Where?" Callie glanced all around.

"A f-few aisles over, I think." My voice was only a whisper.

With Callie's assistance, we crept to the aisle where I thought I heard the voice. My heart pounded in my chest. My breath labored. My pulse throbbed in my head. I peeked around the end of the aisle. The only man there was a short, plump older man. *No, not Gary!*

"It's not him." I closed my eyes and let out a long, deep breath. I leaned against the shelving until I felt my legs were strong enough.

Once I regained my composure, Callie and I continued shopping for a few things for my room as well as some necessities. I wasn't sure why we bought all those things. Quinn and I would have to leave eventually. Good things never lasted—not for me, anyway.

"Let's get home and decorate her room." Callie beamed with excitement.

"Sounds good." I tried to mirror Callie's excitement but knew I fell short.

As we strode back to Callie's Jeep, I took in my surroundings. My eyes flitted in every direction. Goosebumps shot up my arms. Only when I was enclosed in the safety of the Jeep did I exhale. Would being out and about ever get any easier, or would that be what it felt like every day for the rest of my life? I sure hoped not, but it was only our first whole day in Edenton. It would undoubtedly take time. I wished it had been as easy for me to relax as it appeared to be for Quinn.

I was so lost in my thoughts that I hadn't realized we were stopped in front of the cabin. "Ready?" Callie asked.

"Absolutely. Quinn's going to love it." I did what I could

to plaster my best grin on my face.

We brought the bags inside and hurried toward Quinn's room. We waved at Caitlyn as we swept through. Quinn was singing "You Are My Sunshine" in the bathroom. I smiled as it had been quite some time since she had sung that song in such a cheerful tone. My heart swelled.

Callie and I shut the bedroom door and set to work. With the two of us, it didn't take long to hang the curtains, make the bed, and set the stuffed animals against Quinn's pillows. I saved a space for Horsey. Callie leaned the stick horse against the wall in the corner. The last touch was the horse-shaped night-light lamp. I plugged it into the wall outlet and set it on Quinn's nightstand. Quinn had never been able to have a room like this. Tears stung my eyes.

"Oh, Emelia, what's wrong? You don't like it?"

"It's perfect. Gary detests the color pink and wouldn't allow it in his house."

"Shall we surprise her now?" Callie clapped her hands together.

"Yes!" I agreed. Callie's delight was contagious. I opened the bedroom door. "Quinn, we have a surprise for you."

"Surprise?" Quinn squealed. "Come on, Caitwyn. Wet's go see."

"Close your eyes." I swept Quinn up in my arms.

Quinn covered her eyes with her hands as I took the two steps to the doorway. She squirmed with excitement. I lowered her to the floor.

"Okay. You can open your eyes."

Quinn's hands fell to her sides. Her eyes grew wide, and her mouth formed an "o." "This is for me?" She glanced up at me and then at Callie.

"Yes, sweetheart. Do you like it?"

"I wuv it!" Quinn screeched, running and jumping onto the bed. "Thank you so much, Mommy."

"You should thank Callie." I smiled.

Quinn hopped down from her perch, laid Horsey between two of her new animals, and hurried over to Callie. "Thank you, Cawwie!" She wrapped her arms around Callie.

"You're so welcome, sweetie. Glad I could do this for you." Callie ran her hand up and down Quinn's back as Quinn continued to squeeze her.

"Caitwyn, wook at my new room!" Quinn spun around to where Caitlyn had been lingering in the doorway.

"I see it. It's beautiful."

Callie peeked at her watch. "It's almost time for dinner. Would you like to come to the house and meet everyone?"

"Oh—"

"YES!" Quinn exclaimed before I could decline.

I threw my hands and shoulders up in a shrug. "I guess we're coming to dinner." A nervous giggle escaped my lips as we all walked to the door.

"Caitlyn, would you like to join us for dinner?" Callie glanced back at her as we shuffled out of the cabin.

"Thank you, but my parents are expecting me at the café."

"Thank you so much for looking after Quinn." I smiled.

"It was my pleasure. She's a sweet girl. If ya ever need me, just let me know. Even if ya don't, let me know then, too." Caitlyn flashed a pearly smile.

"Aw, well, thank you. So sweet of you."

"See ya later, Quinn." Caitlyn waved as she walked around to the driver's side of her car.

"Bye, Caitwyn." Quinn fluttered her hand above her head.

"Well, shall we?" Callie asked, motioning to her Jeep.

"Yes." My heart pounded in my chest. I wasn't sure what

to expect. Luke would be there, too. My hands started to sweat. I buckled Quinn into her new booster seat and climbed into the passenger side. I slid my hands down my thighs.

"You don't need to be nervous." Callie leaned over as she drove away from the cabin. "These guys are all big softies. But I know how you feel. I was terrified the first time I met everyone, too."

"Okay." I forced my lips upward. "So, how long have you lived here?"

"It's been two years."

As we arrived at a big white house, I inhaled deeply. "Wow! What a house."

"That's pretty much what I said the first time I saw it." Callie giggled.

As we scooted inside, the kitchen was full of men in loud conversation. The first to notice our arrival was a man much taller than my mere five-foot-four frame. He had jet black hair, very defined muscles, and steel-blue eyes. I didn't have to see the ring on his finger to know he was taken. He only had eyes for Callie.

"Hey, darlin'." The man kissed Callie's cheek as he put his arm around her shoulders.

"Hey, babe. I'd like you to meet Emelia and her daughter, Quinn. Emelia, Quinn, this is my husband, Colt."

"Hi, Emelia. Nice to have you here." Colt stuck out his hand for me to shake.

"Nice to meet you, too." I took his outstretched hand. I felt warmth grow on my cheeks.

"Hello, Quinn." Colt raised his hand for a high five.

Quinn smacked her little hand on his. "Hi, Cowt."

Colt slipped his pointer finger and thumb into the corners of his lips. He exhaled, resulting in a shrill whistle that silenced the room. Everyone turned their attention to him.

"Callie has an announcement."

"Thanks, babe. Guys, this is Emelia and Quinn. They will be staying here for at least a little while. Emelia and Quinn, the guy at the stove is Richard Alan. He's a magician in the kitchen."

I giggled. "So I've heard." I waved at Richard. He appeared to be the oldest in the room. His chocolate brown eyes exuded kindness without him ever saying a word.

"That guy is Jon Williams," Callie continued. She pointed toward a slightly pudgy, medium-height man.

"Nice to meet you both." Jon lifted his cowboy hat off his head and plopped it right back in place. I nodded in his direction.

"The guy to your right is Wyatt Glover."

"Hi, Wyatt." I glanced in his direction. If I had to guess, I'd have said Wyatt was about eighteen or nineteen.

"You already know Luke."

"Wuke!" Quinn squealed, bouncing up and down.

I peered over at Luke. A broad smile spread across his lips, and he winked. Blood beelined straight from my pounding heart to my cheeks. I quickly diverted my gaze.

"I see you still have a way with the ladies," the man next to Luke said while jabbing Luke in the side with his elbow.

Luke's jaw tightened as a blush crept up his neck. He stuffed his hands in his pockets and stared at the floor.

"That guy, who thinks he's hilarious, is Austin Collier." Callie rolled her eyes.

Austin grinned, and his chubby cheeks pushed up into his eyes, practically making them disappear. "I *am* pretty funny."

"Last, but certainly not least, is Spencer Wright."

Spencer tipped his hat. I waved. He was almost as tall as Luke but fell an inch or two short.

"Very nice to meet everyone. Thank you so much for allowing us to stay here. Not sure how long that will be." I couldn't let my nervousness show. I didn't want to give any of them any reason to hit me or make us leave.

"You and Quinn are welcome to stay as long as ya like," Colt chimed in.

"Thank you," I replied softly.

"Can we eat now?" Austin whined, which resulted in a round of laughter.

"Make room for our new guests," Colt ordered.

"Wuke, can I sit by you?" Quinn asked, her eyes beaming with hope.

"Oh, Quinn, I don't—" I glanced at Luke, hoping he saw the apology expressed in my eyes.

"Absolutely, you can." Luke grinned and shrugged his shoulders before I could finish.

Quinn ran around the table and launched herself into Luke's arms as she let out a squawk. Quinn was already smitten with the cowboy. *Oh, boy!* It made my heart ache. It was going to crush Quinn when we had to leave.

"Emelia, you can sit by me." Callie jostled me out of my head.

I flinched as I came back to the room. "Oh, thank you."

Once everyone was seated, Colt prayed over the food. So, he and Callie were Christians. *Great!* My shoulders slumped. My parents were Christians, too. So Christian that when I went to them at twenty years old and told them I was pregnant by a guy I didn't really know, they told me that my baby and I were going to hell. They handed me a suitcase with a few of my belongings and said I had to get out and that they no longer had a daughter. They said all my stuff was bought with their money, so it belonged to them, and I wasn't entitled to any of it. They said I should've been thankful for what they did allow me to have. I hadn't spoken to them since. They hadn't ever laid eyes on Quinn.

I felt a slight pain in my side. It jolted me from my thoughts. I glanced in Callie's direction. "I'm sorry. What?"

Callie giggled. "Seems I'm always taking you away from your thoughts. Where are you from?"

Heat rushed to my cheeks. "Pennsylvania." I finally took a bite of food. The meatloaf disintegrated on my tongue. "Mmm."

"I told you." Callie grinned. "Richard is the one who pre-pared the food you had last night."

"Yes, you did. Luke did also." I savored the flavors of an-other bite on my tongue.

I peered over at Luke and Quinn. She had him deep in con-versation. I'd have to be careful with that one. It would serve me no purpose to get romantically involved. As if he would want to be with me anyway. No. I needed to be on my own for a while. At least until I got my bearings. Besides, I knew nothing about him. *He could be just like Gary, for all I know.*

"I'll take your plate." Callie held out her hand at my side.

"Oh, I can do the dishes. I haven't done anything to help yet."

"How about we both do them?"

"Okay." My lips turned up in a grin.

Callie and I cleared the table as the men left to sit outside. I washed the dishes, and Callie dried them as I had no clue where anything belonged. *Everything has its place*, Gary's voice echoed in my mind.

When we were done, I searched the room. My heart plum-meted to the floor. "Where's Quinn?" I asked as the breath left my lungs. I spun around in a circle, tears welling in my eyes, threatening to fall.

47

"Emelia, it's okay." Callie placed her hand on my arm. I jumped back as if I'd been punched. "I'm sorry. I shouldn't have done that. Quinn is outside with Luke and the other guys."

"Are you sure?" My voice squeaked with panic.

"Yes. Come on. We'll go find her."

Callie escorted me out the door. When my eyes fell on Quinn, my heart rate slowed, and the breath that was choking me finally exited my body. I planted my hand over my heart. "I'm so sorry. My nerves are so on edge."

"Hi, Mommy." Quinn flapped her arm in a wave.

I smiled as much as I could muster and wiggled my fingers at her.

"Come to the stable with me," Callie insisted. "I have someone I'd like you to meet." She glanced at me.

"Um. Okay. Quinn, come on, honey." I held out my hand to her.

"Bye, Wuke." Quinn gave him a hug before running over and grabbing my hand.

I peered over at Luke. He was smiling at Quinn, but his eyes screamed sadness or loneliness. Then again, maybe it was just me seeing my own feelings reflected back at me.

Chapter 7

Emelia

"**T**his is Warrior," Callie told us as we stopped in front of one of the stalls in the stable. Scents of horse manure and hay stung my nose.

A tan horse with a white mane poked his head out of the opened part of the door. He turned his head and nuzzled Callie. My eyes were immediately drawn to the scars that seemed to cover the majority of his body. Who would do such a thing? *The same kind of person that did it to you.* My fingers danced along my neck.

"What happened to him?" My words were barely audible.

"He was bred to be a racehorse. When he didn't perform, he was beaten. Of course, that is only our assumption. He was dumped in the woods nearby. When Colt and Jon found him, he was in really bad shape. He wouldn't let anyone near him until he met me. We understand each other."

"Can I pet him?" Quinn begged.

I scooped Quinn up into my arms. Warrior moved his head and looked at me. I peered into his beautiful brown eyes. It was as if he saw my bruised face and neck and offered his understanding.

"Warrior is always here if you need someone to talk to—someone who understands," Callie said. "He's a great listener and even better comforter. I'm always here, too. But I know sometimes humans aren't the ones we want to spill our secrets to."

I lowered my gaze to the ground, still uncomfortable with the topic. Quinn slid slowly down my body and back onto the ground. "Thank you. Everyone here seems so amazing."

"They really are. They changed my life when I got here. This whole town did. I won't be surprised if the same happens for you." Callie flashed a smile that radiated warmth and compassion. "You won't regret coming here. I hope one day you will feel comfortable enough to tell me your story. Until then, feel free to talk to Warrior. He's the best at keeping secrets."

Tell my story? I could barely live with the shame of having stayed in that place for so long, let alone say it out loud. "Thank you. I'll keep that in mind."

"We've been training Warrior to be a therapy horse for children." Callie rubbed the side of his face. "Isn't that right, boy?"

Warrior raised his head. His exhale through his nose was audible. I reached out to touch him but snatched my hand back. It had been so long since I'd been around horses. Since just before I found out I was pregnant. Warrior moved his head toward me. I slowly raised my hand, and he nestled his cheek against it. His fur was stiff and prickly, just like Apollo's. Apollo was my childhood horse. I sighed. I was forced to leave him behind. He was one of the many things I had to leave behind because my parents paid for him.

I felt Warrior's acceptance of me through his contact and his soulful eyes. Yes, he was a horse who understood my pain and the cruelty of the world. I could see it in his scars, and yet, his scars were so much a part of his beauty.

"Now, we just have to see if he will let anyone ride him," Callie explained. "The only person to ride him was Colt, and that was to save my life. Do you think we could let Quinn try and ride him? He's finally allowing us to saddle him." Callie spoke with so much hope in her tone.

"Oh, I don't know about that." My voice crackled.

"Wuke!"

I jumped at Quinn's voice. Luke was standing with his hands on his hips at the back doorway. He wiped his hands on his handkerchief as he walked toward us.

"Hey there, Quinn." Luke bent down as she jumped into his arms. "Oh, I see ya now know Warrior." Luke's eyes met mine, and the electricity was palpable. His smile caused my heart to thump.

What is going on with you, Em? You're not in high school anymore. Get a grip! He's so far out of your league, it's not even funny. Goosebumps prickled my skin as Luke took up space beside me.

"How're ya doin'?" Luke inquired, bumping my arm with his. A spark jolted me.

"I'm okay. How are you?" I glanced up at him, trying to avoid rubbing my arm.

"I'm great. Just livin' the dream." Luke grinned and folded his arms over his chest.

"I can see why everyone loves this place so much. I've never seen Quinn so happy and alive." My gaze moved to the ground as I mumbled, "Not that she's ever been allowed to be a kid."

"What's that?" Luke stuffed his hands in his pockets.

My eyebrows raised in surprise. Did he have supersonic hearing or something? "My ex didn't allow her to do a lot of kid things. He was a firm believer in children being seen and not heard." My shoulders raised in a shrug as I shoved my hands in my pockets.

"Is he her dad?" Luke bit the inside of his lip.

"No. Just someone who took me in when I had nowhere to go."

Luke glanced around the stable. "Would you like to take a walk with me?"

Heat crept up my neck to my cheeks. *What should I do? I really shouldn't be alone with him—no telling what he might do. But maybe I should?* "Su-sure." I turned toward Callie and Quinn. "Callie, would you mind watching Quinn while I take a walk with Luke?"

Callie grinned. "Sure. No problem."

What was that smile about? I shrugged it off as Luke and I strode out of the stable. We didn't walk far before we stopped at a reddish-brown wood barn. It was much smaller than the stable but looked to be renovated. The dim lights inside lit up a few bales of hay as the evening sky darkened. Luke went inside and flopped down on a bale of hay.

Luke patted another bale directly across from him. "Have a seat."

My knees wobbled, and I almost fell off the side of the bale as I sat. Luke's hand came up to my arm. "Ya okay?"

I exhaled deeply. "I'm okay. So, are you from here?" I asked, trying to make conversation.

"No, I was born and raised in Oklahoma. Joined the Marines right out of high school." Luke plucked a piece of hay from the bale.

"Did you see any combat?" I asked softly. "If that's too personal or you don't wanna talk about it, that's okay."

"It's fine. Yeah, I did." He sighed deeply as he tore a piece off the hay's stalk and threw it into the air. I watched as it floated to the ground. "Unfortunately, I saw a lot of it. We didn't all make it home."

"I'm so sorry, Luke. I can't even imagine how that must feel." I placed my hand on his arm. Heat radiated under my fingers. I snatched my hand back as if I'd been scorched by a hot flame. *What am I doing?* The last thing I needed was to get lost in another man. No. I had to find my own way. "I'm sorry. I need to go. It's almost Quinn's bedtime. Good night, Luke."

"Emelia. Wait."

I couldn't turn back. *I'm so sorry, Luke.* I scurried back to the stable—back where I was safe, away from the heat that man evoked.

Chapter 8

Luke

"**W**hat just happened?" I asked aloud as Emelia retreated from me. I inhaled and exhaled deeply. I rubbed my arm where I was sure her handprint was emblazoned. Her touch was electric. It was probably for the best that she ran away. She didn't need my kind of demons. Sounded like she had enough of her own. But she intrigued me. She had just arrived and already left me wanting more.

Guess I should go get some rest. The stallion would be arrivin' the next day. Maybe Quinn could help me pick a name for him. My lips formed a smile. She was a sweet girl.

I made my way to my cabin. Once inside, I took a shower and climbed into bed. *Please, Lord, keep the nightmares at bay.* I prayed that every night, but most nights, it fell on deaf ears. My head hit the pillow, and my eyes closed.

I was in the Humvee. My band of brothers was with me. We pulled over on the side of the road to patrol a small town on foot. All of the guys had gotten out before me. They were huddled together, probably discussing our plan one final time. I hustled the short distance to catch up, but before I reached them, there was an explosion. I flew through the air.

I came to on the hot ground. Chaos was all around. I could barely hear what anyone was saying. The ringing in my ears was so loud. I glanced around at the looks of horror on the faces of the civilians scrambling to get out of the area. Bodies were everywhere. Most of them belonged to my team. I was the only survivor. I couldn't feel any part of my body. Was it still attached? Bile rose to my throat, and my head hit the ground, causing the blackness to surround me.

I shot straight up in bed, my back rigid as sweat slid down it. I gasped for air to fill my lungs. Pain radiated through my left leg. I felt around on my nightstand for the light switch, my eyes fighting to focus against the blinding light.

I fumbled with the lid of the Ibuprofen bottle. When the lid didn't budge, I threw the bottle across the room. A loud growl escaped me as the bottle left my hand. The bottle hit the wall, and the lid flew off, scattering pills everywhere. *Of course.*

I fell back against my pillow and glanced at the clock hanging on my wall. Four a.m. I laid my arm across my eyes. Would the nightmares ever stop? I fisted the bedsheet and slammed my fist against the mattress.

I'd been honorably discharged from the Marine Corps three years prior, havin' served two tours. I just couldn't get my mind right after that day. Why had I survived while everyone else died? My left leg was so damaged it left me unfit for duty. The doctor said I was lucky he didn't have to amputate it. Some days, though, I wasn't sure if that was a good thing or a bad one. Those were the days when the pain was almost unbearable. It was goin' to be one of those days.

My leg was a mangled mess. It was why I wore pants every day. The only time I wore shorts was when I was goin' swimmin'. Even then, I usually waited until there were as few people around as possible. No one needed to see my deformities. Plus, I hated answerin' the questions. Mostly, I hated the looks of pity.

My thoughts took a right turn toward the woman in the cabin across the road. Did she notice my limp? If she did, did she care? I hoped one day she'd feel comfortable enough to tell me more about her past. She definitely had me feelin' things I hadn't felt in a very long time—things I probably had no right to feel.

I ran my hands down my face. "Guess I should get up and get started. The stallion will be here before I know it." I rolled out of bed and dragged myself to my bathroom. I was excited to see the horse again. I still hadn't the first clue what I was goin' to name him. I got dressed and headed for the stable.

"Hey, Warrior," I greeted. He snorted in response.

I led Warrior out of his stall. It was amazin' how far he had come. When Colt and Jon rescued him, he was a bloody mess—kind of like I was after the bomb. Warrior wouldn't let any of us touch him. Until Callie. Callie and Warrior had an instant bond like nothin' I'd ever seen before. He finally allowed others to give him affection.

Callie and Colt were trainin' Warrior to be a therapy horse for kids with physical and mental disabilities as well as those with mental health issues. Or if someone just needed another livin' and breathin' bein' to understand them. Warrior's scars told his story long before anyone else did. I hoped to have that kind of bond with my new horse.

The fact that Colt gave me the horse in the first place filled me with a sense of pride. I had found my place after leavin' the Corps. It was a place I had searched hard to find. I still wasn't sure how Colt found me. The grace of God, I suppose.

When I left the Corps, I wanted to be anywhere but where I was and anyone but who I was. I got lost in the depths of my grief and what I later learned was survivor's guilt. I drank to numb the memories and pain. And I drank a lot. In turn, I tried to find solace in the arms of whatever woman was close by when the bar shut down. Again, there was a lot. Definitely not my finest hours. They left me with more emptiness than ever.

It wasn't until I arrived at Redemption Ranch that I learned there was a God who loved me right where I was, and He hadn't created me to live the life I had been livin'. He had a better future for me, even if I had to fulfill that future alone. God had brought me comfort when I never thought I would have it again.

"Excuse me?" a man's voice said, breaking me from my thoughts.

I looked out the doorway of the barn toward the voice. *When did the sun rise?* I glanced at the man. He looked like one of us, from the cowboy hat perched on his head to his dusty cowboy boots, but I didn't recognize his face. My shoulders lifted in a shrug. I propped the rake up against the nearest wall before stridin' over to the man. "Yes, sir. How can I help you?"

"I'm here to drop off a stallion."

I swiped my handkerchief from my back pocket and wiped my hands. "Oh. Right. How was the drive down? Did he give ya any trouble?"

"Not too bad. It took him a little while to settle down in the trailer, though."

We made our way to the back of the trailer. The door opened, and the stallion backed out slowly. He sure was a beautiful horse.

"Welcome home, buddy." I ran my hand along the horse's side. "You're going to love it here."

"Just need you to sign here, and I'll be on my way." The man pointed to the clipboard in his hand.

"Oh. Sure." I took the pen and scribbled my name across

the page.

"Thank you. Enjoy your horse."

"Yeah. Thanks. Have a safe trip back."

The man tipped his hat before slidin' into his truck and drivin' down the dirt lane. I led the horse into the paddock so he could stretch his legs after bein' cooped up in the trailer for so long. I stood on the bottom rung of the wooden fence, with my arms danglin' over the top. The stallion made short work of the fenced-in area.

The way the stallion's black mane flowed as he galloped made him look majestic. His black tail slapped against his body. His colorin' was somewhere between white and tan— closer to white, except for his legs. His legs and nose were as black as his mane. I couldn't wait to saddle him up and take him for a ride. Maybe Emelia would want to go. I shook that thought from my head faster than it had arrived. Those thoughts had no business bein' in my head.

"Wuke!" Quinn yelled as she ran up to the fence, her mother not too far behind.

"Quinn, you're up early." I helped her up on the bottom rung next to me. I glanced at Emelia. She was standin' on the other side of Quinn, against the fence. She didn't join us on the bottom rung. Instead, she kept her distance.

"She overheard someone say something about a new horse coming today. She heard the truck and trailer and begged me to bring her down. So, here we are." Emelia threw her arms up and let them smack against her legs before shoving her hands into her back pockets.

"What's his name?" Quinn inquired.

"I don't know yet. Wanna help me name him?"

"Yes!" Quinn's lips turned up into the cutest grin. "He looks like a prince." She put her index finger to her lips and tapped her bottom lip as she stared at the horse.

"What about His Majesty?" The word majestic had been dancin' around in my head. "We could call him Majesty for short?"

"Yes!" Quinn softly clapped her hands. "Can I pet him?"

"Oh, honey, I don't think—" Emelia started.

"How about we let him exercise a little more?" I suggested. "When I put him in his stall later, you can pet him. Okay, Quinn?"

"Okay." Quinn's bottom lip poked out.

"Ya wanna go get some breakfast? There should be some left. We can bring our food outside and sit at the picnic table and watch him if ya'd like."

"Can we, Mommy?" Quinn asked in a hopeful tone.

"I don't see why not." Emelia smiled. My heart did a little loop-de-loop.

Did Emelia know just how beautiful of a smile she had? How beautiful she was in general? She was the complete opposite of any of the women I had ever dated. She had short hair; it fell to the middle of her neck. It was light brown in color, almost the color of oak. Her body type was full-figured or plus-sized, or whatever the correct term was. I just called her beautiful, even with a bruised cheek and neck. I wanted to protect her from anythin' else that was bad. Whoa! Where did that come from? *That's a slippery slope there, Luke. Don't get too close to the edge.* The last thing she needed was my kind of trouble.

"Shall we?" I extended my arm in the direction of the house.

Quinn ran ahead. "Don't get too far ahead," Emelia called after her.

"She's so sweet."

"She really is the greatest. The best part of me."

"I wouldn't say that," I stated in a hushed tone.

Pink rushed to Emelia's cheeks. The slightest grin followed. But she never glanced in my direction. Not once. To say I was disappointed would have been a gross understatement. I wanted nothin' more than to be washed away in those greenish-blue tides.

When we stepped into the kitchen, Quinn was the center of every man's attention. She had only been at the ranch for a couple of days, but she already had every one of them wrapped around her little finger. None more than Colt. Or me, for that matter.

"What are you guys going to do today?" Quinn asked, sitting on a chair at the kitchen table, swingin' her legs back and forth.

The men were busy shovelin' food into their mouths, in a rush to finish eatin' to get to their chores. "Well," Colt glanced at us, "today, I have ta go check the fence. Would ya wanna help me?"

"Yes. Pwease, Mommy?" Quinn turned in her chair and flashed her mother a puppy-dog glance.

"Oh, I don't know." Emelia bit her bottom lip. She twisted her clasped fingers and peered up at me for the first time since leavin' the paddock. Concern swam in her eyes.

"Pweeease?" Quinn interlaced her fingers and raised her hands to her chin.

"She's never been on a horse before," Emelia confessed.

"She'll ride Beauty with me," Colt reassured Emelia. "And I'll make sure she wears a helmet, too. I think we even have a safety vest she can wear." Colt perched his hands on his hips.

"Well, okay. I suppose it'd be alright." Once again, Emelia's bottom lip made its way between her teeth.

"Yay!" Quinn yelled as she jumped down from the chair, ran to Colt, and wrapped her arms around his leg.

"We'll get goin' after you eat some breakfast. Okay? Better hurry, though, before your mom changes her mind."

Emelia slid a plate with a waffle and a couple of pieces of bacon in front of Quinn.

"Okay." Quinn pouted and shoved a piece of waffle in her mouth.

After Quinn cleaned her plate and placed it in the sink, Colt took her tiny hand in one of his hands, his lunch bag in the other, and they scurried out the door.

"I hope she'll be okay and not drive him too crazy." Emelia giggled. Soft. Sweet. It caused my lips to turn upward. "Now, what do I do with myself?" Her shoulders rose and fell.

"Ya can help me with Majesty if ya want," I suggested.

"Really?" Emelia's eyes lit up.

"Sure." I shrugged it off like it was no big deal, but I wanted to spend time with her. I had no idea why or how I was feelin' that way after just two days, but I felt it all the same.

"Okay." Emelia's lips parted into a smile that made the room brighter.

"Let's go then." I held the door open so Emelia could pass through as I followed her out.

Once we arrived at the paddock containin' Majesty, we watched as he ran in circles. "Do ya wanna come in, Emelia?" I opened the gate and stepped inside the fence.

"I think I'll stay right here. On this side of the fence. I don't want to distract him." Emelia stepped up onto the bottom rung of the fence.

I twirled on my heel and marched to the center of the paddock.

Chapter 9

Emelia

My eyes were glued to Luke as he removed the wound-up rope from the hook and stepped into the center of the circular paddock. His hat was low on his head to block the already glaring sun. Majesty turned his head as if he was curious about the man who had invaded his space. He moved closer, wanting to trust but not quite sure. *Me, too, Majesty. Me, too.*

Luke slapped the coiled rope against his leg. Majesty began to run around him along the edges of the circle. Luke turned to keep himself facing the horse. Luke continuously struck the rope against his leg. Every so often, a clicking sound would come from Luke's lips. Even though I had no idea what he was doing, I was transfixed on the horse and the man. Before long, Luke had Majesty change directions. This went on for quite a while—or so it seemed.

Suddenly, Luke stood as still as a statue before slowly twirling so that his back was to Majesty. The horse slowed to a stop, staring in Luke's direction as if he were waiting for instruction. He curled his front leg, dragging his hoof through the dirt. With some hesitation, Majesty moved toward Luke. My breath hitched in my throat. Majesty stopped when his head was even with Luke's right shoulder. Luke peeked at Majesty without moving his head. A grin spread across his face.

"Good boy." Luke cautiously lifted his hand and rubbed the side of Majesty's face. He guided the rope over the horse's head. Majesty didn't move an inch. Luke led him over to me. Pride beamed from Luke's entire body.

"That was amazing!" I grinned.

"Thanks. I've watched Colt do that at least a hundred times. First time *I've* had the chance to do it, though." Luke moved his attention to the ground, but not before his cheeks turned a rosy red.

"I would've never known. What *was* that exactly—that thing you were doing with him?" I jumped down off the fence as Luke closed the gate behind him.

"It was a trust exercise. I could tell he was a bit anxious from the ride down as well as his new surroundings. I didn't want to add to that by tryin' to put a rope over his head. I had to let him know he's safe here, and he can trust me." Luke glanced up at me. His eyes locked with mine. It was as if he was digging into my soul. My heart skipped a beat.

I quickly broke from Luke's gaze. I couldn't allow him to see too much. I wished I could trust Luke as easily as Majesty did. But it was just too soon. The wounds created by Gary hadn't scarred over yet. I wasn't convinced they ever would.

As I stepped inside the stable, a snort came from my left. "Hey, Warrior," I greeted softly. I placed my hands on either side of his face and pressed my lips to his nose. I slid inside the stall and ran my hands down his side. "What did people do to you? I'm so sorry you know the cruelty of the world. I know a little something about that, too." I continued to stroke my hands down his side and back to the front.

"My boyfriend, Gary. A few days ago, he tried to kill me. Or at least I thought so. He strangled me. See?" I raised my chin to show Warrior the marks on my neck. The bruises had turned black and yellow. I hoped they would disappear soon. "You must have been so scared each time they hit you. This last time, with Gary, I was terrified. More so for Quinn. I don't know what would happen to her if I wasn't here anymore. We ran. We got on a bus and ended up here. I'm scared he'll find us. I'm scared of what he'll do when he does." I sighed deeply. "Callie was right. You *are* a good listener."

I exited the stall and closed the door. "Thanks for the chat, Warrior."

Warrior lifted and lowered his head in a nod. Then, I glanced to my right and almost jumped out of my skin. For an instant, I saw Gary's face. I flinched and clutched my fist to my chest as a gasp escaped my lips.

My eyes focused on the present and the man standing before me. "Luke, don't do that!" Would that feeling ever go away? Would I ever stop looking in the corners, bracing myself for the beating that may or may not come? My eyes grew large in realization that Luke had probably heard what I had said. Every . . . word. "How long have you been standing there?"

"I'm sorry. I didn't mean to eavesdrop. I just didn't want to interrupt." Luke propelled himself away from the wall with his right foot. "You know you didn't deserve to be treated that way. You have to know that."

"No. No, I don't know that." Why was he saying that? Why did he have to listen to everything I said? I didn't want him to know those parts of me.

Before I knew what was happening—before I could stop him—Luke's arms were swallowing me, drawing me close to him. An odd sense of safety washed over me. I inhaled and exhaled deeply. As I expelled years of pent-up emotions, the smell of his natural scent mixed with hay enveloped me, just as his arms had. I didn't mean to, but I was so overwhelmed.

Tears flooded down my cheeks like waterfalls. Tears for so many things. For the abandonment of my parents. For being a single mother. For Quinn and what she had been subjected to her entire life because of me. For the abuse I endured for far too long. I sank into Luke's embrace.

Once the tears subsided and my wits were restored, my eyes flew open. *What am I doing?* No. No. No. NO! I couldn't get lost in a false sense of security with another man. I wiggled out of Luke's embrace. The warmth escaped with his arms. A cold shiver spread throughout my body. I swiped the remnants of my tears from my cheeks.

"I'm sorry, Luke. I didn't mean for that to happen. I need to go." Every breath I had left in me fought to be free from the prison that was my lungs. I needed to be away from him. Even though the breeze was flowing through the stable, my lungs struggled for air. "Can you have Colt call me when he comes back with Quinn?"

"Su-sure."

I peered up at Luke briefly. I didn't want him to see what was brewing just beneath my surface. What I saw reflected in his eyes confused me. I expected to see pity or disgust. But I didn't see either of those things. I saw hurt, but I saw something else, too. Could it have been compassion or care? I wasn't sure. I had never experienced either of those before to know for sure.

I twirled on my heel and hurried as quickly as I possibly could out of the stable, and Luke didn't stop me. I was relieved yet disappointed. Where did that feeling come from? My breath returned only after I was safely behind the closed door of the cabin.

What is wrong with me? I don't need a man in my life. Not after Gary. I had to keep telling myself that. Never again would

65

I allow myself to be reliant on a man. I would stand on my own two feet. No matter what. Never again would I lose my heart. If I told myself that enough, I would eventually believe it, right?

Chapter 10

Luke

"Ugh!" I kicked out my foot, scooting it across the floor, leavin' a cloud of dust in its wake. "Why does she keep doin' that?"

I guess it was for the best. Emelia didn't need someone like me. That fact didn't make my heart hurt any less, though.

I scratched the back of my head and went to Majesty's stall. "Want to go for a ride, boy?" I slipped the saddle from the sawhorse and flopped it onto his back. I buckled the straps and walked him out of the stable. "Let's go see what Colt and Quinn are up to, shall we?"

Majesty was tamer since his arrival at the ranch than what I had seen in New York. But, then again, I had no idea what his life was like before I met him. Maybe in New York, he was stressed. I shrugged it off.

I lifted my right foot into the stirrup, grabbed the reins and Majesty's mane with my right hand, the horn of the saddle with my left, and hoisted myself into the saddle. I clicked my tongue on the roof of my mouth and squeezed my thighs to Majesty's sides. A grin spread across my face as the horse began to move. "Good boy, Majesty." I ran my hand down the side of his neck and patted him.

Since it was my first time ridin' Majesty, I wanted to take

it slow rather than push him. We needed to get to know each other—learn to be one instead of rider and horse. I started him out walking until we got further from the stable. I didn't want to push him too hard, at first, so I guided him into a trot. He trotted with ease. We rode in sync with each other. I pushed him a little harder into a gallop. The wind blew across my face. That was the part I loved about being on a horse. The fastness. The thrill of the ride.

When I brought Majesty back to a walk, my thoughts drifted back to the bus station in New York City. I had seen Majesty earlier that day and was on my way home. A homeless man was harassin' a woman and her child. I hadn't really wanted to get involved, but the look on her face was pure terror. I had to step in. Then, when I got onto the bus, her face went sheet white. I thought it was odd, but seein' the bruises, it made sense. Never in my life had I wanted to plunge my fist into a man's face as much as I did then. *Emelia*. I had no clue I'd see her again.

On the horizon, I saw Colt and Quinn approaching. "Wuke!" Quinn shouted as she and Colt trotted up to me on Beauty.

"Hey, Quinn. Did you have fun checkin' the fence?"

"Yeah! I even hewped fix it." Quinn's chin jutted with pride. "Cowt made us wunch, too. But I don't wanna go home yet." Her lip stuck out in a sulk.

"Well, if it's okay with Colt, you can ride with me on Majesty for a little bit." I should have hesitated since that was my first time ridin' Majesty. But that little girl had me wrapped around her finger, and I couldn't say no. Plus, she already had a helmet snug on her head and a protective vest on to keep her safe.

"Pwease, Cowt, can I?" Quinn turned her head up to him,

pouty lips in full force. I wasn't sure how anyone could say no to that face.

"I don't see why not. I'll let Emelia know so she doesn't worry."

"Okay." I moved Majesty closer, and he and Beauty touched noses. "Uh oh. Love connection?" I glanced over at Colt and chuckled.

"Maybe so." Colt helped Quinn to stand on Beauty's saddle. I stretched out my arms, and Quinn leaned into my hands. I wrapped my fingers under her armpits and lifted her up and over to sit in front of me.

"See ya both back at the house."

"See you, Cowt! Thank you," Quinn yelled after him as he and Beauty galloped away.

"So, how was riding Beauty?"

"It was so fun." Quinn glanced up at me as her eyes sparkled and her smile brightened. She stroked her hands over Majesty's mane and shoulders. I made sure to keep my grip firm so that she didn't fall off. Emelia would've never forgiven me if anythin' happened to Quinn, but Quinn was a natural on Majesty's back.

"How are ya likin' livin' here at the ranch?"

"I wuv it. I hope we never have to weave."

"Me, too, kiddo. Me, too. Do you miss home at all?" I was curious to know what her life was like before her arrival at the ranch.

Quinn lowered her head. Her shoulders rose and fell with a sigh. "Daddy Gary and Mommy fought aww the time. He scared me."

"I'm so sorry, sweetheart." I ran my hand down her arm.

Quinn's right shoulder lifted in a shrug. "I awways hid in my cwoset when they yewwed. Mommy hasn't yewwed once since we weft." She turned and peered up at me. Her eyes were glassy with tears.

My heart sank. What kind of life had she had? Seemed to have been no life at all for a little kid. I tried to lighten the mood. "Do you want to make him run a little?"

"Yes! Yes!" Quinn squealed and bounced up and down as if our conversation had never taken place.

I tapped the stirrups against Majesty's sides. I repeated the motion, and he moved into a canter. I didn't want him to go any faster because even though Quinn was trapped between my arms, I didn't want her to fall off.

Quinn burst into laughter. She flew her arms straight out to each side and let the wind breeze across her face and through her hair. I couldn't help but chuckle. She was such a wonderful child. I couldn't understand why no man had ever wanted to be her dad. I would have loved it. *Whoa! No need to have pipedreams there, Luke.* I shook my head to make those thoughts disappear.

I pulled on the reins to instruct Majesty to slow down to a walk so he could cool down before we got back to the stable. As the sun began to descend closer to the horizon, I knew we needed to get back. "We should get back to the stable so we can get some supper."

"Awww. Do we have to?" Once again, Quinn's bottom lip protruded from her mouth.

"We can come out another time. I promise."

"Pinky promise?" Quinn raised her little pinky.

"Pinky promise." I linked my pinky with hers, and she beamed up at me.

We rode back in silence. I realized in those moments I was completely smitten with the little girl. I just hoped one day her mother would be smitten with me. *No! Stop havin' those thoughts. Fallin' for you would be nothin' but trouble for Emelia.*

Due to the time, we tied Majesty to the hitchin' post outside Colt and Callie's house. I jumped to the ground and helped Quinn slide down from the saddle. I removed the helmet from her head. Before I could get both her arms out of the vest, she took off like a shot toward the house. My head shook as a chuckle escaped my lips. She musta been hungry. I hung the vest and helmet on the hitchin' post before making my own way to the kitchen.

I started up the steps, but Emelia comin' out the screen door from the kitchen stopped me in my tracks. Would she ever cease to make my breath catch in my throat? I flashed her a lopsided grin.

"I just wanted to say thank you for taking Quinn out longer. She's going a mile-a-minute in there." A small smile spread across Emelia's lips. She turned to go back inside. I started to follow her. Suddenly, she spun around and collided with my chest. "Oomph! I'm so sorry." Emelia splayed her hands across my chest and pushed herself away.

The warmth Emelia's hands emitted left with them. I didn't move; I only observed. I didn't want to say or do anythin' that would cause her to run away again. I seemed to be good at making her run.

"I also wanted to apologize for earlier," Emelia continued. "After what Gary did to me, I . . . well . . ." She motioned toward her neck and face. The bruises were yellowish brown. The physical marks would soon be gone, but the emotional scars would linger for quite some time. "I'd like for us to be friends." Emelia's eyes made their way to mine. Questions swirled in them.

The word "friend" was like a dagger to my heart. "I understand. I'd like us to be friends, too." I shoved my hands in my pockets. I wasn't sure how I was goin' to be just friends with her when my heart was already betrayin' me. Just bein' near her kicked up emotions in me like kickin' up a dust cloud. I knew it was safer for both of us. But it didn't mean I had to like it. "Well, have a good night, Emelia."

"Aren't you going to come in and eat?" Emelia asked, her thumb pointin' over her shoulder.

"I'm not so hungry anymore. Think I'm goin' to put Majesty in his stall and call it a night."

"Oh. Okay. Well, have a good evening." Emelia glanced at the ground before turnin' and disappearin' inside.

A heaviness weighed on my heart. I wasn't sure if it was because Emelia only wanted to be friends or because she looked so sad before leavin' me to stand alone on the porch. Would I always be alone? I left that in God's hands.

I took Majesty back to the stable and made sure he was restin' for the night. I gave him a pat. "Good night, boy." I hung the vest and helmet on the wall where they belonged before makin' my way back to my cabin.

I strode over to my truck, diggin' my keys out of my pocket and climbin' in. I didn't leave the ranch much. There was too much temptation out in the world. I loved life on the ranch. But, in that moment, bein' there had me feelin' suffocated. I had no idea why.

As I drove down the long dirt road to the entrance of the ranch, I rolled down the windows and cranked the radio. Clay Walker began to croon about a woman who caught his attention and how she could hypnotize the moon.

"I can relate, Clay Walker. Oh, how I can relate." I sighed deeply.

I pulled over to the side of the road. "God, what do I do? I know I need to be a better man before I can give my life to someone else. How do I do that? How do I get past the images that are constantly bombardin' me? The sounds that make me jump? I know I'm not as bad as I was when You found me, but I also know I still have so much farther to go. I know the last thing Emelia needs is another man who has . . . issues. Even if they are different ones."

I would never raise a hand to Emelia or Quinn, though. Tears trickled down my face. I was alone, but I still swiped them away as quickly as I could. I pressed my palms into my eyes.

I screamed as loud as I possibly could. I was out in the middle of nowhere, so I knew it wouldn't bother anyone. I had to do somethin' to get my frustration out. I couldn't do what I had always done before. But I had never been a fan of therapists or counselors or whatever they were called. I just couldn't understand why anyone would want to blab their entire life story to someone they didn't even know—to trust someone with their innermost thoughts and feelin's.

But maybe it was time.

A picture of Emelia floated through my mind. I really wanted to tell her those things, but, again, she had enough troubles of her own. She didn't need to try to help me tackle mine.

My stomach rumbled. "Okay. Okay. Enough self-loathin'."

Food was next on my agenda, it seemed. I drove to one of the town's drive-throughs and ordered a burger, fries, and a drink. Typically, I would have gone to have a seat at the bistro, but I didn't want to be around people. I was enjoyin' my solitude for the time bein'.

I parked my truck in town and traipsed down to my favorite spot on the bay. A picnic table sat nestled between two trees, right at the water's edge. The sound of the water lappin' against the rocks and the scent, which was hard for me to put into words—maybe somewhere between fish and moss?—enveloped me like a hug from God. I ate my supper in silence, enjoyin' the sounds of nature. Birds chirpin'. Trees rustlin' in the breeze.

Peace.

"Well, I guess we'll just have to be friends and see what happens," I whispered so only God could hear. I glanced up to the heavens. "I'm leavin' it in Your hands, Father. Whatever Your plans are for our lives, I'll accept and honor You." I stood from my perch at the picnic table, threw my trash into the nearest can, and sauntered back to my truck.

"Hey, Luke," a female voice greeted me from behind.

My eyes closed as I sighed. My head fell back. I didn't want to talk to anyone, but bein' rude wasn't in my DNA.

I turned on my heel. Standin' before me was Alexis Miller. "Oh, hey, Alex. What's up?" I had met her when I first got to town. We'd had a fling. It wasn't long after that I met God.

"Nothin' much. Haven't seen ya around for a long time. Just saw ya truck and wanted to say hi." Alexis's smile said she wanted more than that. And once upon a time, I would have welcomed it. But it wasn't who I was anymore.

"Well, hi. Sorry. I really gotta get back to the ranch." I fiddled with my keys.

"Hope to see ya around sometime." Alexis waved in that flirtatious way. I'd seen it so many times. Hand next to her face, and her fingers wigglin' back and forth. I couldn't get out of there fast enough.

I scurried to my truck and only took a breath once the door was closed and the truck was runnin'. Situations like that were one of the main reasons I didn't leave the ranch. I sped home without worryin' about bein' pulled over.

Most guys would have loved to take a girl like Alexis home for the night. I used to be one of them. With her pearly white smile, beauty queen looks, short shorts, and low-cut tops. But bein' a follower of Christ meant I had to give up things that didn't bring glory to God. He never promised that a life following Him would be easy, but He did promise His hope, strength, truth, and never-ending love. And those things were more important to me than one night with Alexis or any woman for that matter.

Once I parked in front of my cabin, I exhaled deeply as I turned off the ignition. I sat there for a few minutes longer with my head back against the headrest and my eyes closed.

Don't be afraid. Just believe.

I hadn't heard God speak directly to me for a while. Then again, I hadn't been prayin' all that much either. *Thank you, Lord.* With that, I opened the door and slid out until my feet touched the ground.

"Hey, Luke. You were missed at dinner." At the sound of her voice, goosebumps ran up my arms. I closed my eyes. As much as I liked Emelia, I just wanted to go inside and go to bed.

Talk to her.

Okay. Okay. I will. I turned. "Just needed some time to myself to clear my head."

"Oh. Okay. I'll leave you to your evening then." Emelia twisted her hands together and started to turn back around.

Even though Emelia was facing the other direction, I stretched my arm out to stop her. "Would you like to sit outside and talk for a bit?"

"Sure. I'd like that." Emelia turned enough for me to see her face in the light of the setting sun.

Emelia and I meandered over to her cabin and sat in the rockin' chairs on the porch. One of my favorite things about the cabins was the rockin' chairs.

"What do you want to talk about?" Emelia glanced over at me before gazin' down at the ground. Was she as nervous as I was? I had no idea why bein' next to her always made me unsure of myself.

"I dunno." I shrugged. "Anythin'. Everythin'. How's Quinn?"

"She's great. She's already asleep. She couldn't stop talking about her horse rides with you and Colt. She loved every minute of them. I've never seen her so happy."

"Good. I'm glad. I enjoyed it myself." I felt the goofy grin form on my lips.

"Can I ask you a serious question?" Emelia peered over at me, this time not divertin' her eyes.

I locked eyes with her. "Sure. Ask away."

"I know that Callie and Colt are, but are you a Christian, too?" Emelia twisted her hands in her lap.

"Yes, I am. I haven't always been, though. I've done a lot of things in my life that didn't honor or glorify God." I paused to see if I should go further. No one knew a lot about what had happened in my adult life up to that point. Somethin', though, was pushing me to tell Emelia my story to know if I could trust her—trust her with all of my heart. *Where did that come from?* She obviously didn't need or want that. I wanted to stand and go to my cabin, but it was as if I was cemented to the chair.

"What kinds of things?" Emelia asked, almost in a whisper.

"Well, after I was deemed unfit for duty, I was, once again, a civilian. I went back to Oklahoma after I received my discharge. Adjusting back to that life was rough—still is sometimes. I began to drink to drown out the nightmares and physical pain in my leg. The alcohol stopped bein' enough, so it led to more drinkin' and then . . . bein' intimate with women. I've had more than I care to admit. One night, I was at the bar inside a restaurant. I don't really remember what happened. I guess I had hit on a married woman, and her husband was tryin' to fight me. That's what I was told anyway." It seemed that once I opened my mouth, words spewed, and I couldn't seem to stop myself.

"Oh, Luke, I'm so sorry." Emelia's voice cracked as her hand covered mine. Heat radiated from her skin.

I couldn't look in Emelia's direction. I was surprised. I didn't hear pity in her voice. It was compassion—empathy even. But I forced myself to glance at her just in time to catch her gaze. My heart fluttered. I had no idea what that meant. But I liked it.

I stared at my hands as I picked at a loose piece of skin on my left palm. I inhaled and exhaled deeply. "Next thing I knew, I was bein' dragged outside by a man," I continued. "He asked me about my situation. He told me he had a place for me to go to get my life right if I wanted to. That man was Colt, and that place was here. Over the course of time, Colt told me about a God who loved me right where I was. A God that didn't care about what I had done in the past, as long as I asked for forgiveness. He only cared about my future."

I breathed in deep and exhaled before I continued. "I accepted Christ as my personal Lord and Savior not long after that. I haven't been the same man since. I haven't had a lick of alcohol, and I've maintained abstinence. I still have my battles with pain and nightmares, but I trust God has a plan, and I do what I have to do to push through. Some days are easy. Some days are hard. Today has been one of the hard days. Although I have to admit that havin' that ride with Quinn helped." I tilted my head and looked over at Emelia.

"So, God forgave you for everything you've ever done?" Her gaze locked on mine.

"Yes. God's forgiveness and grace are for everyone. You just have to ask for it and receive it." What else was there to say? God had forgiven me. He continued to do so whenever I'd made a mistake and asked for it.

"Wow," Emelia whispered. "I went to church my whole childhood and never knew you could have something like that with God. We were only told about God's condemnation and God's wrath if we ever did anything wrong."

"Emelia?" My eyes lifted to hers once more. My voice broke as I spoke, "I *do* want us to be friends. I could really use one. I think you could use one, too." I stood and ran my hands down my pant legs. "I'm sorry I overtook the conversation, but I appreciate ya listenin'. My heart somehow feels lighter."

As my foot hit the bottom step, I was, once again, flailing my arms up over my head and praying I didn't fall flat on my face. It didn't take long for my balance to be restored. My cheeks burned like a flaming hot fire as I peered over at Emelia. Her hands covered her mouth, but I could see the laughter in her eyes. It gave them a whole other dimension. The sparkle made them even more beautiful.

"Are you okay?" She giggled.

I guffawed. "Yeah. I'm okay. I'll get that step fixed tomorrow."

"Okay. And Luke?"

"Yeah?" I turned my head to face her again.

"I hope you have the sweetest of dreams tonight."

"Thank you. I hope you do, too." I turned back toward my cabin and put one foot carefully in front of the other, hoping beyond all hope I didn't lose my footin' again.

Once I was behind the closed door, I exhaled deeply. "Nice one, Luke." I sighed and rolled my eyes. *Good thing she just wants to be friends.* I propelled myself off the door, changed into my pajama pants, and slid into bed. "Lord, please hear Emelia's request. Please let us both have the sweetest of dreams. Amen." I rolled over and allowed the darkness to overtake me. *Just don't let the nightmares come with it.*

* * *

I woke up to my alarm blaring John Michael Montgomery's "Kick It Up." I had a thing for 90s country. I slapped the alarm off. *Too early in the mornin' for that, John. Too early.*

After changing into my clothes, I wiped the sleep from my eyes before they widened. *Wait! No Nightmares? YES!* I jabbed my fists into the air. Hopefully, it was the first night of many. I jumped out of bed with the brightest smile spread across my face. I couldn't wait to tell Majesty. No, scratch that. I couldn't wait to tell *Emelia*.

I slid my feet into my boots and hustled out the door. Couldn't be late for breakfast. I planted my feet on the porch and breathed in deep. A slow grin crept onto my face. It was a beautiful mornin' already. The sun was just comin' up over the horizon, dancin' in a sky of blue, orange, and red. The grass glistened as the light hit the mornin' dew. I started my trek down to the main house.

"Wuke! Wuke! Wait!" Quinn hollered.

I turned just as Quinn's little body collided with my legs. "Hey, Quinnie!" *Not sure where that nickname came from.* I shrugged. "How are ya this mornin'?" I plucked her off the ground and swung her around before bringin' her in for a hug.

"Wuke, that's too tight." Quinn squirmed. I set her on her feet, and she took off running toward the house.

I turned and found Emelia watchin' me. My cheeks flamed. I cleared my throat. "Hey, Emelia."

"Morning, Luke. How are you?"

"I'm wonderful. No nightmares last night." My chest puffed out.

"Really? None? That's amazing news."

I was taken by surprise when Emelia's arms wrapped around me. I did the same to her. It was in that moment I knew she belonged right there. She pulled away much more quickly than I had wanted, though.

"Ready for some breakfast?" Emelia asked.

"I'm always ready for food." I laughed heartily, probably for the first time in months. Years, maybe.

"Wuke! Mommy! Are ya coming?" Quinn yelled at the top of her lungs from the bottom of the hill.

"We'll be right there! Wait for us!" Emelia shouted down to her.

I kept my walk slow so I could savor the moments with Emelia.

"Finawwy! You took forever." Quinn rolled her eyes as we approached where she stood from her seat on an old tree stump.

I couldn't contain the chuckle that bubbled up and out from my lips. Emelia lightly smacked the back of her hand against my stomach. A slight smile threatened her lips. "Please don't encourage her, Luke."

"Oomph! Sorry." I lowered my head in mock shame.

"You almost made *me* laugh." Emelia tried to stifle her giggle but was unsuccessful.

It wasn't just any giggle, though. It was one that could brighten the darkest of spaces. It brightened the darkest crevices of my heart, anyway—places I never thought would see the light of day again. Yes, it was going to be a great day—one of the best days. I just knew it.

Once we were on the porch, I grabbed the door that was already slammin' shut from Quinn barrelin' through. "After you." I pulled the door all the way open and swept my hand in front of me to usher Emelia into the kitchen.

The men were already seated, with Callie and Colt at the head of the table. Richard was bustlin' about placin' the food on the table.

"Mommy, Caitwyn came to see me." Quinn bounced excitedly.

"Hi, Caitlyn. So nice to see you again. How are you?" Emelia greeted.

"I'm great. Thank you. I wanted to see if Quinn could come with me to my dance class this mornin'."

"Pwease, Mommy. Pwease?" Quinn peered up at her mom with sad, puppy-dog eyes, a pouty lip, and hands folded under her chin.

"H-How much is it?" Emelia asked softly, as if she didn't want anyone but Caitlyn to hear.

"Oh, it's no charge. She'd be my guest. I'd love to have her in my class." Caitlyn did her best to mimic Quinn.

"Well, how can I say no to those faces?" Emelia threw her hands in the air and let them smack against her legs.

"Yay!" Quinn and Caitlyn shouted at the same time before givin' each other a high five.

"Does she need any special clothes or anything?"

"Nope." Caitlyn grinned. "I've got that covered, too."

I glanced over at Emelia. A smile crinkled her mouth, and her eyes glassed over with tears. "What time is class?" she asked.

"Right after breakfast." Caitlyn turned her attention to the table with the large stack of pancakes. Her eyes grew wide as she licked her lips. Laughter erupted around the room. It was a sound I would never get tired of hearin'.

Chapter 11

Gary

My phone rang, startling me out of my drunken stupor. I swiped it from the glass coffee table. "Hello?" The word slurred from my lips.

"Hey, Gary. I found her," Wayne informed me, almost cackling with excitement.

"Who?" My head was in a haze.

"Emelia."

"Right." My eyes grew wide. "Right!"

I sat up straight on the couch. The phone slipped from my hands. I fumbled to catch it before it hit the floor. When I had it securely in my hand, I brought it back to my ear.

"Hello? Gary? You still there?"

"Yeah, I'm here." I cleared my throat, which suddenly was as dry as a desert.

"Did you hear what I said?"

"No. I dropped the phone." My fist tightened as it rested on my thigh. "Where is she?"

"She's in a town called Edenton, North Carolina."

My breath caught in my throat. "Thanks." I hit end. I didn't need to hear anything else Wayne had to say. Most of the time, I wanted to hit Wayne about as much as I wanted to punch Emelia at that very moment. How dare she think she could leave me and there'd be no consequences. She'd learn, though. Oh, how she'd learn.

I stood and shoved my phone into my pocket. Time for a little road trip. First, to sober up a bit. Cold shower would do the trick.

Once I was done in the shower, I threw on some clothes and packed a bag. I slid into my old silver beater of a Camaro, pulled up directions to Edenton on my GPS, and headed down the road. I had plenty of time to concoct plans to mess with Emelia's head before dragging her back home. I chuckled. I could easily just find her and kill her, but I wanted her to know I was lurking and that at any time, I could attack. I liked making things squirm, especially her. I liked the feeling of my fist connecting with her face. *This is going to be fun.*

I stopped overnight at a hotel along the highway so I could spend the whole next day searching for Emelia. When I looked up Edenton online from my room, I decided it shouldn't be that hard to find her in a town so small.

* * *

The next morning, when I got into town, I drove down the main street. *Where to start?* I saw a place called C'est La Vie Bistro just as my stomach growled. Well, breakfast was as good a place to start as any. I parked the car and sauntered inside.

"Have a seat anywhere ya like. I'll be right with ya," the lanky waitress with long light-brown hair and light-brown eyes greeted before she flitted away, her hands carefully balancing a tray full of food.

I slid into a booth and opened the menu. I glanced around the small bistro, hoping to catch a glimpse of Emelia so I could leave the Podunk town without any real effort. *No such luck.*

People were in conversation and laughing. *What are they all so happy about? Bright-colored walls are enough to make me puke. However, the food smells delicious.* My stomach rumbled.

"What can I getcha?" the waitress, who's name tag read *Olivia*, asked a few minutes later.

"I'll have the pancake special." I pointed at the menu.

"Bacon or sausage?"

"Bacon."

"Toast or biscuit?"

"Toast." I sighed deeply.

"White or wheat?"

"White, and can I get some strawberry jam?" Her questions started to grind on my nerves. I did my best to temper my anger. She wouldn't give me any information I wanted if I was rude. People never did.

Once Olivia brought my plate and placed it in front of me, I devoured the food. My appetite was insatiable. I couldn't get enough. It would have to do, though. I knew the only thing that could satisfy my appetite would be to find Emelia.

"Excuse me." I placed my hand on Olivia's forearm as she was withdrawing it from my receipt. "Have you seen this woman?" I turned my phone so she could look at the picture.

Olivia turned her head back to glance at my phone. "Sure. I think I've seen her before. I think she's at Redemption Ranch." She scurried away to wait on more customers vying for her attention.

Just the way I liked it. People who were too busy to pay attention to the details. She'd never remember she talked to me specifically. A smirk appeared across my face. I left enough cash to pay my bill and strode out the door. I googled Redemption Ranch and tapped the "get directions" button. I sped in the direction my phone told me to go.

As the ranch came into view, I slowed to the speed limit. I didn't want to drive too fast or too slow. No need to draw attention to myself in case anyone was outside—too soon for that. I wanted Emelia to know I was lurking but wanted her to look like she was going crazy. Maybe she would think she was going crazy, too.

The wheels in my head churned out ideas like spinning in gravel. I had the rest of the afternoon to devise my first plan. I clapped my hands and rubbed them together. *Oh, Emelia! You're going to regret the day you left me.*

Chapter 12

Caitlyn

"**A**re you ready to go, Quinnie Bear?" I asked as Quinn and I walked toward the door of the cabin.

"Who's Quinnie Bear?" she asked, her nose scrunched in confusion.

"You are, silly. I wanted a nickname for ya. How do ya like it?"

"I wuv it!" Quinn exclaimed before wrapping her arms around my waist. "I've never had a nickname before. Wuke cawwed me Quinnie a wittwe bit ago, though," she continued as she climbed into the back seat of my car and buckled her seat belt across her booster seat.

I couldn't help the grin that formed on my lips as I shut the door. Quinn was definitely something special. It was only the third time I had spent time with her since she first came to the ranch, but she crept into my heart quickly. I had signed up to teach another dance class, same as the day before. I decided to invite Quinn again. I wanted to be like her big sister. I had always wanted a little sister, but I got a brother instead.

"After class, we can go to the café for lunch. Would you like that?" I asked as I slid into the driver's seat and buckled my own seat belt.

"Yes!"

A soft giggle escaped my lips. "Great. We'll do that, then. I can introduce you to my mom and brother. My mom and dad own the café."

Quinn's eyes grew larger. "The whowe thing?"

"Yep." I peered at her through the rearview mirror.

"Wow!"

Quinn's awestruck wonder amazed me. When, as we got older, did we lose that sense of wonder? I hoped spending more time with Quinn would help me get some of it back.

I pulled into the parking space in front of the dance studio. "Are you ready to dance?" I glanced back at Quinn.

"Yes!" Quinn squealed with her hands in the air. Her excitement about everything left me wondering exactly what her life had been like before.

I stood from the car and opened the door for Quinn. Her tongue protruded from her lips as she reached for her buckle. She slid down from the seat, and we glided through the door of Dance City Studios. "My class today is on the left."

Quinn turned the knob and pried the door open. Already, the room was filled with the laughter of little girls excited to learn dance. As much as I dreamed of being a nurse, dance was something I would've loved to teach all the time.

"Mornin', girls. Quinn, here are some more dance clothes for you. You can change right through that door over there." I extended my arm to point to the door at the far end of the room.

"Thank you." Quinn scurried off to change her clothes. When she returned with her leotard inside out, I covered my giggle with my fingers.

"Quinn, honey," I whispered. "You've got this on inside out. Let me help you." We hurried back into the changing room. Once Quinn's outfit was on correctly, we joined the class again.

I addressed the class. "Girls, for those of you who weren't here yesterday, we have a new dancer with us. Her name is Quinn."

"Hi, Quinn," everyone greeted at once.

Quinn's cheeks became rosy as she held her hand up in a wave. She didn't say a word. I hoped the girls would make her feel comfortable and welcomed again.

"Who wants to learn some Hip Hop dance moves?" I asked.

"We do!" several girls responded in unison.

"Are y'all ready to get started?"

"Yeah!" they all shouted, again in unison.

Quinn stood rooted in place. One of the girls from the day before, Lainey, took her by the hand. "Quinn, you can dance by me."

"Thank you, Lainey," I said. She was a sweet girl, and I was so proud that she took the lead in welcoming Quinn back to the class.

I turned on the music and stood at the front of the class, facing the mirror. "Ready? So, our first move will be to stand and put your hands to your right, like this." I put my arms out with my hands straight up and down. "We're gonna slide our left foot to the left, and as we slide our foot, we're goin' to look to the right, at our hands. Also, as you step to the left, you'll slide your right foot over. Let's give it a try." I twirled and faced them. "One, two, three, four. That's great, everyone."

None of them got all of the steps correct, but my class was about having fun with dance, not perfection. I wanted my students to love dance as much as I did. If I harped on them, at four and five years old, to get things right each and every time, they might have ended up hating dance. And if that happened, what kind of teacher would I have been?

"Let's try the next set." I spun around and faced the mirror. "We are gonna do just the opposite. So, swing your hands around to your left. With your right foot, you'll step to the side and slide your left foot over." I continued to demonstrate the steps for them. "Are we ready to try all of the steps together?" I asked, facing them once more.

Some of the girls nodded while others glanced around the room, fear dancing in their eyes. "Let's just give it a try, okay? It's not about perfection. It's about trying your best and having run, right?"

The girls nodded.

I turned on my heel back to the mirror. "Ready? One, two, three, four, five, and six." Quinn and Lainey, along with Emma and Grace, all collided at once. Arms and legs flew in every direction. "Oh no! Are you—" Bursts of laughter erupted. I placed my hand over my heart. *They're okay.*

We continued to work on the steps for the rest of the hour. Each time we went through them, the girls performed better and better. Their excitement bubbled up and out every time we finished. It was contagious as I got excited for them, too. Quinn was a natural. Her huge, bright smile told me I had made the best decision to invite her. I hoped she would stick with it after I left for school.

"Are you ready to go get some lunch?" I asked Quinn after we had changed back into our street clothes. I checked my blood sugar while I was changing. I had one of those monitors attached to my arm. Because I was just active and hadn't had a snack, I knew my blood sugar was low before my monitor told me. I knew I needed to eat as soon as I could.

"Yep." Quinn glanced up at me before grabbing my hand.

Warmth spread through my chest as Quinn held tight to my

hand. I wasn't sure what was happening, but as my grandmother would always say, "My cup runneth over."

"Let's go, then. I'm excited for you to meet some of my family."

The studio was right down the street from the café, so Quinn and I skipped down Broad Street. As we approached the café, the aroma of pastries and coffee floated through the air. I inhaled deeply. I would miss those scents when I left for college.

I was scheduled to move into my dorm room in August. *Two short months.* I had been accepted into the nursing program at Indiana University in Bloomington, Indiana. It was the only school I had wanted to go to, so I was super excited when I received my acceptance letter. My parents, though, not so much. They worried about my Diabetes. I knew I could handle it on my own, but I understood why they would be concerned since Indiana was so far away.

The bells on the door jingled and knocked me back to the present. "Hey, Dyl," I greeted my younger brother. He was two years younger than me, but he had towered over me since he was eleven. I attempted to ruffle his light-brown hair he wore in a mullet as he leaned on the front counter, but he suddenly stood, so I couldn't reach.

"Hey, Sis." Dyl grinned back at me. Then, he motioned toward Quinn. "Who's this?"

"Dyl, this is my friend, Quinn. Quinn, this is my brother, Dylan. Everyone calls him Dyl."

"Hey, Quinn. Nice to meet ya."

"Hi, Dyw." Quinn flashed her pearly white baby teeth.

"Is Mom here, Dyl?"

"Yeah, she's in the kitchen." Dyl nodded to the right.

"Great." I grabbed Quinn's hand and led her back to the

kitchen. "Hey, Mom."

My mom turned from the oven and put the mitts on the big island in the middle of the room. "Oh, hey, Sis." My entire family called me Sis more than they called me by my name. "How was class? This must be Quinn, who I've heard so much about." Mom opened her arms toward Quinn.

"Yeah. Quinn, this is my mom, Marci."

"Hi, Mrs. Marci." Quinn fell into Mom's embrace.

"How did you like dance class?"

"It was awesome!" Quinn extended both arms over her head. Her little hands made fists before she lowered them to rub her belly in a circular motion. "It made me *so* hungry."

"Well, let's get you something to eat, then. What would you like?" Mom put one hand on her hip and leaned the other on the island.

"What do you have?" Quinn glanced up, her brow furrowing in question.

"Well, we have grilled cheese and french fries. Or hot dogs."

"Griwwed cheese and french fries, pwease." Quinn beamed up at Mom.

"Comin' right up. Why don't you girls go have a seat, and I'll bring it out to ya."

"What about me?" I asked in a whiny tone.

"I already know what you want." Mom threw a towel at me.

I giggled as Quinn and I left the kitchen. But then, a wave of sadness washed over me. I was really going to miss those moments with my mom and brother.

Quinn and I sat at a table, and she stared at the wall. It was my favorite wall anywhere. Joshua Chapter One, Verse Nine was written on it. It was one of my top three Bible verses. It was why the café was called Courageous Café and Bakery.

"What does that say?" Quinn pointed to the wall.

"It says, 'This is my command. Be strong and courageous. Do not be afraid or discouraged. For the Lord your God is with you wherever you go.'"

Quinn peered up at me. "What does it mean?"

"Well, it means that God wants us to be strong and brave, especially when bad things happen, and to also remember that when we *are* afraid, we can be strong and courageous *because* God is *always* with us. No matter where we are."

"Oh," Quinn replied. I could see her mind trying to work through all of that.

Mom set our plates in front of us. "Enjoy."

"Thanks, Mom." I grinned up at her. She put her hand on my shoulder and gave it a gentle squeeze.

"Thank you." Quinn smiled as she plucked a fry from her plate and took a bite.

"You're most welcome."

I said a silent prayer, thanking God for the food, for my family, for my newest friend, and for the day. Quinn didn't talk much while we ate. Her eyes darted from her plate to the wall more times than I could count. Did she believe in God? Had she accepted Jesus as her personal Lord and Savior? I had no idea. A conversation for another time.

Chapter 13

Luke

As I mucked out Majesty's stall, my mind wandered to thoughts of the woman who was stayin' in the cabin that was across from mine. Those thoughts had taken up permanent residence since her arrival at the ranch almost a month before. As my ringtone bellowed, I pulled my cell phone from my back pocket. "Hello?"

"Luke . . . help . . . someone . . ." Emelia stuttered, her words riddled with fear.

"I'm comin'. Where are ya?"

"Cabin."

"Stay inside. I'm at the stable. I'll be right there." I bolted out to my truck as I hung up with Emelia and hurriedly punched in Colt's number.

"Colt, meet me at Emelia's cabin. Somethin's wrong," I barked into the phone.

"What's goin' on?"

"I don't know, but she's scared. I'm on my way there now."

"I'm on my way, too."

I hit end and tossed my phone on the passenger seat. I peeled my truck out on the gravel outside the stable and sped up the dirt road to the cabins. I slammed the truck into park in front of Emelia's cabin and jumped out before it even stopped movin'.

"Emelia!" I rushed through the door. I listened. Nothin'.

I headed to the back of the cabin. As I got closer to the back bedroom, I heard whimperin'. My heart leaped from my chest and into my throat. I glanced down at Emelia, crumpled on the floor below the window. "Emelia, what happened?" I sat next to her, examinin' her for wounds. Air filled my lungs but didn't reach my mouth. "Are you hurt?" When I saw no visible injuries, my heart slowed, and I enveloped Emelia in my arms. My breath finally expelled from my body.

"I saw . . . someone . . . across . . . the road in the trees." Emelia's body shook. I ran my hand up and down her arm in an effort to comfort her.

"Are you sure it wasn't an animal?"

"I'm sure." Emelia burrowed her face into my chest. I loved the feel of her in my arms but hated the reason for it.

"Luke! Emelia!" Colt shouted from the front door.

"Colt, back here."

Colt entered the bedroom. "What's goin' on?" His eyes were filled with concern as he focused on Emelia.

"She said she saw someone across the road, in the trees. Can you go take a look?"

"Absolutely." Colt quickly disappeared from the doorway.

"Do you want to move to the couch in the living room?" I asked softly.

Emelia only nodded in response. Her body still physically shook but not quite as much as when I first arrived. I held out my hands to help her stand. "Do you want some tea or somethin'?"

"I'll take some warm milk," Emelia mumbled, her voice barely audible.

"Okay." I fumbled toward the kitchen and looked for a

cup. I carefully poured the milk and slid it into the microwave. "Here you go, sweetie," I said as I handed the cup to Emelia. I don't know where that term of endearment came from, but I mentally shrugged it off and sat next to her on the couch. I didn't want to do or say anythin' she didn't want, so I just sat with her. My hands twisted in my lap. I just wanted her to know I was there for her.

About twenty minutes later, Colt knocked on the door before enterin'. "Did ya see anythin'?" I asked him as I sat up and rested my elbows on my knees.

"Some of the foliage was disturbed. I found a Marlboro cigarette butt and a crushed Michelob can, but I didn't see anyone. I searched in all directions, but whoever was there left." Colt's shoulders lifted and lowered in a shrug.

The cup slipped from Emelia's hands and crashed to the floor.

"What is it?" I inquired.

"Gary." She swallowed hard. "He smokes Marlboro . . . and drinks Michelob." Emelia's face was sheet white.

Colt looked at me, concern filling his eyes once again. "We'll have to keep an eye out, then," he said. "But hopefully, it's just a coincidence. Maybe it's just some kid with his dad's beer and smokes."

"Yeah." Emelia's chin hit her chest. "Maybe you're right. Thank you for coming."

"You're safe here, Emelia," Colt reassured her. "We'll make sure of it." He sat on the coffee table directly in front of Emelia and placed his hand on her arm. "Ya'll gonna be okay? I have a few things I need to finish up before supper. Or do ya need me to stay here and stand guard?"

"No. No need to stand guard," I assured Colt. "We'll be fine. Thanks for ya help."

"No problem. If ya need anythin' else, let me know." Colt walked to the door and grabbed the doorknob.

"Will do."

With that, he opened the door and left.

"We should call the cops," I suggested. I dug my phone out of my pocket.

"No." Emelia placed her hand on my arm. "It won't do any good. They won't do anything."

"What do ya mean?" I swiveled to face her.

"I've called them before. If there aren't any bruises or there isn't any proof, they can't do anything." Emelia inhaled and exhaled deeply. "And it just makes things worse."

"Well, I'm gonna camp out on your couch, then."

"You don't have to do that."

"Emelia." I placed my hands on her shoulders. "Look, I know you're tryin' to get through a man controllin' ya, and I don't want to be another one of those guys. It would just make me feel better to know you and Quinn are safe. You'd be doin' me a favor. Really." I covered my heart with my hand.

"Fine." Emelia sighed and lifted her shoulders in a shrug.

"That's settled then." *Glad she didn't put up much of a fight.* "I'll be back in a little bit. Will you be okay until then? I just need to get Majesty in his stall and settled for the evenin'. Or would you like to come with me? Then, after, we can get some supper at the house."

"I think I've had enough alone time for now. I'll come with you. Caitlyn should be dropping Quinn off soon."

Good. I didn't really want to leave her there by herself. I knew, though, if I insisted she go with me, I would've said the wrong thing.

97

Chapter 14

Luke

Over the next few weeks, Emelia stuck to me like glue. I can't say that I minded it at all. It was nice gettin' to know her even more just by the little things we did together. I helped with Quinn, and they both helped with chores. Quinn was never without one of us or Caitlyn close by.

It was the Fourth of July. It used to be one of my favorite holidays as a kid, but after the Corps, it was a nightmare. Every firework was like a bomb goin' off in my mind, taking me back to combat. That year, though, I had Quinn and Emelia. I wanted to do my best to push through for them. I was excited to spend time with Emelia and Quinn and to see the fireworks through Quinn's eyes.

"Wuke!" Quinn exclaimed, jumpin' into my arms.

"Hey, Quinnie!" I twirled her around. "How's my favorite girl?"

Quinn squealed with laughter. "I'm good."

"Are you ready for the festival and fireworks?"

"Yeah!" Quinn turned in my arms to glance in Emelia's direction. "Mommy, Caitwyn asked if she couwd take me to the festivaw."

"Are you sure you want to go?" Emelia asked.

Quinn nodded.

"Okay, I'll give her a call."

I set Quinn down on the ground. "So, does this mean you're my only date for the festival, Em?" I bumped her shoulder with my own. A lopsided grin spread across my face as Emelia's cheeks turned crimson. "Is it okay if I call ya Em?"

Emelia lowered her head as a slight smile formed on her lips and nodded. "I suppose it does."

"I'll see ya later, then."

"Yes, you will. I told Callie I'd help her around the house today. But I guess I'd better call Caitlyn first."

"I look forward to seein' ya later." I wanted to kiss her so much.

Patience, My son.

I know. Thank you, Lord. I was gettin' used to hearin' God's voice again.

I walked back into the paddock and continued workin' with Majesty. My heart did a pitter-patter as I thought about Em. She truly was one of the most amazin' women I had ever met.

After I finished workin' with my horse and put him back in his stall, I headed to the main house in search of Colt. As I approached the house, Colt and Callie were sittin' on the porch in conversation. I needed to talk to someone, and I wasn't quite ready for therapy. With Em and Quinn around, I needed to be better or at least headed in that direction. I had no idea if I'd ever be back to the way I was before I went to war, but as long as I was workin' toward it, I knew I'd never go back to the way I was when I came back. That much I knew for sure.

"Hey, Colt. Hey, Callie." I waved as my foot hit the top step.

"I'll leave you boys to chat." Callie rose from her rockin' chair and skirted inside.

"How does she always know?" I asked.

"Know what?"

"When one of us needs to talk."

Colt shrugged. "That's just Callie. What's up? How are ya?" Colt motioned for me to sit.

"I'm doin' okay. Just wanted to talk somethin' out since today is the Fourth and all."

"We were just fixin' to go to the festival. You goin'?"

I ran my sweaty palms down my legs. "Well, yeah. I kinda have a date with Em. Not a real one, but we are goin' to the festival together and then to the fireworks." I sighed heavily. *Fireworks.* "The fireworks were what I wanted to talk to you about. I know they usually cause an episode. What can I do? I mean, to help me through the fireworks without lookin' like an idiot in front of Em and Quinn?"

"Well, the only thing you *can* do is breathe through it. Stay in the present as best ya can, and just ask God to guide you through it." Colt paused to glance at me. "And remember to breathe."

I inhaled and exhaled deeply. I smacked my hands on my knees before risin' from my seat. "Okay. I will give it my best shot. We shall see how this goes." My cheeks puffed up as I blew the air out of my mouth.

"Great." Colt chuckled. "We'll see ya there. If not, we'll see ya at the beach later."

I headed back to my cabin to get cleaned up for Em. *Oh, how I wish this was a real date.* I wanted to hold her hand as we strolled around the festival and wrap my arm around her as we gazed up at the fireworks. I would just have to be content with what she was offerin'. I would've rather had her as a friend than not have her in my life at all.

Chapter 15

Caitlyn

I arrived at Redemption Ranch to pick up Quinn. I also wanted to ask Wyatt Glover if he wanted to join us. Wyatt had been my best friend since he arrived in Edenton when he was sixteen. He was just a year older than me. I moseyed over to his cabin and rapped my knuckles on his door.

"Hey, Caitlyn. What're ya doin' here?" Wyatt's smile warmed my heart. It always had.

"Hey, Wyatt. I came to see if you wanted to join Quinn and me at the festival."

"I'd love to." Wyatt stepped out onto the small porch beside me and pulled the door shut.

"I'm on my way to get Quinn." I motioned toward her cabin with my thumb over my shoulder.

"Great. Let's go." We stepped off Wyatt's porch and started toward Quinn and Emelia's cabin.

"Caitwyn!" Quinn hollered as she ran out the front door.

"Hey, Quinnie Bear," I greeted as she fell into my arms.

"I'm so excited for the festivaw," Quinn told me, bouncing up and down. She glanced around me. "Is Wyatt coming with us?"

"He's agreed to be our date. Is that okay?" I was suddenly worried she would be upset. I didn't want to ruin her first

Fourth Festival.

"Yay!" Quinn grabbed our hands in each of hers. "Wet's go!"

"Wait. Did you remember your swimsuit? We're all going swimming later."

Quinn lowered her head. "I don't know how to swim." Her voice was so soft I barely heard her.

"I can teach you," I reassured her as I squeezed her hand.

"Reawwy?" Her bulging eyes met mine.

I giggled. "Of course, I will."

"Pinky promise?" Quinn lifted her pinky.

"Pinky promise." I hooked my pinky around hers.

"Okay!" Quinn ran back inside and returned a few minutes later with her swimsuit and towel. "Wike my new towew?" She held it up and smiled proudly at the mermaid with a bright multicolored tail. "My swimsuit matches. Just wike a mermaid!"

"I can't wait to see you in it."

We all crowded into Wyatt's truck with Quinn in the middle in her booster seat. By the time we arrived at the festival, it was in full swing.

"Wow!" Quinn twirled around, gazing at everything taking place around us. There were vendors selling their paintings, jewelry, and more—everything anyone could possibly want. A few food trucks were scattered about, with smells of sausages and funnel cakes filling the air around us. A few of the local eateries had booths as well. Mom and Dad had one for the bakery somewhere, but they gave me the day off, even though I had offered to help.

"What do you want to do first, Quinn? I think Dyl is defending his watermelon-eating championship." I couldn't help but giggle.

"Wet's go watch." Quinn grabbed my hand and dragged

me over to the event.

The contest had already started. All four contestants were sitting in a single line behind a long white plastic table, shoveling watermelon into their mouths straight off the rind. Juice was dribbling down their chins and hands. No need for spitting seeds out as they had already been removed for the seed-spitting contest. What people got out of spitting seeds, I would never understand.

"Go, Dyw, go!" Quinn shouted as she threw her arms up over her head and bounced up and down. "Woooo!"

Over the course of the previous couple of months, Quinn had managed to win over the hearts of my entire family.

With my hands cupped around my mouth, I hollered, "Go, Dyl! You got this!"

"And the winner of this year's watermelon eatin' contest is . . . defendin' champion, Dylan Logan!" The announcer raised Dyl's hand above their heads as the crowd cheered.

"Hey, Quinn. Do ya wanna learn how ta spit watermelon seeds?" Wyatt asked with a mischievous grin on his lips.

"YEAH!"

What kid wouldn't want to learn that? I rolled my eyes and followed them to the next event area.

"Okay, Quinn. First, ya want to find the biggest seed ya can," Wyatt instructed as he sifted through the bucket of seeds.

"Wike this one?" Quinn asked, holding a seed between her thumb and pointer finger for inspection.

"That's perfect. And I'll use *this* one." Wyatt held up a seed twice the size of Quinn's.

I enjoyed watching Quinn get excited about spitting seeds. If I was being honest with myself, I enjoyed the time spent with Wyatt, too.

"Okay. Now, ya want to put the seed with the pointy end

on the end of your tongue."

"Ike 'is?" Quinn asked, her tongue sticking out with a seed on the end of it, waiting for Wyatt to approve.

"Yep. Just like that. When you get ready to spit the seed, curl your tongue into a tunnel like this. Now, you want to inhale through your nose. Careful not to choke on the seed. Make sure you lean back as you inhale, and then, let 'er rip!"

Quinn tilted her head back as her chest rose. She lunged forward, and the seed flew from her mouth. It bounced just in front of her before coming to a stop. "That wasn't very good." Her head lowered.

"Quinn, that was ya first time. I bet with practice and a little bit of faith, ya can make that seed fly. Ya know, God says in Matthew Chapter Seventeen Verse Twenty that, 'If you have faith as small as a mustard seed, you will say to this mountain . . .' or in this case, this seed, 'move from here to there, and it will move, and nothin' will be impossible for you.'"

"Is that true?" Quinn glanced up at me.

"If God says it, then it's definitely true. Why don't you try again?"

"But how do I have faith?"

I kneeled beside Quinn and placed my arm around her shoulders. "You just have to close your eyes and say, "God, I believe you can help me spit this seed sooo far."

"What are you teaching my daughter?" Emelia spoke up from behind us.

I felt my cheeks grow hot, and it wasn't because of the weather. I wasn't exactly sure what to say. I turned to face Emelia and Luke. "Um . . ." But then, I saw the amusement in her eyes.

"Um. W-we were . . ." Wyatt stammered.

"They are teaching me how to spit watermewon seeds!"

Quinn placed her fists on her hips with a proud grin plastered on her face.

"Are they now?" Luke asked with a chuckle. "How'd ya do?" He kneeled next to Quinn.

"Not very good." Quinn gazed down at the ground as her bottom lip stuck out. "But Wyatt said if I have faith as smaww as a mouse seed, then . . . What did you say, Wyatt?" She peered up at Wyatt, her face scrunched in confusion.

Wyatt chuckled. "Mustard seed."

"Yeah. If I have faith as smaww as a mustard seed, I can do better. I don't know how big a mustard seed is, though." Quinn scratched the side of her head.

Emelia sucked her bottom lip between her teeth. What was that about? I made a mental note to ask later.

"Well, you see this watermelon seed?" Luke grabbed one from the bucket and held it out for Quinn to see.

Quinn nodded. I glanced over at Emelia. A smile formed on her lips as she watched Luke with Quinn.

"See the tip here?" Luke continued. "A mustard seed is just a little bit smaller than that."

"Wow! That's smaww!"

"It sure is."

Quinn repeated the motions of putting another seed on her tongue and spitting it. "I spit the seed way far this time!" Quinn jumped with excitement.

"That's awesome, Quinnie Bear." I patted her shoulder.

"We ready to move on to somethin' else?" Wyatt asked.

"Yes." I sighed heavily. "Thank you."

"What? You don't like spittin' seeds." Wyatt peered over at me.

I rolled my eyes and lightly pushed his shoulder. "Um. No, I don't. I'd much rather be doin' something else. Emelia, Luke, would you like to join us?"

"No. That's okay. You kids go have fun." Emelia shooed us away with her hand.

"Come on, Wyatt and Caitwyn." Quinn grabbed my hand as I quickly grabbed Wyatt's, and she pulled us away.

"See ya later!" I shouted over my shoulder, with laughter bubbling in my throat.

"Don't forget to meet us at the beach later for swimmin'!" Luke bellowed.

I could only wave our linked hands in response.

Chapter 16

Emelia

I wasn't sure what to think about Wyatt and Caitlyn talking to Quinn about God.

"What's on your mind?" Luke inquired. "You've been quiet since we stopped to talk to the kids."

"I'm just not sure about them telling Quinn about God. I'm trying hard to change my views and experiences, but it's hard."

"What do you mean?" Luke pressed. I caught a glimpse of his face twisted in confusion.

"My parents were Christians. I had a decent childhood. But it wasn't until I found out I was pregnant from a one-night stand that I realized Christians are so judgmental."

"We aren't all that way," Luke stated softly, almost as if someone had squeezed his heart.

"I'm starting to realize that. When I told my parents I was pregnant, they told me they no longer had a daughter. They packed me a suitcase, and I haven't seen or talked to them since. They said we were both going to hell. They've never met Quinn. Not long after that, I met Gary, and he took me in."

Luke sighed. "I'm so sorry, Em. You didn't deserve to be treated that way. Your parents' views are not the same as God's views. God loves all of His children, and He wants a relationship with all of them, no matter what bad things they've done. He wants His children to have forgiveness and grace and mercy and, most importantly, love." Luke wrapped his arm around my shoulder.

I did my best not to flinch. I don't think I succeeded because Luke immediately removed his arm. His arm falling back to his side brought relief, but it also brought sadness—emptiness, really. Without knowing how much longer Quinn and I would be at the ranch, I couldn't let myself fall for the cowboy, no matter how much my heart wanted it. I couldn't possibly be his type anyway. He was the epitome of a good-looking, red-blooded, American male, and I was . . . well, I was me, in this body. I glanced down at my plus-sized frame. Besides, he had his own worries. He didn't need mine on top of that.

"Thanks." I tried my best to smile, but it fell short.

I realized, though, that when I was with Luke, I wasn't checking my surroundings as much. I felt safe with him. The thought immediately made the hairs on the back of my neck stand at attention. *You always have to be on guard, Em. You can't let Gary get to you. More importantly, you can't let him get to Quinn.* I did what I could to stuff those thoughts deep into my mind. *Not today. Not now.* I just wanted to enjoy the time with Luke. I wasn't sure how many more chances I would have to spend with him. I had an uneasy feeling almost every day—a feeling Gary was close by. It would only be a matter of time.

"You don't have to talk about any of this if you don't want to, and I can't even imagine what you've been through, but how long did he mistreat you?"

"You mean terrorize me?"

Luke lifted his shoulders and let them fall.

"It didn't start until after I had Quinn. I guess that was the good part. Gary never hurt me while I was pregnant. And he never hurt Quinn."

"Why didn't you leave?" Luke asked quietly.

I lifted one shoulder. "I didn't have anywhere else to go. But the last time, he raised his hand to Quinn . . ." I sucked in my tears. "I got between them. He threw me against the wall and wrapped his hands around my neck. He could've killed me. I'm not sure why he didn't. I was almost unconscious. He let go right before I blacked out. I knew, then, that I had to get out. It was just a matter of time before he hurt Quinn and/or killed me."

I ran my fingers across my neck. The marks were gone, but I could still feel Gary's hands there, squeezing. I shook my head, willing the nauseousness to disappear. *Why am I unloading on Luke?* "I'm sorry." I shook my head again and gazed at the ground. "I shouldn't be telling you all of this."

"It's okay. I asked. Em, I want you to feel like you can tell me anythin'. You can trust me. I know convincin' you of that will take time, but I wanted to tell you."

"I appreciate that. It will definitely take more time for me to trust anyone again. But I'm starting to feel I may be able to trust some of the people here." I tilted my head and glanced up at him.

"I'm glad. Have you decided if you're goin' to stay or not?"

"I want to stay." I glanced down at my hands, trying to swallow the lump that lodged itself in my throat. "I'm not sure it's safe to stay . . . for anyone."

"You didn't ask my opinion, but I think Redemption Ranch is probably the safest place you could possibly be. No one is goin' to let anythin' happen to you or Quinn."

"I believe that you want that to be true, but I'm not so

sure." I kept my gaze on my interlocked hands.

"You'll see."

Luke had such confidence. I wished he could've transferred some of that to me. I'd have given just about anything to feel safe and secure.

Luke and I walked around the festival for a few more hours, visiting with vendors. I wanted so much for him to reach out and grab my hand. *No, Em. No, you don't.* I wasn't sure where the want came from or whether I liked having it at all. Yes, I did. I knew exactly where it came from; it came from the depths of my being. Luke was everything I could have ever wanted in a man. He was kind and caring. He was great with Quinn. He had a good heart. I shrugged off those thoughts. *Wishful thinking again. Remember, Em, he's out of your league. He wouldn't want someone like you.*

On occasion, I found myself searching my surroundings. My heart leaped to my throat when I saw a man who resembled Gary. I kept that to myself, though.

"Well, are you ready to head to the beach?" Luke leaned down and softly asked. His breath brushed my ear, creating goosebumps up and down my arms.

I inhaled and exhaled deeply. "Su-sure." I faltered.

"Let's go, then." Luke grinned. He grabbed my hand and led me to his truck. A tingling burn crept up my hand and into my arm, leaving another trail of goosebumps. My body shook with a shiver.

"You cold?" Luke asked, peering over at me. "I have a blanket in the truck."

I wished that had been the cause. "I'm okay. Thank you."

When we arrived at the beach, everyone was already there—the whole Redemption Ranch crew, including Caitlyn and Quinn. Quinn was laying her towel down on the light-brown sand. It was rough on my feet—grainy like the beaches back home. There were trees along the perimeter, creating shady spots here and there. The water was a dark blue. Fish and moss scents filled the air.

"Hey, Quinn." I scooped her up in my arms.

Quinn squealed with laughter. "Hi, Mommy. Caitwyn said she's gonna teach me how to swim."

"She did? That's very kind of her. Make sure you listen to her closely so that you don't get hurt. Okay?"

"Okay." Quinn squirmed out of my arms. The sand splattered at the intrusion of her feet.

"Here's the floaties we bought," Caitlyn said to Quinn, holding up two deflated arm floaties.

"Okay." Quinn's bottom lip stuck out.

"You won't have to wear them forever. I promise. Just until you feel safe in the water, and you can keep your head above the water," Caitlyn told her in between breaths blowing up one of the floaties. Wyatt was busy blowing up the other one.

How did I get so lucky to end up in this place? With these people? A piece of the wall around my heart began to crack.

Quinn stuck her arms out as Caitlyn and Wyatt pushed the floaties on. She squealed again once they were in position. She dragged Caitlyn and Wyatt to the water. That seemed to be the common theme of the day—Quinn dragging Caitlyn and Wyatt.

I stifled a giggle. I sure did love that little girl with everything that was in me. This was the life she should've already been living. She should've already known how to swim and ride a bike and . . . just be a child. I swiped at a tear that threatened to fall to my cheek. I sighed heavily.

"You okay?" Luke asked, bumping me with his arm.

How did he always know? Was he psychic or something? "Yeah. Just doing the 'should've' thing."

"Oh, I know that thing all too well." Luke chuckled.

I glanced over as Callie walked toward the water. She was a little thinner than me. She had on a black, one-piece suit with a coral-colored flower on it. Her wild, red curls were plucked on top of her head and held in place by a hair tie. Her back was completely exposed. What I saw made my knees buckle. Scars cascaded all over her back. Long ones. Short ones. Some overlapped others. I wondered what had happened to her. Callie really did understand some of what I had gone through. My left hand flew to my heart while my right hand caught a tear before it had a chance to fall.

"Her aunt," Luke whispered from behind me.

"What?" I flinched.

"Callie's aunt did that to her back. It's not my story to tell, but she understands more of what you have been through than most people."

"I see that."

"Do you want to go in the water?" Luke asked, grabbing my hand.

My heart skipped a beat. *Stop that!* "Yes, let's." My lips parted in a fake smile.

I gasped at the cold water as it rushed over my feet. I paused to allow myself to grow accustomed to the temperature before taking another step forward. My heart raced, but not because of Luke. Oh, how I *wished* it was because of him. I walked out into the water up to my waist. *Thump! Thump! Thump!* My heart pounded in my chest. Someone splashed me, and water covered my entire face. My breath caught in my throat. I couldn't get enough air to breathe. *Am I drowning?* I felt Gary's hand holding me under the water. *Wait, no.* It was Luke's hand, trying to pull me up.

"Mommy!" Quinn yelled, riddled with fear.

Before I could get my footing back and catch my breath, arms were around me, pulling me out of the water. I gasped, trying to fill my lungs with air.

"Are you okay?" Luke helped me down to the towel laying in the sand. He pushed my hair from my face and ran his hand down my cheek. "It's okay, Em. Breathe."

Once my lungs were filling, I wrapped my arms around Luke and all but pulled him down to the ground. His arms were around me as he sat next to me. "It's okay, Em. You're safe. I've got you." He softly reassured me in my ear, making those goosebumps return.

"Thank you." That was all I could manage.

"What happened?"

I shook my head. I didn't want to talk about it. I didn't want to think about it. Ever.

"Em, look at me." Luke put his index finger under my chin and lifted my head so our eyes locked. His eyes pleaded more than his words did. "Talk to me."

I diverted my eyes because I was about to tell Luke something no other soul knew besides Gary and me. If I looked into his eyes, I knew I wouldn't have the courage. Inhaling deeply, I gathered up what strength I could find to get the words out.

The breath seeped out of my mouth. "Well, one night just after Quinn was born, I didn't clean the kitchen quite the way Gary expected. While I was taking a bath, he barged into the bathroom, told me how lousy of a housekeeper I was, and shoved me under the water." I gulped air into my lungs so I could finish. "That was the first time I thought I might die."

Luke pulled me a little closer, enveloping me. I knew I could get lost in him. It wouldn't hurt for a little bit, right? He did have a way of making me feel safe. Not safe enough to give him my heart, but safer than I had felt in a very long time.

Quinn ran up to me and leaped into my lap, wrapping her arms around my neck. "I'm okay, honey," I assured her.

"You scared me." Quinn nuzzled her face into my neck. I rubbed my hand up and down her back to soothe her.

"Someone just splashed me in the face, and I couldn't breathe. Luke made sure I was alright."

At the mention of Luke's name, Quinn jumped into his arms and hugged him. "Thank you for hewping Mommy and making sure she was safe."

"Always, Quinn. Always," Luke spoke softly next to her ear. It was amazing how quickly Luke had become one of Quinn's favorite people. It wasn't hard to see why, but the fact that she could trust anyone was evidence of how resilient she was. "Are you ready for some fireworks?"

"Yeah!" Quinn had already gotten dressed in the midst of my meltdown.

Suddenly, shame and embarrassment washed over me. The last thing I wanted to do was watch fireworks, but Quinn had her heart set on it. She'd never really seen fireworks, except the ones the neighbors set off. I dried myself off and tossed my clothes over my swimsuit. Luke had his shirt and jeans back on and slipped his feet into his shoes. "Everyone ready to go?" he asked.

"Mommy, can Caitwyn and Wyatt sit with us?"

"Oh, honey, I'm sure they'd rather be off by themselves for a bit."

Quinn's face filled with disappointment.

"Actually, we'd love to. If it's okay with you, of course," Caitlyn chimed in.

Quinn bounced up and down. How could I say no? "Of course, it's okay."

Chapter 17

Luke

I wasn't exactly thrilled to see the fireworks display. I'd had an issue with them sendin' me into a PTSD nightmare. I hoped this time would be different. I wanted to experience the fireworks through Quinn's eyes, and I prayed I could at least enjoy them a little bit—like I used to. I didn't hold out much hope, though.

Quinn ran ahead and picked a spot for all of us to sit. I laid a blanket on the ground. When the first firework sailed into the air, I braced myself for the pop. The first couple weren't so bad. The colors were beautiful, and the noise wasn't very loud. I prayed they'd all be that way. *Nope.* As soon as it whistled into the air, I knew it was goin' to be like a bomb explodin'. *Stay in the present, Luke; you're not over there anymore.*

I gripped the blanket next to me until my knuckles turned white as the next couple of fireworks shot into the air. *Breathe, Luke. Just breathe.* I squeezed my eyes shut, willing the bile to retreat from my throat. I felt a hand on top of my own, and everythin' seemed to melt away—the people, the sounds, the nightmares, the iron taste of blood in my mouth. When I opened my eyes, Em's face was the only one I saw.

"It's okay, Luke. *I've* got *you* this time," Em comforted me.

My skin tingled and grew warm. *What is this woman doin'
to me?* Em's hand curled around mine, and I knew I was goin'
to be alright watchin' the rest of the show. Interestin'. She
calmed my demons yet again. I wondered if I did the same for
her. I sure hoped so. Except her demons were still out there.
Somewhere.

My mind stayed in the present for the rest of the night.
Quinn's eyes and expressions were priceless, and I was so
happy I was able to see them. She ooh'd and aah'd, her eyes
growing wide when the fireworks exploded into a huge array of
colors.

"Wuke, did you see that one?" Quinn asked as she plopped
down in my lap. Em removed her hand from mine. My heart
sank to my stomach, and my hand suddenly felt cold.

"I did. Wasn't it cool?" I asked with a chuckle.

"So coow!" Quinn settled into my lap.

Nothin' was goin' to wipe the smile from my face. For the
first time in my adult life, I felt like havin' a family of my own
could be within my reach. I was growin' way too attached to
Quinn and Em. What would I do if Em chose to leave? I
couldn't beg her to stay. I couldn't make her stay. It had to be
her choice. She deserved that much. I would just have to pray
without ceasin' that she would choose the ranch as their home.
And maybe that she would choose me, too.

*God, help her to see that the ranch is her home, but only if
it's in Your will. If it's not, help my heart to be okay with it.*

The only thing I knew in that moment was that my life
would never be the same. No matter what Em decided to do.

"Are you ready to go?" Em broke me from my thoughts.

"Oh. Yeah. Sorry." I stood and started to fold up the blanket.

"Caitlyn and Wyatt already left to take Quinn home."

"Then, we'd better get goin'." I wasn't ready for my time

with Em to be over, but those moments couldn't last forever. *Wishful thinkin'.* We piled back into my truck, and I did my best to drive slowly on the way home.

"So, where did you go when the fireworks started going off?" Em asked softly.

"I was right next to ya. I didn't go anywhere." I tried to deflect the question, knowin' full well it wouldn't work on her.

Em's breath escaped her lips in an audible sigh. "You know what I mean."

I paused a minute to gather my thoughts. "Well, usually, hearin' them takes me back to the day I was injured. The day I lost my team."

"What do you normally do when that happens?"

"Well, you already know what I used to do. Bars. Drinkin'. Women. Now, I just pray my way through it. The last few months, the nightmares and moments have been fewer and farther between. Tonight, though, you seemed to erase it from my mind. So, thank you."

"I did? Well, you're welcome, I guess."

I glanced over to see a satisfied smile spread across Em's lips. It caused mine to turn upward, too. The bruises on her face and the red marks on her neck had gone away. I hoped the memories had started to fade also. But I knew the mental part was harder to get through. Oh, how I knew.

"Well, here we are," I announced. I couldn't hide my disappointment.

"Would you like to come in and say good night to Quinn? I know she would love that." Em leaned her head back on the seat and flashed her pretty greenish-blue eyes in my direction.

My heart fluttered. "I'd love that, too," Em added.

"Mommy! Wuke!" Quinn ran up to the truck.

"Hey, baby girl. Did you have a good time today?" Quinn

leaped into Em's arms as soon as Em's feet were on the ground.

"I had the best time." Quinn giggled before jumpin' down and runnin' over to me. I scooped her up into my arms. "Thank you for hewping Mommy earwier," Quinn whispered in my ear.

"Always will, Quinn. I always will. I promise," I whispered back.

"What are you two whispering about?" Em asked as her cheeks turned a light shade of pink.

"It's a secret." Quinn tried her best to look innocent.

"So, I've been replaced, I see." Em's bottom lip stuck out as she flashed Quinn her puppy dog eyes.

"Never, Mommy." Quinn reached out to Em. A smile spread across Em's lips as she swooped Quinn into her arms.

So, Quinn comes by it naturally. I shook my head as a chuckle escaped my lips. "Well, good night, Quinnie. Sweet dreams." I planted a kiss on her cheek.

Quinn wrapped her arms around my neck and squeezed. "Night, Wuke. I wuv you." She jumped down out of Em's arms and ran back inside the cabin.

My heart skipped a beat. Never in a million years would I have thought a little kid would have said that to me, or that it would make my heart react the way it did.

"Wow. She's never said that to anyone but me." Em placed her hand over her heart, her eyes glassy.

"No one has ever said that to me before. Besides my parents."

"Really? I find that hard to believe."

"Well, it's true. Right out of high school, I joined the Marines, so I never had the opportunity to meet anyone. Since I've been out, I haven't felt like I was worth lovin', so I never allowed myself to be in a position to. Until now." I glanced over at her.

What? What was I sayin'? Where did that come from? I still had demons. Too many demons. Demons that were too much for her. Then again, just a touch of her hand at the fireworks made them disappear. I shook my head. With my fists, I stuffed my thoughts down into my pockets.

I felt the electricity surge through my body as Em's hand caressed my cheek. "You *are* worth loving, Luke. Good night and sweet dreams." Her hand drifted away as she stepped onto her porch and opened the door.

I placed my hand on my cheek, and the floodgates of my heart broke open. As much as I tried to stop it from happenin', it did, whether I wanted it to or not. Em and Quinn had somehow snuck through the barriers and into my heart. I knew they would reside there forever—no matter if they called Redemption Ranch home or not.

Chapter 18

Emelia

"Caitlyn, I can't thank you enough for hanging out with Quinn today. I know it meant the world to her."

"No problem. It meant a lot to me, too. She's a great girl."

"Thank you." At least I had gotten something right in the world.

"I brushed my teeth, Mommy. I'm ready for bed." Quinn scampered in from the bathroom, rubbing her eyes with the backs of her hands.

"Good night, Quinnie Bear." Caitlyn held out her arms for a hug.

"Night, Caitwyn." Quinn wrapped her arms around Caitlyn's waist.

"Night, Emelia." Caitlyn waved as she strode out of the cabin.

"Alright, munchkin. Let's get you all tucked in." I followed Quinn to her room. She jumped in her bed, scooped up Horsey, and pulled the top sheet over her body. I tucked the sheet under her legs, leaned down, and kissed her forehead. "There. Snug as a bug. I love you, sweet girl. Sweet dreams. Sleep tight. Don't let the bed bugs bite tight."

"Night, Mommy. Don't let the bed bugs bite tight." Quinn yawned, turned on her side, and closed her eyes.

I wasn't sure why Quinn said the rhyme like that. I had taught her the way it went, but she always added the "tight" at the end. It wasn't long before I was saying it that way, too.

I turned off the overhead light. Quinn's nightlight left a soft glow in the room. I stood in the doorway, watching the sleepy form in her bed. My heart overflowed with love for her. A smile crept to my face as I closed the door. Once upon a time, our nightly ritual was the only bright spot of my day. Being at Redemption Ranch, though, made every day a bright spot. I smiled.

I headed to the kitchen with a little spring in my step. It had been a good day. Better than any day I'd had in years. I made a cup of warm milk and went out to sit on the porch. I couldn't get over how clear the sky was here—so many stars. My mind reflected on the day. Luke. He was such a sweet man. He tore through my nightmares and brought me back to the present that afternoon. So easily. It would have been easy to fall in love with him.

Gary was sweet, too. At first.

No. I squeezed my eyes closed. Luke was *nothing* like Gary. Not even a little bit. But I couldn't fall in love with Luke. That would be putting him in too much danger. And he had his own nightmares to deal with. I just couldn't do that to him. I sighed heavily.

I wished I believed in the same God as Luke. I had at one time. But I wasn't sure I could again. I wasn't sure God wanted someone like me back in his family. Not sure he wanted someone who was battered and broken. He could never forgive me for the things I'd done and subjected my daughter to.

I rocked back and forth in the rocking chair, savoring the quiet and the warmth of my drink. I needed something to soothe my mind, and warm milk always did that. I knew if I didn't, the nightmares would appear as soon as my eyes were closed. I spent so many nights lying in wait—waiting for Gary to realize I had done something wrong and come to punish me in whatever way he saw fit. Or if he decided he wanted something else from me, whether I was willing to give it or not.

The hairs on the back of my neck stood at attention as footsteps dragged in the dirt to the left of my cabin. My heart raced before it felt as if it had stopped altogether. My breath hitched in my throat, and my palms began to sweat. My mug slipped from my hands and crashed to the wooden floor of the porch. I didn't dare inhale or make a sound.

Callie came into view, and my lungs gasped for air as my heartbeat returned. My hand flew to my chest. "Callie, you scared me."

"I'm so sorry." She rushed to my side. "Let me help you pick up the pieces."

Somehow, that statement sounded like a lot more than just the mug. My hands were shaking so much that it was impossible to pick up the shards. "I'll get it tomorrow, Callie. Would you like to sit down?" My hand trembled as I motioned to the other chair. I wasn't sure my wobbly legs would hold me up much longer. "What brings you by?"

"I just wanted to see how you're doing. I saw what happened at the beach today."

My cheeks became emblazoned, and I diverted my gaze to my feet. "I'm fine. Just had a flashback when someone splashed me in the face."

"I'm so sorry that happened to you." Callie placed her hand on top of mine. "I know how those feelings can bubble up almost out of nowhere. Happened to me at church one Sunday."

"Yeah, I saw . . ." I wasn't sure if it was okay to finish my sentence.

"My scars?"

I nodded.

"Yeah. My aunt used to beat me with a whip. When she was mad. When she was sad. When I seemed too happy. For any reason at all, really. When I first arrived in Edenton, I was quite the mess. The people here, especially Colt, helped me realize that I am worth loving and that *they* love me. I hope we are helping you to see that you are worth loving, too. And that we love you."

I glanced down at my hands as they played with a string hanging from the bottom of my shirt. "I just don't know if it's safe for us here. For any of you, either. I wouldn't be able to live with myself if anything happened to any of you because of my presence here. I will stay until I feel like Quinn and I are in danger or putting you all in too much danger. Although, I'm worried about being distracted too much to see when we are, in fact, in danger."

"You mean Luke?"

I nodded my head.

"He would do just about anything to make sure the two of you are safe. That man is smitten with both of you. Tell me you don't see it."

I lifted a shoulder in a shrug. "He has his own things to deal with. The last thing he needs is a woman who has a kid and is on the run from an abusive ex-boyfriend."

Callie placed her hand over mine once more. "You should really let *him* decide that, shouldn't you?"

"Maybe, but for now, it's my decision. It *has* to be."

"Okay." Callie sighed. Her hand smacked against her leg before she stood. "I just wanted to make sure you were okay. See you tomorrow for breakfast?"

"Sure." I did my best to smile, but I knew it didn't even

come close to convincing her I was okay.

"Have a good night." Callie waved.

I ran my hands over my face. *How can these people see me so clearly when my vision of myself is so foggy?*

They trust in Me.

What? Who said that? I sat up straight, and my eyes darted in every direction. *Now, you've done lost your mind, Em. You're hearing things that clearly aren't there.* I sighed heavily before stepping inside to get a broom and dustpan. I needed to get those pieces picked up, along with my broken pride, before Quinn woke up. As I carried the broom onto the porch, my eyes grew heavy, and I stifled a yawn. I swept up the broken cup. There was a rustling sound at the side of the cabin. Our cabin was on the end of the row, so it would be easy for the boogeyman to get to us if he wanted.

"Who's there?" I clutched the broom handle close to my chest.

More rustling sounded, but no one spoke. I didn't hear any animal noises either. I wasn't about to get off the porch and look. That's how people got killed in movies—being too curious. I hurried inside and locked the door. I finally took a breath as I leaned against the door. I emptied the dustpan into the trash and returned it, along with the broom, to the closet on my way down the hall to my bedroom. My eyes were heavy once again, but my racing heart, I knew, would keep me from sleeping.

Chapter 19

Gary

I had planned on messing with Emelia just a little, but from my perch in the woods across the dirt road, I saw her friend come up from the side of the cabin. With my binoculars, I saw the look on Emelia's face and watched as the cup shattered on the ground. *She thought it was me.* I chuckled.

When her friend left and Emelia went inside, I decided to keep playing my little game by saddling up to the side of her cabin to rustle the bushes against the wood underneath the window on the end. It made a nice sound. Music to my ears, really. Nothing like the terror in her voice when she called out to see if someone was there. *It's me, darling. Coming to get you. To punish you for leaving me.* But I remained silent.

I could have jumped out of the shadows and dragged Emelia back with me. I had some chloroform in the car, but I was having too much fun watching her squirm. I could do this forever, but I had no intention of that.

I waited until I saw Emelia through the bedroom window. By the look on her face, I knew she wasn't going to sleep, and if she did, she would only be dreaming of me. A satisfied smile spread across my lips. I slithered back to my car and drove back to my hotel. *Until next time, my sweet.*

Chapter 20

Caitlyn

The first of August came too quickly, yet somehow, not quickly enough. I had already packed everything I was taking to Indiana for school. I wanted to make sure I spent my day with Quinn before I had to work at the café. I was set to leave the next morning. It was going to be hard for me to say good-bye to her. She had become the little sister I never had.

"Are you ready to go for a walk with Tinkerbell?" I asked Quinn as I helped her jump off the small step of the porch of her cabin.

Tinkerbell was a horse that had arrived at the ranch a week prior. She was chestnut brown with a long blonde tail and mane. Quinn said the mare reminded her of Tinkerbell from Peter Pan, so Uncle Colt and Aunt Callie decided that would be her name.

"Yeah. Wet's go."

We made our way to the stable. Once inside, Quinn went over to Warrior's stall. She had made it a habit to stop and say hi to every horse there. I'm sure the horses appreciated the extra attention. I grabbed the lead rope and met her at Tinker-bell's stall. I showed Quinn how to place the rope on.

"Do you want to lead her out and on our walk?" Tinkerbell had been one of the gentlest and easy-going horses I'd ever met.

"Can I?" Quinn's face lit up like a Christmas tree.

"Of course." I giggled.

"Come on, Tinkerbeww." Quinn pulled gently on the rope, and the horse followed her out of the stall. Quinn continued until we were all outside. "Where do you want to go?" she asked, glancing up at me.

"Let's go this way." I motioned to the left. Going to the right would take us to the creek where Aunt Callie was hurt two years before. I wasn't going to take any chances where Quinn was concerned.

"I'm gonna miss you when you weave tomorrow." Quinn's bottom lip stuck out as she talked.

"I'm gonna miss you, too. I promise I'll write as often as I can, and I'll call ya at least once a week."

"Promise?"

"Pinky promise." I stuck my pinky out to Quinn. She hooked hers with mine and grinned.

"I wanna be wike you, Caitwyn."

"What do you mean? Ya want to be a nurse, too?"

"No." Quinn giggled. "I'm not owd enough to do that. I want to be wike you and God."

"Oh. Well, that's easy enough to do." I stopped walking and turned to her as Tinkerbell huffed softly.

"It is?" Quinn scrunched up her nose.

"Yep. All ya have to do is ask God into your heart. Is that what ya wanna do?"

"Yeah." Quinn tilted her head and glanced up at me.

"Okay, then. Do you understand what you'll be doin'?"

Quinn shook her head.

"Well, one of my favorite verses is John Chapter Three Verse Sixteen. That verse tells us that God loves us so much, He sent His Son, who He loves just as much, to die on the cross for the things we've done wrong in our lives. If we tell Jesus anything that we've done wrong and ask for forgiveness and ask Jesus into our hearts, He will forgive us."

"And that wiww make me be wike you? What's it cawwed again?"

"A Christian?"

"Yeah, a Christian."

"Yes, it will. Do ya wanna do that?"

"Yes," Quinn admitted softly.

"Close your eyes and repeat after me." I waited for her to close her eyes. "Dear, Jesus, thank you for lovin' me so much you died on the cross for me."

Quinn repeated every word slowly. I took hold of her hand and gently squeezed to let her know she was getting the words right.

"If I've done anythin' that was wrong in your eyes, I ask that you forgive me."

I listened as Quinn repeated those sweet words.

"I want you to be Lord of my life." I paused again. "Please come live in my heart so that we can be best friends forever and ever. I love You. Amen."

"Amen. So, I'm a Christian now?" Quinn asked, opening her eyes.

"Did you mean the words you said?"

Quinn nodded.

"Then, yes, you are."

I opened my arms, and Quinn fell into them. My heart overflowed with gratefulness that God had brought this little girl into my life so I could lead her to Him. "Wanna finish the walk now, Quinnie Bear?"

"Yes, pwease. Can we not teww Mommy about what we did? I'm not sure she wikes God very much."

Quinn's request confused me, but I had to honor it. "I won't tell a soul." I pinched my thumb and forefinger to my closed lips and dragged them across my mouth to the other side like a zipper. A person's relationship with God was theirs alone. If someone didn't want others to know about it, that was up to them, no matter their age.

"Okay. Let's finish our walk with Tinkerbell. I think she's getting annoyed at us for standing around so long." I laughed heartily.

Quinn and I both glanced back at the mare. She was staring at us. The look in her eyes told us I was right. Quinn giggled. "Wet's go, Tink."

She must have shortened the name because "bell" was too hard. I was going to miss Quinn's speech impediment. But at least I'd get to hear her voice when I called.

We ventured a little further away from the stable. Once the sun was almost in the middle of the sky, I suggested, "We should probably head back for lunch."

"Yeah." Quinn rubbed her belly. "I'm getting kinda hungry."

"Me, too."

We led Tinkerbell back to the stable, where we put her in her stall before heading to the house for lunch. Quinn grabbed my hand as we skipped to the house.

"Mommy!" Quinn exclaimed when Emelia came into view. She was sitting on the porch reading a book.

"Hey, honey. How was your walk?"

"It was good, but I'm so hungry."

"Well, go wash your hands for lunch. Are you staying, Caitlyn?" Emelia rose from her chair.

"I have to go meet my parents to work at the café. One final shift before I leave tomorrow." Sadness filled my voice.

"Bye, Caitwyn." Quinn squeezed me before bolting into the house.

"Thanks for all you've done for her," Emelia said when Quinn was out of sight.

"You're welcome. I'm not sure if it's been more of a blessing for her or for me. I'm really goin' to miss her. I told her I would call and write as much as I can."

"Thank you. That's very sweet of you. We know you'll be busy." Emelia stretched out her arms and wrapped me in a hug.

I waved as I stepped off the porch and slid into the driver's seat. *I sure am going to miss this place. These people.* I sighed, swiped away the tear at the corner of my eye, and drove to the café.

Chapter 21

Emelia

It had been hard for me not to tell Caitlyn she wouldn't be working at the café that night. Her parents, along with Colt and Callie, had planned a huge surprise party for her.

Everyone had forgotten about what happened at the beach on the Fourth of July, or at least no one ever mentioned it. As I stared in the mirror, I studied my reflection. For the first times in four years, the image held no bruises. It was finally free of Gary's rage. If only the memories would disappear just as easily. But with Gary still lurking, no such luck. When would his grip on my mind finally let up? I shrugged it off and finished washing my hands. No more dwelling on the past. We had a barn to decorate.

I knew that night was going to be hard on Quinn. She had to say goodbye to Caitlyn. They had become almost inseparable. I opened the bathroom door and found myself alone in the cabin. I swallowed the panic and headed outside. *Stay calm, Em. She's safe here.* I tried my hardest to believe that lie.

"Quinn!" I hollered when I didn't immediately see her.

"I'm over here with Wuke and Wyatt! Wet's go!" They were on the dirt path leading down to the barn.

"I'm sorry, guys. I had no idea she'd come out here. She's just excited about the party." *UGH! Why am I apologizing for*

131

Quinn's presence? I always had to apologize to Gary if Quinn "got in his way." But not to these guys.

"No need to apologize," Luke responded. "We all love having you both here."

Luke's lopsided grin was almost irresistible. I wanted to kiss it. What? No. *You will do no such thing. He is much too good for the likes of you.* I stiffened my back and raised my chin. I didn't dare glance in his direction. "Shall we get going to the barn, then?" I did my best to plaster a smile on my face.

Luke extended his arm. "After you."

Quinn had already grabbed Wyatt by the hand and dragged him down the hill toward the barn. He didn't appear to mind. His head bent back with laughter, and even though I didn't know what they were talking about, Quinn was talking a mile-a-minute.

My heart sank. Quinn was getting too attached to everyone. We had been there almost two months with no definite sign of Gary, but I knew he was out there. Even though everyone else chalked it up to coincidence—or at least that was what they kept telling me, perhaps to make me feel better—I felt in the pit of my stomach that it was only a matter of time. But if we left, would he find us somewhere else? I really had no clue.

Was Luke right? Were we safer at the ranch? I wasn't sure about any of my options. All I knew was Luke made me feel safe—when we were together, anyway. I wished I could always feel that way.

"Earth to Em." Luke waved his hand in front of my face.

I closed my eyes and shook Gary loose from my thoughts. "I'm sorry. I was just thinking."

"I can see that." Luke chuckled. He tried to make eye contact. "Wanna clue me in?"

Telling Luke my innermost thoughts would be letting him

get too close. I had already told him too much. As long as I kept him at arm's length, *he* would be safe. I couldn't allow any other bad things to happen to him. He'd been through enough.

"Oh, it's nothing." I waved him off.

"Okay. If that's how ya wanna play it." Luke sighed and shoved his hands into his front pockets.

Luke didn't pry, but he also didn't say anything else on the way to the barn. Not. A. Single. Word. I glanced up at the beautiful mixture of blue, red, orange, and yellow that made up the evening sky. The sun was setting on the horizon. An owl hooted in the distance. The crickets were starting to chirp. I continued to be in awe of how much brighter and clearer things were at the ranch.

Once we got to the barn, decorating was already in full swing. With the whole ranch there to help, we set everything up in record time. The place looked beautiful. Caitlyn was going to love it.

Callie stepped forward. "Okay, everyone! Thank you so much for helping. See you all back here in an hour for the party. Caitlyn should arrive shortly after that."

Quinn and I skipped back to the cabin alone. Luke had chores to finish. Colt and Callie had to pick up the cake and balloons. I was relieved and disappointed all at the same time. I enjoyed just *being* with Luke. But keeping the distance was a good thing. Right? Out of sight, out of mind? I wished that were true.

Quinn barreled through the front door of the cabin and ran to her room. I sauntered to mine and slid a dress shirt and clean pair of jeans out of my closet.

"How do I look, Mommy?" Quinn appeared and twirled around in a baby pink dress she had picked out herself. She paired it with a cute pair of Mary Jane pink flats. Tears

133

brimmed in my eyes. She looked so pretty. So happy.

"You look beautiful. Let's fix your hair." I pointed Quinn toward the bathroom.

"Can I have braids?" She glanced up at me.

"Of course."

"Yay!" Quinn's excitement never got old. She had spent so much of her childhood being "seen and not heard" and not truly able to be a child. It broke my heart but made her excitement and happiness, now, that much sweeter—one of the reasons we hadn't left Redemption Ranch yet.

Quinn and I hurried down the path to the barn as we were running a little behind. I had trouble getting Quinn's braids just right. She said they had to be perfect. For Caitlyn.

The barn was glowing with twinkle lights and balloons of all shapes, sizes, and colors. It seemed as if the whole town was there. The community really showed up for people. It was comforting to see. I wished I'd known this kind of place existed long before. Maybe I wouldn't have been in the predicament I was in.

"Okay. Marci just called to tell me Caitlyn and Dylan are on the way! They should be here in about ten minutes," Colt announced to the crowd.

Wyatt stood guard at the door as the lookout. A short time later, he shouted, "They're here!" The car doors shut, and footsteps sounded against the dirt and rocks outside.

"Wyatt, what's going on?" Caitlyn asked as she stepped inside, guided by her brother, who had blindfolded her.

"How did you know I was here?" Wyatt asked.

"I smell your cologne." Caitlyn giggled. Wyatt's face turned bright red. "Can I take this blindfold off now?"

"Yeah. Let me help." Wyatt stepped behind her and untied it.

As soon as the cloth was removed from Caitlyn's eyes, everyone yelled, "Surprise!"

Caitlyn placed her hand over her heart. "What's all this?" She spun around the room laughing.

"It's your going away party," Colt informed her.

"Uncle Colt, y'all didn't have to do all this." Caitlyn waved her hands and twirled around in a circle.

"Yes, we did. You're going away to college tomorrow. We're all gonna miss ya. We wanted ta give ya a proper send-off."

Caitlyn wrapped her arms around her uncle's waist. "Thank you." Her white smile beamed from across the barn.

The band started to play, and the dance floor filled. Quinn found her friends from dance class, and they all did their best to dance to the beat of the music. I covered my mouth and giggled. When a slow song began to play, Wyatt led Caitlyn to the dance floor, followed by Colt and Callie and other couples.

"May I have this dance?" A hand appeared in front of me.

With hope filling his eyes, Luke stood before me. How could I say no? I smiled and laid my hand in his. He escorted me to the dance floor and wrapped his arms around my waist. I slipped my hands behind his neck. Being this close made my knees wobble. Were those butterflies in my stomach? I swallowed hard.

"Did I mention how beautiful ya look tonight, Em?" Warm breath brushed my neck, Luke's mouth inches from my ear. Goosebumps prickled my arms. I sucked my bottom lip between my teeth.

"Thank you." My cheeks grew hot. I glanced up at Luke. His face was so close to mine. My breath failed to leave my lungs. My head became light. *What is this man doing to me?*

Luke placed his hands on either side of my face. His lips

were so close to mine. My heart fluttered. And then, it happened. Gary's face appeared. "Gary, stop." I pushed away.

"I'm not him, Em," Luke whispered through his clenched jaw. Hurt filled his voice. His brows furrowed.

My hand clapped to my mouth. "I'm so sorry, Luke." I ran from the barn before anyone could see the first tear fall. The last thing I wanted to see was Gary's face when Luke was about to kiss me. Maybe it was a sign—a sign that Luke was better off without us.

"Stupid. Stupid, girl," I chastised myself. What was I going to do? How would I ever be able to face him again? Footsteps echoed from behind me. I closed my eyes and sucked in a breath, my feet frozen in place.

"Em, what happened?" Luke asked, his voice full of worry.

My head fell back. "I don't know. I'm so sorry." I covered my face with my hand as my body began to shake with sobs.

Arms wrapped around me. "It'll be okay. I promise." Luke sucked in a breath. "I'm fallin' in love with you, Em," he blurted out. "I'll wait as long as I have to for you. As long as it takes."

"No!" I broke free from his comforting arms. "You can't do that. It's too dangerous for you. You deserve someone better. Someone who doesn't have all of the issues I have."

Luke's brows furrowed again. "You assume I think there's someone better than you. There's no one better than you and Quinn. I've fought these feelin's since the day I first saw you at the door of your cabin. These feelin's aren't goin' anywhere. *I'm* not goin' anywhere. Ever."

"Are you sure?" I peered into his eyes.

"Em." Luke placed one hand on my shoulder and the other on my cheek. "I've never been more sure about anythin' in my entire life." He leaned in. I braced myself. His lips were almost touching mine.

"I'm so sorry. I just can't do this," I whispered breathlessly. I pushed away once again. "I'm going to go say goodbye to Caitlyn and gather Quinn to go home." My heart sank at the thought of leaving him, but I needed distance. My brain was in a fog.

Luke stepped to the side to allow enough space for me to get by, his shoulders slumped in defeat. "Okay." He dropped his hands to his sides before stuffing them into his front pockets.

I could feel Luke's eyes on me as I returned to the barn. I couldn't look back. If I looked back, I would run to him and do the very thing he just tried to do. I. Just. Couldn't.

Chapter 22

Luke

As Emelia disappeared into the barn, my heart retreated with her. "Son-of-a . . ." I kicked an invisible rock and strolled over to lean my arms against the corral fence.

"God, what am I doin'? Am I fightin' a losin' battle?" I rested my head in my hands. "What do I do?"

I have heard you. Now, be patient, My son.

"Thank you, Lord, for hearin' my prayer." I inhaled and exhaled deeply. Patience had never been my strong suit. But then again, not havin' patience always got me into a heap of trouble. That was as good a time as any to start practicin' patience.

Footsteps sounded behind me. I didn't bother turnin' around. I didn't want to talk to anyone in that moment. I thought it might have been Emelia and Quinn. *Wishful thinkin'.*

"What are you doing out here all by yourself?" Callie asked.

I rubbed my hands over my face. "I have no idea."

"What's wrong? What happened?" Callie asked, layin' her arms on the fence.

"I told Em I'm fallin' in love with her." I closed my eyes and sighed. "And then, I tried to kiss her again." I shook my head. I was so stupid.

"What did she say?"

"She said I can't fall for her. It's too dangerous. Imagine that. Too dangerous for a Marine." I chuckled softly. "I just told her I'd wait for her, no matter how long it takes. And then, she ran away. Again."

"Aww, Luke." Callie ran her hand across my back. "It's going to take her time. And a lot of it. You just have to be patient. I see the way she looks at you. She's fighting it. She'll come around."

"If it's in God's will for us to be together, I know He'll make it happen." I shoved my hands in my pockets once again. "I think I'm just goin' ta go home and go ta sleep."

"Are you sure?"

No. But I nodded.

"Keep your chin up, Luke. It'll happen. In God's time."

I sighed deeply. "I know. I'll talk to ya tomorrow, Callie. Enjoy the rest of the evenin'."

I traipsed back to my cabin with my head low and an awful ache in my heart. I stood at the door, starin', willin' it to open. I didn't have the energy to turn the knob. Why did the place always feel so empty after spendin' time with Em and Quinn? It never felt that way before they came into my life.

I closed my eyes, and my head fell back. My almost kiss with Em played over in my mind. A lump formed in my throat at the thought that it might've been the closest I'd ever come to feeling my lips on hers. I've never had a woman not want to be with me. Then again, there'd never been one like Em. I finally opened the door and stepped inside.

Never before had I wanted this cabin to be full of life. Of laughter. Of love. *Please, God, let my life be filled with those things. No matter how long it takes.* I flopped down on the couch, closed my eyes, and let my mind wander until sleep overtook me.

139

* * *

The next mornin', I woke to a stiff back. I stood up like a ninety-year-old, hunched over and clutchin' the small of my back. Once my feet were firmly underneath me, I straightened up and stretched to get the kinks out. With no appetite and with emptiness in my heart, I showered and dressed for the day. It was my day to give the horses a bath.

I'd thought about asking Em and Quinn if they wanted to help with the horses. *Maybe I should just leave them alone for a bit.* Before I knew what I was doin', I sauntered over to their cabin. *Okay, God. I feel you pushin'. I'm goin'.*

As I put my hand up to knock, the door flew open. Quinn bounced right off my legs. I reached out to grab her so that she didn't fall. "Quinnie, are you okay?" I did my best to stifle my laugh.

"Hi, Wuke! I was just coming to see you."

"You were?" I placed my hands on my hips. I peered behind her, hoping for a glimpse of her mother.

"Yep." Quinn nodded, mimickin' my stance.

I chuckled. "Why's that?"

"I wanted to see if I couwd hewp with anything today?"

"Well, as a matter of fact, I was comin' to see if you and ya mom wanted to help me give the horses their baths."

"I'd wuv to! Mommy!" Quinn hollered, runnin' to the back of the cabin. "Wuke wants us to hewp him with the horsies today. Can we? Pwease?"

Em stepped out of the bedroom. My breath caught in my throat. She always had a way of takin' my breath right out of me. "Well, I don't see why not."

Em glanced at me, and her cheeks turned a lovely shade of pink. A goofy grin spread across my face. *Don't be such a dork, Luke.* I slid my thumbs into my front belt loops.

"Yay!" Quinn zoomed back to the door and straight out on-to the porch.

"Good mornin', Em." I smiled.

"Morning, Luke." She didn't even peer in my direction. She walked out the door. My heart sank. *Maybe I blew it last night. Should I apologize? Apologize for her tellin' her I'm fallin' in love with her?* Never. We would see how the day unfolded. But sayin' I'm sorry wasn't goin' to be part of it.

"Let's go, then." I swung my arm in a large circle.

We made our way down to the stable. I was goin' to have to try my hardest not to let my disappointment show on the outside, even though it was crushin' me on the inside.

Patience.

Give me Your patience, Lord. I closed my eyes and took a few deep breaths. "You ready to have some fun, Quinnie?"

"YES!" She threw one fist up in the air before grabbin' my hand and skippin' alongside me to the horses.

As we stepped into the stable, I instructed, "So, first, we need to gather the supplies we'll need to get them brushed and combed before their baths. I like to do things in stages. That way, you don't have too many things crowdin' the workspace."

I scurried about gettin' everythin' together. "We need to groom the horses before we bathe them. We use this comb right here. It's called a currycomb. This comb helps to loosen the dirt that may be in their coat. Who should we start with? The only horse we won't be bathin' is Warrior. Callie has a special groomin' ritual she does with him to help his scars."

I glanced over at Em, who was starin' at the wall. She reached out her hand and glided her fingers over the words. Painted on the wall was Colossians Chapter One Verse Thir-teen and Fourteen. "For He has rescued us from the dominion of darkness and brought us into the kingdom of the Son He loves, in whom we have redemption, the forgiveness of sins," she read aloud.

That verse had been vital to all of us at the ranch. We all needed God's redemption. I hoped Em would find it, too.

"Wuke!" Quinn pulled on the side of my pant leg. "Did you hear me?"

"I'm sorry, Quinnie. Which horse did you want to start with?" I leaned down so that she knew I was listenin'.

"How about Tink?"

"Sounds good."

I led Tinkerbell out of her stall and over to the combin' area. I handed a comb to Quinn. "Em?" I glanced behind me and held out a comb to her. "Would you like to help comb Tink?"

"Su-sure." Em joined us beside the horse.

"You each can do one side. Let me show ya how to do it. Ya want to start at her ears and work in a circle motion down to her tail. Make sure ya don't press too hard or too soft."

"Just right? Wike Gowdiwocks and the Three Bears." Quinn grinned.

"Exactly like that." I pressed my fingertip to Quinn's nose. "Ya wanna give it a try?" I handed the comb back to her. Quinn stepped up on the stool I placed next to Tinkerbell. I put my hand over hers. "Just like this. Do ya feel how much pressure I'm puttin'? Ya see the dirt comin' up to the top of her coat?"

"I do. I do. Wet me do it." Quinn pushed at my side with her arm.

"Yes, ma'am." I held my hands up in surrender. I turned to Em. "Ya wanna try on the other side?"

"Sure." She followed me around the horse.

"Let me show you," I said, softer than I meant to. I reached around so that my hand covered hers. I breathed in deeply.

142

Electricity surged through my entire body. I could smell the floral scent of her shampoo. *Get yourself together, Luke.* We moved our hands in a circular pattern, startin' at Tinkerbell's head. We slowly moved the brush down her body. I coughed slightly to clear my throat. I removed my hand from hers, and a chill made its way up my spine. I shivered. "I think ya have it, Em."

Em turned her head and smiled. I saw the pink in her cheeks that I knew was reflected in mine.

"Remember to always be in contact with Tinkerbell so that she knows where ya are. Helps to keep her calm." I spoke loud enough for both Em and Quinn to hear me but not loud enough to spook the horse.

"How's it goin' over here?" I asked, walkin' around the mare. "Lookin' good, Quinnie." I placed my hand on her back, and she beamed up at me. "I know this isn't super fun, but it's part of ownin' horses. Ya have to do everythin' so that your horse stays safe, healthy, and happy."

"Is Tink happy?" Quinn asked with questions in her eyes.

"Yes, I believe she is. She likes ya."

Once Quinn and Em were done with the currycombs, I put those away and retrieved the hard brushes from the workbench behind me. "It's also important to put everythin' away in its place so the next person can find it," I continued. "So, these are hard brushes. We are goin' to sweep off the dirt that ya just brought to the top of her coat. Like this." I demonstrated by placin' the brush on Tinkerbell's neck and flicked my wrist in a short, sweepin' motion.

"Ya don't wanna do this with the mane and tail. We will use a wide-toothed comb for those. Ya also don't wanna do this on the head or lower legs. Work ya way down her body so that the dirt moves backward and off her as ya move along. Okay.

Let's see what ya got." I watched as Quinn's tongue barely protruded from her lips as she flicked her wrist.

"Not too long of strokes, Quinnie. Otherwise, the dirt could get pushed back in. There ya go!"

Quinn was such a good girl. She loved workin' with the horses and tried her best to do things right. I had no doubt her doin' her best to do it right was from the years of livin' with Gary and seein' how things went if it wasn't right. My heart ached. I was so happy they were at the ranch but was sad because of the reason why.

"How ya doin' over here?" I asked Em.

"I think I'm doing this right." She glanced up at me.

"Ya are." I grinned, which made Em's face brighten.

As Quinn and Em finished the task of gettin' the dirt off, I held up the wide-toothed comb. "Who wants to comb the mane and tail?" I held the comb up and raised my brows. I knew Quinn would want to and that Em would let her.

"Meeee. I do! I do!" Quinn waved her hand in the air.

"Okay. Here's the comb. Just make sure ya comb it like ya would comb ya hair. Em, ya could help by runnin' ya hands through the mane to make sure ya get all the tangles out."

I stood back and observed how Quinn and Em moved and interacted with each other and Tinkerbell. I wanted them to be my family. I was done fightin' it. It was too exhaustin'. I crossed my arms and leaned against the door jamb. They were both so gentle with the mare. My heart grew warm with love.

"Aww done, Wuke. What do we do now?" Quinn turned in my direction from where she stood on the stool.

"Now, my dear, Quinnie, it's time to give her a bath." I clapped my hands together. "Let's collect the supplies we'll need for this part of the job."

"What do we need?" Em asked.

"Well, we need some towels. They're on the shelf over there." I pointed over Em's shoulder. She twirled around and took some off the shelf. "Now, we have to have the sweat scraper." I waited.

Quinn scrunched her nose. "Eww! What's a sweat scraper?" She cocked her head.

I scanned around me. It wasn't in its usual place. *Ah, there it is.* I plucked it from the table against the wall. "This is it." I held the contraption in the air. It resembled a window squeegee, except it was curved. "We also need the hose, clean sponges, and cloths. And shampoo, of course." We skirted around the room, collectin' all the supplies. "We're gonna take her just outside the stable."

We led Tinkerbell outside and tied her to the hitchin' post. I grabbed the hose. "We, first, have to hose her down. We want to start at the hooves and move upward. Do ya wanna help?" I bent down to Quinn.

"Yeah." She nodded.

"Okay. I'll help with the hose because the nozzle can be powerful."

I had Quinn stand between my arms. I put the hose in her hands and wrapped my fingers around hers. We pressed the trigger together and guided the water to Tinkerbell's hooves before movin' the water flow up her back, makin' sure to spray away from her face.

"Now, we want to wash her with shampoo," I continued.

We dunked the sponge in the bucket of water I had warmin' in the risin' sun. I squeezed some shampoo onto the sponge and rubbed it between my hands to make it sudsy. A bubble formed on the sponge and dislodged itself. Quinn poked it with her finger. When it popped, she let out the loudest laugh I'd ever heard from her. It was one of the sweetest sounds I'd ever heard.

"We don't want to wash Tink's face or her backside with soap. We'll just use a cloth and warm water to wipe her down in those areas. Okay? Em, do ya wanna help, too?"

"Sure," Em responded with more confidence than she had before in the stable.

I threw Em a sponge. "Ya wanna go in a circular motion like ya did with the currycomb. That's it, Quinn; good job. We can alternate sections. Once Quinn gets done with this section, we'll rinse it off and move on to the next." We continued the ritual until Tinkerbell was completely clean and dry.

"Well, we're all done." I raised my hands in the air and let them fall back to my sides. "I'll finish up with the rest of the horses after lunch."

"Did you like helping out, honey?" Em placed her hand on Quinn's back.

"Yeah!" She jumped in the air.

"Thank ya both for ya help. Shall we clean up? Then, we can go see if lunch is ready."

"Yeah. 'Cause I'm hungry." Quinn rubbed her belly.

My stomach roared. "Guess I need to eat, too." I patted my stomach.

Quinn doubled over in a fit of giggles.

"First, we have to make sure everythin' is back in their proper places for the next person that has to do this job. Again, that's a very important rule. If we don't place things back where they go, it takes more time for the next person. Understand?" I knew I'd be usin' them after lunch but wanted Quinn to know the importance of the lesson.

Quinn nodded.

After all the supplies were back in their proper places and Tinkerbell was back in her stall, we strolled the short distance to the main house. Quinn ran ahead just like she always did.

"Thank you for that, Luke. She really is smitten with you. I appreciate you being so kind to her."

"It's not hard to do. She's a wonderful little girl. I have to admit that I'm just as smitten with her. I'm really glad both of ya are here." I smiled. I really wanted to remind Em that Quinn wasn't the only one I was smitten with, but I didn't want to send her runnin' for the hills for a third time.

Em's cheeks turned pink. I saw a hint of a smile. "Thank you."

A lot of laughter and chatter was goin' on in the kitchen as we walked through the door. Austin was tellin' a story about somethin'. I chuckled. He was always tellin' a story. Most of the time, it was exaggerated so much I could never tell what was true and what wasn't. Quinn was perched on his lap. He made a comment, and Quinn squealed with laughter. The whole room erupted. She had that effect on everyone at the ranch. She really was somethin' special.

"Okay. Everyone is here. Let's all have a seat," Colt spoke over the bunch.

Once everyone was seated, Colt prayed over the food. The scent of barbecue chicken filled the air around the table. My mouth salivated. I was hungrier than I had thought.

Just like every other night since I arrived at the ranch, the same people were present at the long wooden table. I glanced across the table at Em. We were surrounded by people—people I cared deeply about. But I wanted nothin' more than to be alone with her. I knew it was better this way. Temptation wouldn't come into play. I wouldn't allow it. But I'd have liked to have had a quiet conversation with her.

I wanted to do whatever I could to make Em feel the same way about me. But I also wanted that to be her decision. She may have called me Gary at Caitlyn's goin' away party, but I was *nothin'* like him. I would do whatever I had to do to prove that to her. Even if it took a lifetime.

In My time.

I closed my eyes. *Thank you, Lord. I trust in You. I trust in Your timin'*. I opened my eyes and found Em's directed at me. My cheeks flamed. I diverted my gaze to my plate.

"Mommy, can I spend the night with Cawwie and Cowt? Pwease?" Quinn begged as she ran over to Em's chair.

"Oh, honey. I don't know. I'm sure Callie and Colt have other things to do."

"They towd me to ask you."

"We did. We'd love to have her," Callie reassured Em.

"If you're sure, I guess I don't see why not."

"Yay!" Quinn threw her arms around Em.

"I guess I'll go to the cabin and get your things and bring them back, Quinn."

"Don't forget Horsey."

"I'd *never* forget him. He would be pretty upset if you had a sleepover without him." Em stood from her chair. "I guess I'll be back in a little while then."

"We'll be here, won't we, Quinn?" Callie bumped Quinn lightly.

"Can I walk you home?" I asked. Anticipation and hope flowed through me. *Please say yes.*

"If you'd like." Em ducked her head.

I opened the door and stuck my hand out as if to say, "after you."

Chapter 23

Emelia

I wasn't sure how I felt about Quinn sleeping over at Callie and Colt's house. A shiver ran down my spine as goosebumps prickled my skin. With Gary out there somewhere, I was uneasy about not having her with me. I guess she wouldn't be *that* far away. I had to learn to let go a little bit. *Kids have sleepovers, Em.*

"Are you cold?" Luke asked.

"No. It's just a chill that ran through me. It happens from time to time." I ran my hands up my folded arms as I glanced up at Luke, flashing him a half-smile.

Luke shoved his hands in his pockets. I wasn't sure what to say or talk about. It seemed like forever ago he told me he was falling in love with me. I didn't know how I felt about that either. How could he love someone like me? *No, Em, you're not going to think like that anymore. Get Gary out of your head.* Easier said than done.

"So . . ." Luke started.

"So . . . what?"

"What are ya goin' to do with ya afternoon and night all to yaself?"

"You know," I glanced up at the sky, "I have no idea. I haven't had this much time to myself in four years."

149

"Would you like to take a horse ride with me?"

"Really?"

Luke peered into my eyes. "I'd love nothin' more than to spend the afternoon with ya."

My cheeks burned from the heat of his stare and his words. *I shouldn't go. I should go back to the cabin. I should keep my distance.* "Um. Sure. I think that would be nice." *What are you saying, Em? You were supposed to say no.*

Once back at the cabin, Luke insisted on remaining on the porch while I grabbed everything Quinn would need for her sleepover, including Horsey. I'd never admit it to anyone, but I was terrified to spend the night alone. Alone with the sounds the cabin made. The sounds of the bushes brushing against the outside just under the window. So many boogeymen in the dark. A tear made an appearance on my cheek. I quickly swiped it away. *Get yourself together, girl. Luke doesn't need your problems. None of them do. Maybe it's time to move on.*

On the stroll back to the house, I enjoyed the chill in the fall air. Autumn was my favorite time of year, and the weather in Edenton didn't disappoint.

After dropping Quinn's things off at the main house, Luke and I went to the stable, but only after Callie reassured me that Quinn would be fine. She and Colt were already engrossed in a battle of Candyland.

"You can ride Tinkerbell, Em. She was very tame when I rode her the other day. I'll ride Majesty, of course."

"Okay. It's been so long since I've been on a horse. I have to admit I'm a little nervous."

Luke placed his hands on my shoulders. "You used to ride?"

"Yes. I used to have my own horse, Apollo. But I had to leave him behind just like everything else." I sighed and lowered my gaze to my feet.

"I'm sorry." Luke paused. "You'll be fine. I'll be right beside ya. It's like ridin' a bike."

"Okay. Do you have that stool I can use? I'm afraid I'm not as thin and able to jump up on a horse as I used to be." My cheeks flushed.

"Sure." Luke flashed a sly grin. "But I'm sure you're just as beautiful."

My face grew hotter. I covered my cheeks with my hands as he strode into the stable.

"Here ya go." Luke set the stool down next to Tinkerbell.

I put my foot in the stirrup, grabbed the reins, and pulled myself up so I could flop my leg over the horse. "Ha! I did it!" I held my head a little higher.

Luke chuckled before jumping onto Majesty. "Let's go." He clicked his tongue, and Majesty trotted off.

I clicked my tongue and squeezed my thighs into Tinkerbell's sides. *That much I do remember.* Tinkerbell took off to catch up with Majesty and Luke. "So, where are we going?" I asked once we were side by side.

"Just wanted to show ya more of the ranch."

"Is it safe?" I glanced around, suddenly feeling more vulnerable out in the open.

"Yeah. Not really anywhere for a person to hide for miles once we get away from the cabins."

"Okay." I exhaled deeply. I hoped he was right. I scanned the landscape in every direction. "This place really is gorgeous. I can see why you never leave it."

"What's that supposed to mean? I leave the ranch." Luke's voice was sharp with offense.

"I just meant . . . I'm sorry. I didn't mean it the way it sounded." I hung my head.

We continued in silence. I was afraid of sticking my foot further into my mouth. *Why do I always get so tongue-tied around him?* It frustrated me so much.

I glanced around. The grass wasn't quite as green as it had been just a few months ago. The leaves on the trees were changing to orange and brown. The ranch was the most beautiful place I'd ever seen.

When we came to a creek, Luke finally spoke. "Do ya want to take a break?"

"If I get down, I'm not sure I'd be able to get back on." I giggled.

"We can always walk them back." Luke lifted his shoulders in a shrug.

"Okay. I might need help down, though. Short leg problems." I wiggled my legs.

Luke slid out of the saddle and jogged around Tinkerbell. He clapped his hands and spread his arms out toward me as he broadened his stance. "Alright. I'm ready." He flashed a grin.

My body shook with laughter. I stood in the saddle, leaned forward, and hoisted my leg over Tinkerbell's back. My foot started to slip from the stirrup.

"Watch out!" I warned Luke.

Before I knew it, Luke and I were both on the ground. "Oh my gosh! Did I hurt you?" I glanced up to find Luke's face inches from mine. The world around us seemed to disappear. It was only us. I sucked my bottom lip between my teeth. "I'm sorry. I didn't mean to fall on you. I hope you aren't hurt."

"I'm fine." Luke stood and brushed off his jeans before extending his hands to help me up. A surge of heat raced up my arms. He dragged me up as if I were as light as a feather. As soon as I was firmly upright, his jaw clenched as he turned away.

"I'm sorry," I replied softly as I swatted at my pants to remove the dirt.

"Really, I'm fine."

"No, not for that." My voice cracked. "For not being able to feel for you what you feel for me." I plucked a piece of grass from where I stood, my feet cemented to the ground. I tore the grass apart, piece by piece—just like the conversation was doing to my heart. "I just can't. Not right now. You have your own stuff to deal with. You don't need my stuff, plus a child that isn't yours." I didn't dare look at him.

"Shouldn't that be *my* decision?"

"Not while I can't ensure we're safe. At the very least." My lip quivered.

What is happening to me? I cared for Luke. Deeply. He made it impossible not to. But was it *love*? I couldn't have been sure. Looking back, I suppose I had never truly felt love before.

"I understand, Em. I meant it when I said I'd wait as long as it takes." Luke leaned against a tree, lifted his hat off his head, and with the same arm, wiped his forehead with the bandana wrapped around his wrist.

"I can't ask you to wait like that."

"Then, I guess it's a good thing I wasn't askin'." Luke flicked the brim of his hat at me before plopping it back on his head. He propelled himself off the tree with his foot. "We'd better get back."

"Okay." I dropped what was left of the blade of grass.

We grabbed the reins of each horse and led them back to the stable. In silence. Somehow, though, it wasn't a completely awkward silence. It was just a state of being together. Being in the expanse of the ranch. Being beside an incredible man who apparently was in love with me. I wasn't sure what to think of it all. For the first time in years, I felt free. It was a wonderful feeling, but I wasn't sure it would last. Gary would strike at some point. I was surprised he hadn't yet.

Upon our return to the stable, I helped Luke get the horses settled for the evening. I really did enjoy our ride. *How do I put that into words without betraying myself?* My heart wanted so much more, but my mind knew what was best.

"Well, thank you for the ride, Luke. Have a great evening," I said quickly before anything else could escape—like, what I was truly starting to feel.

"Wait. Can I at least walk you home?"

"I'd rather spend some time alone. If that's okay."

Luke didn't bother masking the disappointment in his eyes. "Yeah. Of course."

I hurried out of the stable and to the dirt road that led to the cabins. Snapping sticks sounded from the woods beside me. I spun around in all directions, but I was completely alone. "Luke?" I called out.

Luke didn't answer. *Of course, he won't answer.* I rolled my eyes. *You told him you want to be alone.* Goosebumps formed on my arms, and my heart fell to the pit of my stomach. A breeze picked up, and a faint whiff of Marlboro slammed into me. Gary was there. I ran my hands up my arms and willed my legs to move faster, even though they felt like Jell-O. I didn't take a breath until I was behind the closed and locked door of the cabin.

Chapter 24

Gary

I ogled Emelia from the woods as she made her way to her cabin. A smirk spread across my lips as she glanced all around and ran her hands up her arms. A low chuckle escaped me as she yelled for the man. The real surprise was that she was alone. Where was Quinn? Never in my wildest dreams did I ever think Emelia would let her guard down enough to leave her brat with someone else. Not that I cared. One less loose end to worry about when I dragged her mom back with me. If I decided to let her live.

I took a swig of my beer, crushed the can, and threw it on the ground, just like I had done before. I wanted someone to find it. I was sure Emelia had already figured out I was watching, waiting in every crevice of the dark. I would strike when she least expected it. When her guard was completely down.

If Emelia thought what I had done to her before, in warning, was bad, it was nothing compared to what was in store for her. But I wanted to watch her squirm just a little bit more. She had heard me outside her cabin a couple of times. Once, she had called those guys, so I had to skedaddle. Definitely didn't want to meet them in a dark alley. They were almost twice my size. The one with brown hair was a little too close to Emelia for my liking. If I got the chance, I'd just have to take him out,

155

too—no ifs, ands, or buts about it. Emelia was mine and always would be.

I wanted to go closer but needed to wait until the coast was clear. I darted out from the trees and skulked in the shadows, taking cover behind the bush just under Emelia's bedroom window. The light turned on. I wished I could see her face and the fear that would be gushing from every inch of her when she found my little present. Too bad no one ever locked their doors here. They really should. Any crazy person could just waltz right in. Emelia needed to remember who she belonged to.

When Emelia found what I'd left for her, everyone within earshot would know. I chuckled. She probably would think it was me at first, but then, after input from others, she'd just think a rat had found its way inside—like it was nature being nature. I scoffed.

I slithered up to the window. I peered in at the corner so I wouldn't be seen. Emelia slowly made her way down the hall to the bathroom and disappeared from sight. I cackled softly and waited with bated breath.

A few seconds later, Emelia screamed a blood-curdling scream. *Sweet victory!* Sounds of running footsteps filled the air. As much as I wanted to stick around for the show, I hightailed it out of there, through the woods and back to my car.

I'd gotten a room in a neighboring town. Edenton was too small a town to stay there unnoticed. I'd already been seen too much just at the bistro with that waitress.

When I got back to my room, I took the envelope of money out of my pocket and slid it onto the small desk. I'd forgotten I'd left it under the seat. I chuckled. Emelia hadn't known my gambling had finally paid off. I'd hit the jackpot—enough money to live on for a year or two. For me, anyway. I wasn't like those other losers at the casino who couldn't stop when they'd made enough money. No. I was nothing like them.

Chapter 25

Emelia

When I saw the rat, dripping wet and dead in the bottom of the bathtub, I screamed so loud and couldn't catch my breath. I wasn't sure if anyone heard my screams. My first thought was Gary. Would he really have taken a chance of being seen going into my cabin? I knew he would.

I heard pounding. Was that the door, or was it my heart pounding out of my chest? I begged my feet to move forward. I took one step, two steps. My eyes were glued to the door. My breath stuck in my lungs like hair matted to a forehead during a hot, humid day.

"Em, it's me. It's Luke. Let me in." His voice was muffled by the door between us. Was it really him? Or was it Gary trying his best to sound like Luke? I took a few steps closer. "Come on, Em, open up! Or I'm gonna break the door down."

I crept to the door and peeked into the peephole. The air finally expelled from my lungs. I turned the lock. My mind and body were in a fog. Luke turned the knob and barreled through the door. "What happened? What's wrong?" He, once again, scanned everywhere for any signs of injury on my body. "Are you hurt?"

I opened my mouth to speak, but the words wouldn't come out. I shook my head and pointed to the bathroom as the tears rained down my cheeks.

Luke disappeared into the bathroom long enough to look in the tub. When he returned to my side, he tried to calm me with his gentle voice as he ran his hands up and down my arms. "It's just a dead rat."

"Gary . . ." It was all I managed to get out.

"It was only a rat that got in somehow. It happens around here."

I shook my head. "He told me once," I swallowed hard, "that if I ever tried to run away, he'd drown me like a rat."

Luke's jaw clenched. His hands balled into fists. "Okay. Get your stuff. You're not stayin' here tonight. You can stay in my cabin. I'll sleep on the couch."

"No. I couldn't impose like that. I'll be fine here." Fear trembled in my voice.

"Em," Luke spoke sternly, "you're comin'. I just want to make sure you're safe." He closed his eyes. "Please," he begged softly.

"Fine." I huffed, slightly relieved Luke wouldn't take no for an answer. I grabbed my pillow. I could come back when it was light out. It wasn't completely dark outside but dark enough for the boogeyman.

"Ya know, I have pillows in my cabin."

"Yeah, but they aren't *this* one," I sassed as I walked by Luke to the front door. My arm brushed the front of his shirt, sending a shiver of a completely different kind down my spine. He scoffed just before I felt his presence behind me as we strolled over to his cabin.

"I'll just apologize now. My cabin isn't much, but it's home." Luke opened the door and allowed me to step over the threshold first.

It wasn't as big as my cabin, but it was cute. No, scratch

that. Nothing about Luke was cute. The cabin was handsome. The thought forced a giggle to escape. I ran my fingers across the back of his couch, the faded brown leather smooth under my touch. It was very worn in, just like his boots that sat by the door. The cabin was rustic and screamed cowboy. A framed picture of a cowboy riding a bronc hung on the wall. I noticed there wasn't a television. That wouldn't have stood with Gary. He *had* to have a television. *UGH! Luke is not Gary!* I covered my face with my hands.

"What's wrong?" Luke asked, placing his hand on the small of my back. I jerked in response. "I'm sorry." His hand fell away.

My eyes fluttered closed. The disappointment of Luke's hand not residing on my back radiated through me. *Will I always have this reaction?* I sure hoped not. Luke didn't deserve that. The reaction was just a reminder that I didn't need to get close to him. "Thanks for letting me stay," I softly said, regret filling my voice.

"I'll always be here for you, Em. No matter what. I mean that." Luke's hand grazed my arm.

I peered up at Luke. Looking into his eyes, I knew he meant it. "Thank you."

"The bedroom is this way." Luke raised his arm to show me the way. "Bathroom is here." He motioned to the left as we walked by. Then, we stopped at the bedroom door.

"Are you sure it's ok for me to take the bedroom? I can sleep on the couch instead of you. It's no problem. I don't want to put you out in your own home."

"It's fine, Em. I've slept many nights on that couch." Luke flashed a lopsided grin as he scratched the back of his head.

"Thank you, again, for letting me sleep here." I lightly kissed Luke's cheek before entering the room and closing the door.

I leaned against the door, closed my eyes, and exhaled deeply. *I can do this.* I glanced around the room. It was a perfect example of a bachelor's bedroom. Rustic. Simple. Queen-sized bed with wood frame, wood dresser against the wall.

I laid down on the bed and let my head sink into the pillow. I rolled over onto my side. My pillow was swallowed by Luke's enormous king-sized pillow. I slid my hand under his pillow and drew it closer to my face. Luke's scent invaded my nose. Earthy. Musky. I breathed in deeply. The scent comforted me far more than I thought it would—more than it should have. My eyelids grew heavy, and even though the threat of Gary lingered, I felt safe. Secure. Sleep swarmed and lulled me into dreamland.

Chapter 26

Luke

My head fell against the closed door. I closed my eyes and sighed deeply. I placed my hands on the door and leaned into it. "Please, Lord, help Em to feel safe. Not because I want her and Quinnie with me, but for her," I whispered.

I pushed myself away from the door and, with a heavy heart, trudged to the couch. I flopped down and rubbed my hands over my face. Why would a man put a dead rat in someone's tub? No one could be *that* cruel. Could they? I let my head fall back against the back of the couch.

God, help me to keep Em safe. I don't know what I'm up against. But You do. Give me the strength and the wisdom to make sure Em and Quinnie are secure. I'm not sure what I would do if I lost either of them.

Before, it would have been about this time I'd have chosen to go to the bar to get a drink. I always drank when I felt lost, among other things I felt. Then, I'd end up in some hotel room with a nameless woman I wouldn't remember the next day. My throat felt dry. My tongue stuck to the top of my mouth. I stood and went to the kitchen to get a drink of water. I gulped it down.

All I really wanted to do was hold Em. Hold her tight and never let go. But all I could do was wait. Would she ever love me the way I loved her? I looked up at the ceiling to acknowledge God because I knew it was in His timin'. All in His hands.

Chapter 27

Emelia

It had been a few weeks since I found the rat in my bathtub. The thought still made me shiver. Neither Luke nor I spoke of the incident again. Nothing else happened in the weeks following, so I thought maybe it really had been a rat that had gotten into my cabin—especially since the tub had been empty of any water.

It was the first day of the Harvest Festival. The last week of September. Quinn and I helped some of the vendors set up. There was so much build-up to the day, Quinn couldn't wait.

"Wuke, are you gonna wawk with us?" she asked with hope-filled eyes.

"Not today, Quinnie. I have to help with the horses. But another day, okay? I promise." Luke kneeled next to her and placed his hand on her shoulder. "At least one day this week, I'll spend with you and ya mom."

"Okay." Quinn's bottom lip stuck out. She definitely had perfected her pout. "Pinky promise?" She held up her pinky.

Luke linked his pinky with Quinn's. "Yes. Pinky promise. Now, where's my best girl's smile?"

Quinn flashed a toothy grin.

"That's better." Luke opened his arms and swallowed Quinn in a hug.

Seeing them interact further tugged at my heartstrings. I felt more for the man every day, but it still wasn't safe. Even though my eyes hadn't seen Gary, I felt him around me. It was unnerving, to say the least. Exactly what he wanted, I was sure. I ensured Quinn and I were around people as much as possible. Gary still hadn't made an appearance. With everything that was in me, I hoped I was wrong and was just being paranoid.

"Come on, Mommy. Wet's go wook at the booths. I wanna see Mrs. Marci." Quinn tugged on my hand.

"I guess we'll see you later, Luke." I glanced up at him.

"Yes, ma'am." Luke held his index finger up to his hat and flicked the brim before sauntering away.

Quinn pulled harder on my hand, forcing me to put one foot in front of the other. "Okay, baby. I'm coming."

We stopped at booths along the way. There were so many: paintings, baked goods, jewelry, the local inn, and more. Of course, the deliciousness of the baked goods filled my nose. I wanted some, but my body didn't need any of them. Laughter and chatter wafted through the air. Everyone talked to Quinn like she was a part of their family. It made my heart happy to know everyone accepted her. Eventually, I hoped they would accept me, too. Or maybe it was *me* who needed to accept *them*. It was a constant battle between my head and my heart.

"Hi, Mrs. Marci!" Quinn's giggly squeal brought me out of my thoughts.

"Hey there, Quinn." Marci's face lit up as Quinn wrapped her arms around Marci's waist.

"Have you heard from Caitwyn watewy? I miss her."

"She called earlier. She said she was going to call you tomorrow morning. She knows the festival is going on, and she doesn't want to keep you from it. It's one of her favorite times of the year. She's sad she's missing it, especially because you're here this year." Marci tapped Quinn on the nose. A giggle escaped Quinn's lips. "Hi, Emelia. How are you doing?" Marci turned her attention to me.

"Oh. I'm okay." A sudden chill spread throughout my body. I wrapped my arms around myself. I scanned as far as I could all around me without twisting my entire body.

"Everything okay?" Marci asked, placing her hand on my arm.

Don't flinch. "Yeah. I just had a chill. I'm fine."

Marci's face was marked with concern.

"Really. I'm okay." I touched my hand to hers.

"Okay. Bye, Mrs. Marci." Quinn waved and moved on. We didn't stop until she had visited every booth.

"Now what?" I asked.

"Um. Can I ride a horsey? Pwease?" Quinn placed her hands under her chin in a praying position.

I threw my hands in the air and let them smack against the outside of my thighs. "I don't see why not."

Secretly, I think Quinn wanted to see Luke. If I was being completely honest, I did, too. He truly was the most beautiful man I had ever met in my entire life. Why he was interested in *me*, I had no clue. I gave up trying to figure out the why of it all. I hoped one day I could feel the same way about him. My problem was I just didn't trust men. Maybe it was more that I didn't trust my instincts about men. Not after Gary, anyway.

Quinn and I strode over to the horse corral. Luke and Wyatt were helping kids get on and off horses. Callie stood in the background with Warrior. None of the kids seemed interested in riding him.

"Hey, Callie. How are you?"

"I'm great, Emelia. How are you?" Callie ran her hand down the side of Warrior's face.

165

"I'm good. Hey there, Warrior. How're you doing, boy?" I gently moved my hand down his back. He whinnied in response. I wasn't sure I would ever get used to Warrior responding in a way that made me feel he knew exactly what I was saying and feeling at any given time. He was such a special horse.

"Quinn, would you like to be the first to ride Warrior?" Callie bent down to ask.

"Oh, I don't—"

"Yes!" Quinn interrupted. "Pwease, Mommy? I'ww be carefuw. I promise."

Callie glanced at me. "She'll have a helmet on. I'll have Luke take her around the corral. I really need someone to ride him to see if he is completely ready to be a therapy horse."

Who was I to argue with that? "Okay." I turned to Quinn and kneeled beside her. "You be careful and listen to everything Luke tells you, okay?"

"Thank you, Mommy. Thank you." Quinn's grin was so wide her eyes almost disappeared. Any decision I made that resulted in that grin was well worth it. She wrapped her arms around my neck and kissed my cheek.

"Now, go before I change my mind." I giggled.

Quinn squealed and ran over to Luke. I smiled as Luke fitted her with a helmet and scooped her into his arms.

"You sure about this?" Luke asked as they stood next to Warrior.

No. But I nodded. A lump formed in my throat, causing my words to lodge.

"Okay, Quinnie. Are you ready?"

"Yep!" Quinn nodded.

Luke lifted Quinn and plopped her in the saddle on Warrior's back. He leaned in close. Only Quinn heard what he said. Luke took the lead rope from Callie and started down one side of the corral.

"He really is a great man," Callie remarked. "Next to Colt, of course. Luke is amazing with Quinn."

"He really is," I agreed.

My eyes never left Luke, the horse, or Quinn. I always had to be ready for the unexpected. I spent so much time never knowing when or if a punch or shove was coming. I braced myself for anything bad that could happen.

"He cares so much about both of you," Callie continued.

I sighed deeply. "I know. I care about him, too. Just not the way he wants me to. Not right now, anyway."

"How come?"

I closed my eyes for a brief moment. "Because I have to be prepared for if or when we have to leave. Gary is around here somewhere. I feel it with every fiber of my being."

Callie's arm wrapped around my shoulder. I made a conscious effort, once again, not to flinch.

"I wish my life was simpler so I could just fall in love with Luke, with all of you, and with this town and stay here forever. But I have to be realistic."

"I understand. I wish there was something I could do or say to help. To make it so you feel safe here."

"You're doing it—the best you can, anyway. You're being a great friend. I haven't had one of those in a very long time. So, thank you." I glanced at Callie and flashed a grin.

"No problem. I hadn't really had one until I moved here, either." Callie gave me a warm smile. "Oh. Here they come."

"Mommy! Mommy! Wook! Warrior wikes me!"

"I see that! He's a great horse, isn't he?"

"You did so well, Quinn," Callie complimented her. "You're a natural cowgirl. Now, all you need are boots and a hat."

167

"Don't get her started, Callie." I laughed.

Luke placed his hands around Quinn's waist and hoisted her off Warrior's back. When her feet hit the ground, she wrapped her arms around Luke's leg and squeezed. "Thanks, Wuke. I wuv you."

"Aww, Quinnie." Luke squatted down and enveloped her. "I love you, too."

A tear threatened to fall. I quickly swiped it away. It made my heart ache in a way it never had before. *Why couldn't life just be different?*

"I'll see ya later, Quinnie. I gotta get back and help with the other kids, okay?"

"Okay. Bye, Wuke." Quinn waved as she grabbed my hand with her other one.

Quinn and I spent the rest of the evening walking around, taking in all of the sights and people. I didn't think Gary would show up there since so many people were around, but I couldn't have been sure. If he showed up, the people there would instantly know he wasn't one of them anyway.

"Well, I think we've seen and done everything, Quinn. Are you ready to go home to our cabin and get some sleep so we can come back tomorrow?"

Quinn yawned and rubbed her fists into her eyes. "Yeah."

I gathered Quinn into my arms and started on the path to our cabin.

"Can I walk you home?" Austin asked as he came up beside us.

I hadn't talked with Austin much, but he knew how to make Quinn laugh. He seemed harmless enough. "Um. Sure. I guess that would be okay." I glanced around.

"Would you like me to carry her for you? She's knocked out already." Austin held out his hands.

"No. Thank you. I have her." I ran my hand up and down Quinn's back and held her a little tighter. Suddenly, having Austin so near made my skin crawl. I couldn't exactly pinpoint what it was. He hadn't done anything to warrant the feeling.

"Well, thank you for walking us home," I said when we reached the cabin. "I really appreciate it." I slathered on my best polite smile.

As I turned the doorknob, Austin asked, "Aren't ya gonna invite me in?"

"Excuse me?" I tried to hide the horror in my voice.

"You let Luke come in. I just thought—"

"Well, I don't know what you thought, but I'm not that kind of woman."

I could feel the heat rise to my face. Not out of embarrassment but anger. Outrage, even. How dare he think that because Luke entered my cabin because I was terrified, I would just let any man in for any reason at all.

"Are you sure?" Austin asked snidely. He ran his finger up my arm.

My skin felt as if it was filled with creepy crawlers. I didn't even respond. I couldn't. My blood was boiling. I opened the door and quickly slammed it in Austin's face. My hand trembled as I turned the deadbolt lock. I hurriedly went to Quinn's room to lay her down in bed. I was so wobbly with rage, I worried I would drop her.

After tucking Quinn in, I took the couple of steps to the bathroom to splash some water on my face, hoping it would temper my anger. My heart stopped as someone knocked on the door. When it sounded again, my heart raced. My palms became clammy. My breath expelled from my lungs faster than air could be taken in. A bead of sweat made a beeline down my spine.

Chapter 28

Luke

As I was helpin' get the horses back in the stable, out of the corner of my eye, I spotted Austin walkin' alongside Em and Quinn. Quinn appeared to be fast asleep on Em's shoulder. I watched as Austin held out his hands. My jaw clenched tight. I didn't have a good feelin' about it. My pulse quickened.

"What's that about?" Colt nodded in the direction of Austin and Em.

"I'm not sure, but whatever it is, I don't like it."

Colt's hand landed on my shoulder. "Be careful, Luke. She may not take too kindly to ya punchin' Austin in the face."

"I wouldn't do that." My jaw flinched once again.

"Your fists say different." Colt nodded to my clenched fists at my sides. I immediately relaxed my hands. "Go make sure she's okay. I'll take care of the horses. But, Luke, be careful."

"I will." I bolted away down the path in the direction they'd gone.

When I arrived at the cabins, I hid in the shadows of the cabin directly across from Em's.

"Aren't ya gonna invite me in?" Austin asked.

I wanted to pummel him. *Control yourself, Luke. Don't be stupid. Em's seen enough violence in her lifetime.* I continued to lurk in the shadows, listening.

"You let Luke come in. I just thought—"

Em's voice was too soft to drift over to me. As soon as the door was closed, I stepped out of the shadow of the cabin. "What's goin' on, Austin?"

Austin jumped, his eyes as wide as saucers, and his mouth formed an 'o.' "No-nothin'," he stuttered.

"Didn't look like nothin' to me. Looked like ya were tryin' to get somewhere with her." I jammed my hands in my pockets to prevent myself from doing what I really wanted to do with them, which was slam them into Austin's face. *Lord, give me strength to keep my cool.*

"Well, *you* got somewhere with her. So, I thought I'd give it a try."

"You might give *what* a try exactly?" My eyes narrowed, and my jaw tightened.

"Ya know." Austin shrugged.

"I don't know what you think might or might not have happened between Em and me, but I suggest you pack your bags and leave the ranch before you find out what I might or might not want to do to your face." My temper was in full flare. I needed to walk away because if I didn't, everythin' would go black.

"The only one who can make me leave here is Colt," Austin retorted in a whiny tone.

"Do ya really wanna explain to Colt what happened here tonight? Do ya really think he would be okay with what ya just tried to do?" I towered over Austin, standing toe-to-toe.

Austin's eyes widened more as he craned his neck to look up at me. He swiped his arm across his upper lip to erase the sweat. He didn't speak. Not a single word. He ran, kickin' up dirt as fast as he could until he reached his cabin. I wasn't sure if he would leave in the middle of the night or not, but I knew I had to make sure Em was okay.

I stepped up to the door of Em's cabin and raised my fist. I hesitated. *Is she gonna think I'm a crazy, jealous maniac? I mean, I did follow them. I guess I won't know unless I knock.* I rapped my fist against the door. No answer. My heart fell to the pit of my stomach. I thumped on the door again.

"Who is it?" Em asked softly through the closed door.

"It's me, Em. It's Luke." I placed my hands on either side of the door frame.

The door slowly opened. The fear on Em's face matched her voice. Once she saw it was me, she flung the door open and leaped into my arms, wrapping hers tightly around my neck.

"It's okay, Em," I softly responded, tryin' to soothe her.

"Please don't leave me," Em whispered in my ear. The way she asked, along with her breath against my ear, had goosebumps pricklin' up and down my arms.

"I won't. Not if ya don't want me to." I ran my hands up her arms. "Let's get ya inside."

Em nodded, pried herself from my neck, and led me inside. She flopped down on the couch. I hesitated before sittin' in the chair. After what had transpired, I didn't want to crowd her.

"I'm so sorry that happened to you, Em. I've told Austin to pack his things and leave the ranch." Her body softened with relief. "If he's not gone by tomorrow, Colt and I will take care of it."

"Quinn and I will stay inside until we know he's gone." Em ran her right hand up her left arm.

"I can understand that. I'll let you know when I'm sure he's gone."

Em's eyes grew wide. "You aren't leaving, are you?" Her hand rested on my arm. Heat seared my skin. Panic filled her voice.

"No. I said I'd stay. I'll sleep on the couch."

Em exhaled sharply. "Thank you. I was so scared, Luke." I looked down at my hands. "Gary always took what he wanted whether I wanted to or not," she continued. "I was terrified Austin was going to do the same."

"Oh, Em. I don't even know what to say to that. Except that a real man—a loving and kind man—would never do that to you."

"Thank you for staying. I'm going to get ready for bed. I was going to stay up for a while and read, but after that, I'm exhausted. I don't want to be too tired for the festival tomorrow. I couldn't do that to Quinn."

"I understand. Go try to get some sleep."

Em stood and tiptoed down the hall. I ran my hand down my face. I plucked my phone from my pocket and hit Colt's number. "Hey. Can you come to Em's cabin?" I asked while sneakin' out onto the porch.

"Yeah. I'll be right there."

"Thanks." I pushed my phone back into my pocket and sighed deeply. *How's she ever gonna trust me when guys keep mistreatin' her?*

It wasn't long before Colt was on the porch next to me. "What's goin' on?"

I lifted my hat off my head and ran my hand through my hair. "Well, Austin tried to get Em to let him into her cabin. She was horrified. He outright admitted to me what he was tryin' to get from her. I told him he needed to leave the ranch."

"Oh, man. Like she needs that after everythin' she's been through." Colt scoffed and rubbed his foot on the plank underneath him. "You did the right thing." He rubbed the back of his neck. "Dang it, Austin."

"We can't save everyone, Colt. I'm sure ya know that."

173

"Yeah." Colt sighed. "He's just always been a good kid. We'll check his cabin in the mornin' to make sure he's cleared out, and we'll escort him out if he hasn't."

"That's what I told Em. She said she isn't comin' out until she knows he's gone."

"I can't say I blame her. Thanks for lettin' me know, Luke. Sorry ya had to deal with that on your own."

"Ah, it wasn't a problem. Austin was more scared of what I might do to him than anythin' else."

"I bet he was." Colt chuckled. "I guess I'll meet ya in the mornin'."

"Sounds good. Em asked me to sleep on the couch."

"I figured as much." Colt strolled over to his truck. "I'll see ya in the mornin'." He jumped in and skidded away.

I let out a deep breath. I wasn't sure how Colt was goin' to react to my split-second decision. It made me feel good to know he backed me on it, though. He trusted my decisions. A satisfied smile formed on my lips.

I opened the door and scuffed back inside. *Guess I'd best try to get comfortable on the couch.* I stood starin' at the couch with my hands on my hips. *How am I goin' to sleep on this thing?* It was definitely not long enough for my six-foot frame. I scratched the back of my neck. I leaned the pillow up against the arm, flopped down, and sprawled out. My feet hung over the end. *Oh well.* I would sleep as well as I could. It was worth it to make sure Em felt safe and to know for myself that she and Quinn were safe. I closed my eyes.

* * *

"**W**uke," Quinn whispered.

I jumped and fell straight off the couch, causin' Quinn to bend forward in a fit of giggles.

174

"Sorry." Quinn placed her fingers over her mouth.

"It's okay, Quinnie. How did ya sleep?" I asked, standin' from the floor. I stretched my back. It cracked like a walnut in a nutcracker.

"How'd *you* sleep?" Em asked, sauntering into the room from the back of the cabin.

"Oh, I slept about as good as to be expected on a couch that is too small."

Em stifled a giggle. "I'm sorry. I should have taken the couch and let you sleep in the bed. I didn't think about the couch being too short."

"It's really okay, Em. I think I'll run home, take a shower, and get ready for the day. I'll keep ya posted about Austin." I grazed Em's elbow with my fingertips.

"Okay. Thank you, again, for staying."

"Not a problem." I flashed her a lopsided grin and left the cabin.

Chapter 29

Emelia

"**W**hy do I have to stay inside?" Quinn whined.

"It's not safe outside right now, sweetie. Do you want to watch cartoons?"

"Why isn't it safe, Mommy?"

"There's just someone Luke and Colt have to get off the ranch."

"Okay." Quinn slumped down onto the couch. I turned the television on to her cartoons. I plopped down next to her and snuggled her close.

A few hours later, there was a knock on the door. I slowly pried the door open and found Colt and Luke hovering outside. "Hey, Colt. Hey, Luke." I smiled.

"Just wanted you to know he's gone," Colt informed me. "Sorry for what happened and that we can't stay to chat, but we've gotta get goin' to get things ready for the festival."

"Oh. Yes. Don't let me keep you. We'll see you both later, I'm sure."

Quinn was in her room getting changed for the festival. "Are you ready to go?" I asked her as I stood in her doorway.

"Yeah. We can go outside now?"

"Yes. Luke and Colt just stopped by to let me know it's okay. And just in time to go to the festival."

"Do you think Wuke wiww ride the hayride with us?" Quinn asked with hopeful eyes.

"I'm not sure. I suppose if he has time. We will have to ask him. Alright?"

We opened the door and found Luke lingering with his fist in mid-air. "Hey, you two."

"What are you doing here?" I asked, trying to hide my smile.

"Well, I have a surprise for Quinnie." Luke grinned until his teeth showed.

"What is it? What is it?" Quinn bounced up and down with excitement.

"You didn't have to do that." I sighed.

"I know. I wanted to."

Luke's sweet smile knocked down another piece of the wall around my heart. If that kept happening, the wall would be gone in no time. I somehow had to stop it. If that was even possible. He held out two wrapped boxes he had been hiding behind his back.

Quinn squealed with delight. She ran to the couch and tore at the wrapping paper. She ripped off the lid. "It's a cowgirl hat!" Luke helped her take it out of the box and plopped the white hat on top of her head. "I wuv it! Thanks, Wuke." She jumped into his arms and wrapped hers around his neck. Luke caught the hat before it hit the floor.

"Open the other one." Luke's smile was almost as bright as Quinn's.

Oh, lord! This man!

Quinn made light work of the second box. She pulled out one pink cowgirl boot and then the other. "Wuke, hewp me put them on?" She stuck her feet out to him.

"Of course. Do you like 'em? I hope I got the right size."

177

Luke grabbed one of the boots with one hand and Quinn's foot with the other.

"I wuv them."

"Oh, good. They fit." Luke scratched the back of his head and chuckled. "Now I know how the guy from Cinderella felt having to put the shoe on all those women's feet."

After the boots were properly on her feet, Quinn kicked her legs back and forth.

"Now, you're a proper cowgirl, Quinnie." Luke flicked his index finger on the brim of her hat.

"How do I wook, Mommy?" Quinn stood and modeled her hat and boots for me.

"You look so pretty."

Quinn shot out the door.

"Quinn, wait . . ." I waved from the door. "Oh, it's no use. Luke, you really didn't have to do that."

"I know." His cheeks turned pink. "I wanted to."

"Well, thank you. You just made her the happiest girl on the planet."

Luke's chest puffed out, and he grinned like the Cheshire Cat.

"Oh. Quinn wanted me to ask if you would join us on the hayride and at the bonfire."

Luke glanced in my direction, and heat rushed up my neck. "Quinn, huh? What about you?"

I sucked my bottom lip between my teeth. "I suppose I'd like that, too."

"Suppose, huh?" Luke's body shook with a chuckle. "Then, I *suppose* I could arrange that. For my best girl, Quinn, that is." He winked.

I laughed and rolled my eyes. "I'd better go find Quinn."

I opened the door and hurried out. I wasn't sure why my

heart fell to the pit of my stomach when Luke responded, but it had. I was glad he and Quinn had such a good bond. On the other hand, though, they might have gotten *too* close. With Gary lurking around and us not knowing when he would strike, it still left me wondering if it was safer to stay or to go. My mind constantly went back to staying or going. I wanted to do what was best for everyone, but I had no idea what that was.

I glanced around outside. Quinn was nowhere in sight. Panic bubbled up in my stomach. Where did she run off to? In pure Em fashion, my first thought went straight to Gary taking her. I cupped my hands around my mouth and hollered, "Quinn! Quinn! Where are you?" When she didn't respond, panic rose to the surface. I scrunched my hair in my hands and turned in every direction. Tears stung my eyes.

"I think I saw her headin' to the stable," Jon called out from the porch of his cabin. He raised his cup to us before bringing it to his lips.

I waved a shaky hand at him. "Thank you."

I walked as quickly as I could without running down the path to the stable. My short legs were no match for Luke's long ones. Sure enough, there was Quinn in deep conversation with Colt. From where I stood, it looked as if she were showing him her new hat and boots. I couldn't help but softly giggle as relief washed over me.

"Before the festival gets in full swing, I'm gonna go finish my chores." Luke tapped my arm with his fingertips.

"O-okay." When I finally composed myself, I went over to Quinn and Colt. "Quinn! Don't run off like that without telling me where you'll be." I placed my hand over my heart.

"I'm sorry, Mommy. I just wanted to show Cowt my presents." Quinn lowered her head.

"They're mighty nice, Quinn." Colt smiled. He leaned over

to me and whispered, "I helped pick 'em out." Quinn sure did have Colt and Luke wrapped around her little finger. "Are ya goin' to the hayride in a little while?" Colt directed his question to Quinn.

"I think so." Quinn remained somber.

"Yes, we are." I gave Quinn's shoulder a light squeeze.

"Well, I'm the driver, so maybe you'd like ta sit up front with me and help guide the horses?"

"Reawwy?" Quinn's entire face lit up like a sunbeam as she peered up at me. "Can I, Mommy?"

"I don't see why not. Are you sure, Colt?" I grabbed my bottom lip with my teeth.

"Of course." Colt chuckled. "Do ya want ta help me get the horses ready to pull the wagon? And get the hay ready?"

"Yeah!" Quinn pumped one fist into the air. "See you water, Mommy." She waved me off.

"Well, it seems I've been replaced by *two* cowboys." I stuck out my lower lip. What was I going to do with myself before the hayride?

I decided to head to the main house and see if Callie needed me to do anything. "Hey, Callie," I greeted as I let the screen door to the kitchen clap shut behind me. Callie had large pitchers of ice sitting on the dinner table.

"Oh, hey, Emelia. How are you?" Callie turned from the sink, where she was slicing a few lemons.

"I'm doing okay. I came to see if there was anything I could do to help."

"Sure. I'm just making some lemonade for the hayride and getting the s'mores stuff ready for the bonfire. Here, you can start pouring into the pitchers." Callie handed me some lemons already cut in half and the lemon squeezer. As I squished the first lemon into the squeezer, Callie commented quietly, "I'm really sorry about what happened with Austin."

"Thanks. I'm just glad Quinn was asleep. I sure know how to attract them, don't I?" I rolled my eyes and poured the lemon juice into the pitcher, filling it the rest of the way to the top with water. I added some sugar and lemon slices.

After Callie and I finished with the pitchers, we gathered the cups, pitchers, candy bars, marshmallows, and graham crackers. Callie and I loaded up her Jeep and headed to an area behind the cabins where the bonfire was to take place.

"I truly can't thank Colt enough for spending so much time with Quinn. She adores Luke and him." I glanced over at Callie.

"He really loves it. Seeing him with her solidifies my thought that he will make the best daddy."

"You won't get any argument from me."

"This is going to be so much fun. This is the first year we've done the hayride and bonfire." Callie grinned. "I can't believe I've been married to Colt for a year. We got married on the last night of the festival last year."

"Oh, that's so sweet. I'm not sure I'll ever get married." I sighed.

"I can understand your hesitation. What Gary did to you was wrong on so many levels. Same goes for Austin. I hope you know not all men are that way."

"I'm beginning to see that." Luke's face danced around in my mind.

In time, daughter.

"What was that?" I glanced around me.

"What was what?"

"Didn't you hear that voice?"

"No, I didn't hear it." Callie grinned.

"Why are you grinning?"

181

"I think you just heard the voice of God."

"There's no way. God doesn't waste his time on people like me." I shook my head from side to side.

"God talks to everyone, Emelia. You just have to listen. Most people are too busy or caught up in the things of the world to notice when God is speaking to them. They never realize what they miss out on, including opportunities." Callie shrugged.

"I'm not sure He cares that much about me at all. My parents told me that my daughter and I were going to hell because I had her from a one-night stand."

"Don't you dare believe that, Emelia. Not for one minute. God loves you. He thinks the world of you. And if I'm being completely honest, everyone around here does, too. *Especially* Luke." Callie placed her hand on my shoulder.

"You really think so?" I glanced at her out of the corner of my eye as a tear threatened to fall.

"I know so. You just put what your parents said out of your pretty head. They *are* allowed to be wrong, you know."

"The hayride is about to begin. If you want to ride, be sure to get in line," Colt announced over the loudspeaker.

"Oh. We'd better go get our spots." Callie grabbed my hand and dragged me over to the front of the line. The scent of hay invaded the air.

Luke was the first person in line. "Someone really wants a hayride," Callie teased him.

"I just want to make sure I get the best seat on the wagon." Luke's eyes managed to pierce my soul. My cheeks flared. He held out his hand. "After you."

I placed my hand in Luke's and climbed up onto the wagon. "Thank you."

I slid onto a bale of hay. It prickled my legs. I wiggled so the hay would give way and be more comfortable. Luke sat down next to me. He was so close his thigh was touching mine. Electric charges surged through my leg, up my stomach, and straight into my heart. I wanted to move my leg away, but it was as if it was glued in place. Right. Next. To. His. I closed my eyes. *Just breathe.*

The feelings Luke evoked were unnerving. I wasn't even sure what those feelings were. I just knew if I wasn't careful, my heart would take control over my mind. And that just couldn't happen.

"You okay?" Luke leaned in. The air from his lips pricked my ear.

"I'm fine," I answered a little too quickly, causing Luke's head to fall back in laughter. My elbow collided with his side.

"Oomph!" Luke clutched his side. His smile never faded from his lips. "What was that for?"

"For laughing at me." I stuck my bottom lip out.

"Now you look like Quinn. Except even prettier." Luke tapped my nose with his finger just like he always did to Quinn.

My cheeks grew warm. I couldn't help but smile.

"That's better." Luke bumped my shoulder with his.

As the wagon lunged forward, I was tossed almost into Luke's lap. "Whoa!"

"Don't worry. I've got ya." Luke's voice was sultry against my ear as he wrapped his arm around my shoulder. I felt the statement meant more than just in that moment. I was almost certain of it.

"Can we go faster, Cowt?" Quinn asked in a squeal of laughter.

"No." Colt shook his head before it fell back, and a laugh rumbled from his lips. "Everyone will end up falling out. That wouldn't be good, would it?"

"No. I don't think so," Quinn agreed.

Luke's arm remained around my shoulders for the rest of the ride. I wanted to overthink the moment just like I always had, but instead, I closed my eyes and lived in it because what if it didn't last or it never happened again? I soaked in every moment. Luke's scent. His security. His love. Everything.

"Well, the ride has come to an end, but we hope you'll stick around for the bonfire," Colt bellowed so everyone could hear.

No, I don't want to leave this spot.

Luke stood, and with him, he took his scent, his security, and his warmth. A heaviness unlike anything I'd ever experienced filled my heart. A few sparks flew as Luke offered his hand to help me descend from the wagon. "Are you ready for the bonfire?" he asked.

"Yeah, I think so." I tucked my hands into the front pockets of my jeans.

"Shall we then?" Luke bent over, one arm over his stomach and the other extended out toward the bonfire.

I giggled. "Let me go grab Quinn, and then we'll be ready." I lifted my thumb and pointed it over my shoulder.

"I'll be right here waiting."

Thankfully, I had already turned away to go after Quinn, so Luke didn't see the blush on my cheeks.

Chapter 30

Luke

I stuck my thumbs through the loops of my jeans as I waited for Em and Quinn. *How am I ever goin' ta wait patiently for her?* Everythin' in me wanted to shake her and scream that we were right for each other—that we belonged together. But I knew I couldn't do that.

Em and Quinn arrived next to me and broke my train of thought. I just had to enjoy what I had with them, whether it was ever more than that or not. God would work that out. Eventually.

"Do ya wanna make some s'mores?" I asked Quinn.

"Yes." She grinned

I never knew I could care so much about a kid in my life. She was everythin' I could ever imagine my child to be. I squeezed my eyes shut. *No! Not the right thinkin'!* Not. At. All.

"What's a s'mores?" Quinn scrunched her face in curiosity.

"Ya don't know what a s'more is? Oh." My eyebrows raised in surprise as a laugh erupted from my belly. "You're in for a real treat. It is the most amazin' thing *ever*."

Em giggled from behind me. I grabbed Quinn's hand and pulled her over to the table.

"So, first, you take a marshmallow, and you put it on a stick like this," I instructed. "Then, we take it over to the fire. I like mine burnt, but we'll make yours slightly golden brown, okay?"

Quinn nodded. I placed the marshmallow near the fire, and we waited for it to turn brown. When it was the perfect shade of brown, I lifted it from the fire.

"Now, we go back over to the table. We take the graham cracker square like so, and a piece of chocolate. We put the chocolate on the square and the marshmallow on top of the chocolate. Then, we cover it with another graham cracker." I glanced over at Quinn. Her eyes were wide with anticipation as she licked her lips.

"We'll share, Quinn," Em told her.

"Aww, do we have to?" Quinn whined.

Em giggled. "Yes. You don't need quite that much sugar this late at night. You'll never get to sleep."

"Okay." Quinn's shoulders slumped. Her face was covered in disappointment.

"Here you go." I handed Quinn the square.

Quinn opened her mouth as wide as she could and chomped down. Her eyes grew wider, if that was even a possibility. "Mmm. This is good," she said, talking with her mouth full. She handed the s'more to Em.

Em took a bite and closed her eyes. "So much better than I remember."

"That's because *I* made it." I grinned and puffed out my chest.

"You want a gold star or something?" Em playfully stuck her tongue out at me.

"No, but I'll take a kiss on the cheek." I tapped my cheek with my index finger.

Em's eyes rolled to the top of her head. She lifted herself onto her tiptoes and planted her lips on my cheek. "Happy now?" She giggled.

"You have no idea." I lifted my fingertips to my cheek. It tingled long after her lips departed. Never in my wildest dreams did I think a kiss on the cheek could feel so good. My heart did a flip-flop in my chest. I wondered if Em's lips tingled, too.

Quinn giggled.

"Oh, ya think that's funny, do ya?" I gathered Quinn into my arms and tickled her.

Quinn shook with laughter. After a few minutes, she breathlessly pleaded, "Wuke, pwease stop! My tummy hurts." She burst into another fit of giggles. "I surrender! I surrender!" Laughter bellowed all around us.

"Where did you hear that word?" I asked.

"From TV." When Quinn's feet were firmly planted on the ground, she placed her hand on her heart.

As the night wore on, the crowd dwindled, and my heart sank to my stomach. I wasn't ready for my time with Em and Quinn to end. I *never* was. Would it ever get any easier not bein' the one to tuck Quinn into bed at night? To get to spend the evenin' cuddlin' on the couch with Em and talkin' about our days? But I had to wait on God. I sighed. I knew He was in control.

"What's wrong?" Em asked from next to me.

"It's just been such an amazin' night. I'm not ready for it to end yet."

"Yeah. Me neither. But Quinn is knocked out. I should get her to bed."

"Can I walk ya home?" I asked softly.

"Um. Sure." Em stood from where she had been sittin'.

"Here. I'll take her."

"Oh. Thank you."

Em lifted Quinn into my outstretched arms. Quinn barely

moved. She nuzzled my neck and wrapped one arm around me. My heart swelled.

"She's the sweetest kid I've ever met, Em. I have to admit that I'm smitten with her. But she's not the only one." I chided myself as soon as the words left my mouth. *Smooth, Luke. Real smooth.*

"She really loves you, too. Maybe that's partly because she's never really had a dad," Em responded somberly.

"I'm sure that's been hard on both of you."

"It really has." Em glanced down at her clasped hands.

As we approached Em and Quinn's cabin, I grasped at straws for just a little more time with them. "Do ya think I could tuck her in?"

Em twitched her lips to the side. "I guess that'd be okay."

Yes! Why did that excite me so much? What have these two done to me? I'm a Marine, and here I am excited about gettin' to tuck Quinn into bed.

Love. The love I put in your heart for them.

I hear You, God. I hear You.

Em opened the front door and allowed me to enter first. I took the few strides to Quinn's room. My heart ached. It ached for the little girl who never had a dad. It ached for the woman who didn't know what love truly felt like. It ached for me because the thought of never havin' them as my family was almost too much to bear.

I didn't notice when Em came into the room. She pulled the covers down. I laid Quinn on the bed and nestled her horse into the crook of her arm and removed her boots from her feet. I kissed her forehead and whispered, "Good night, sweet Quinnie. Sweet dreams."

A small smile formed on Quinn's lips as she turned over, taking her horse with her. Em kissed her on the side of her head and ran her hand over Quinn's hair. I stepped out of the room as Em turned off the light. We both peeked in and watched her sleep by the glow of her nightlight. Then, Em broke the trance by closing the door.

"Thank you for walking me home." Em kept her voice soft.

"No problem." I pushed my hands into my pockets for fear I would gather Em up in my arms and kiss her. It was the only thing I wanted to do. I didn't want it to go further than that, but I longed to know what her lips felt like against mine.

"Thank you, again, for today. Especially for what you did for Quinn with the boots and hat. You truly made her decade. It was one of the best days I've had in a long time."

"It wasn't a problem. I had a lot of fun." I felt the lopsided grin coming long before it appeared on my face.

Before completely leavin' the doorway of the entrance to the cabin, I turned and faced Em. She looked so beautiful washed in the glow of the moon. I placed my hands on her cheeks and gazed into her eyes. My eyes lowered to her lips as I leaned in.

Em closed her eyes and whispered, "Luke . . ."

I changed the direction of my path and pressed my lips to the middle of her forehead. Oh, how I had wanted to kiss her lips. I wanted to more than anythin' in the world. But that wasn't what God wanted. It wasn't what Em needed. She needed me to be the kind of man who was patient and would wait until she was ready—the kind of man who would let *her* decide. I ran my thumbs along her cheeks.

"Sweet dreams, Em. See ya tomorrow." I dropped my hands to my sides and briskly headed back to my cabin. A cold shower was in store. My entire body was inflamed. I had never had a woman affect me the way Em did. The jury was still out on whether I liked it or not.

Chapter 31

Emelia

It was the last night of the festival. There was a dance that doubled as Colt and Callie's wedding anniversary party. Callie and I had gone shopping to find dresses for Quinn and me. Callie insisted on buying them for us. I was grateful because I had run out of money long before. It didn't stop me from arguing with her about it, though. She told me not to rob her of her blessing, so what could I say to that? Nothing. I just threw my hands up in surrender.

"Quinn," I called out from the living room. "It's time to get ready for the party."

Quinn squealed and came barreling out of her room. "I'm so excited to wear my new dress." She had picked out a dress that matched her boots. I pulled the dress over her head as she stuck her arms and head through the correct holes. It slid down her body to just about her knees.

"Alright. Go get your boots on, and then I'll fix your hair."

"I want braids, Mommy."

"Okay. I'm going to get ready while you get your boots on." I retreated to my room.

I was so nervous to wear the dress we had picked out. It was well out of my comfort zone, but Callie was adamant that I looked perfect. She said the dress brought out the green in my eyes. The A-line, emerald-green, lace dress had a V-neck, three-quarter sleeves, and scalloped edges along the bottom. It was banded just below the bust, so it took the focus away from my protruding stomach. *I wonder if Luke will like it.* I ran my hands down the dress as I stared at my image in the mirror.

Quinn gasped from the doorway of my bedroom. "Mommy, you wook so pretty!"

"I do?" I looked down at the dress. "Are you ready to do your hair?"

"Yeah." Quinn skipped into the bathroom to get rubber bands and her hairbrush.

I pulled the chair out from the kitchen table. "Have a seat." I braided two French braids into Quinn's hair. "Okay. You're all done. I'm going to put on some makeup and fix my own hair. You can watch some TV if you want." I turned on the television and changed the channel to cartoons.

After I was ready to go, I stepped into the living room. "How do I look, Quinn?"

Quinn jumped up from the couch. "You wook beautiful." She twirled around. "How do *I* wook?"

"You'll be the prettiest girl there. Shall we go?"

Quinn nodded and ran to the door.

"Stay with me, though. It's getting dark, and we don't want your dress to get dirty before anyone has a chance to see you in it."

Quinn took hold of my hand. As soon as the evening air grazed my skin, the hairs on the back of my neck stood up. A chill ran down my back.

Entering the barn was like stepping into a daydream. The tiny string lights glistened from every corner. White roses adorned every table.

"I told you; you look gorgeous in that dress." Callie pulled

191

me out of my trance.

"You really think so?" I glanced at Callie, sliding my hands down the front of my dress.

"Yes. And I'm not the only one who thinks that." Callie nodded. I peeked in the direction of her nod. Luke was strutting toward us. The look on his face was one I'd never encountered—not directed at me, anyway.

"Wow, Em. That is some dress." Luke took my hands in his and stretched my arms away from my body.

Heat quickly engulfed my cheeks. "Thank you."

"Hi, Wuke!"

"Hey, Quinnie. How's my best girl?"

"I'm good. How do I wook?" Quinn twirled around for him.

"You look absolutely beautiful," Luke told Quinn before returning his attention to me. "I have to make a pass around the room. I'll be back, okay?"

"Su-sure. Okay."

"Mommy, can I go say hi to my friends?" Quinn tugged on my hand.

"Of course."

Quinn scampered off to the other side of the barn. Knowing she had friends brought a smile to my face. I had wanted that for her for so long.

I took a seat at a nearby table and scanned the room. My eyes stopped abruptly when I saw Luke talking to a gorgeous woman. She was petite and thin with long, flowing blonde hair. She was laughing about something and laid her hand on Luke's arm. Something bubbled in the pit of my stomach. Anger? No. Was it jealousy? I had no idea. I'd never been one to be jealous, but that had to be what I was feeling. I wanted to look away, but it was like watching a car accident. I just *had* to watch. The woman leaned in close to him before her head fell back with laughter.

I couldn't watch anymore. I stood and scurried right out of the barn. I couldn't breathe. When I was out in the fresh air, my chest heaved, attempting to get air to fill my lungs. Heat radiated throughout my entire body. I had no right to feel the way I did. Luke wasn't my boyfriend. Even if he was, he could talk to whomever he chose.

"Em?" I froze at the sound of Luke's voice behind me. "What are ya doin' out here?"

I swallowed the lump that was lodged in my throat. "I just needed some fresh air."

"What's wrong?" Luke's fingertips grazed my shoulder.

"Shouldn't you be in there with your friend?" I spewed out with more disdain than I had intended. I closed my eyes.

"Em. Look at me."

My feet were cemented to the ground.

"Em, please," Luke begged.

I slowly turned around.

"That woman is a part of my past. Not my present. And certainly not my future."

Music to a slow song danced through the air. Clay Walker began to croon the first few chords of "Watch This." I loved that song.

Luke held out his hand. "May I have this dance?"

"Su-sure." I briefly smiled.

If Luke and I were dancing, we wouldn't have to talk. I wouldn't have to admit that I was jealous for the first time in my life. I didn't like feeling jealous—not one bit.

I laid my hand in Luke's, and he slowly pulled me closer. We swayed to the music. He whispered the words to the song in my ear. My eyes welled up with tears. The song was about a man telling a woman that he would show her the love she always dreamed about. It talked about the fear of falling in love after having a broken heart and about how the man would make the feelings disappear. I *did* want to feel the world stand still because of one kiss.

I leaned back enough to be able to see Luke's eyes. They were glistening just as I knew mine were. I gazed into his eyes and knew he meant every word in that song and every word he had ever spoken to me. I lifted my hands to his cheeks and brought his face close to mine. My eyes closed as I pressed my lips to his. It wasn't a hot, passionate kiss. It was tender. And kind. And loving. And right. Everything and everyone around us melted away. It was just Luke and me. I felt like we were floating on a cloud. When I moved away, my chest was once again heaving. Luke's was, too.

"Wow," Luke gasped as he leaned his forehead against mine.

"You can say that again."

"Wow."

We both chuckled.

"What does this mean, Em?"

"I don't know." I lifted my shoulders in a shrug. "I know I still need more time. I just had to know what that felt like. I'm sorry. Maybe I shouldn't have done it?" My gaze moved to the ground.

"Ya don't have anythin' ta be sorry about. I will give ya all the time ya need. Ya wanna hear somethin' funny?" Luke scratched the back of his head.

"Sure. I can always use a good laugh."

"The couple of months since the Fourth of July—since we've gotten close . . ." Luke cleared his throat before continuing. "I haven't had a single nightmare about the war."

"Really?" I peered up at him. "That's not funny. That's wonderful news."

"Yeah." Luke wrapped his hand around the back of his neck and squeezed a few times before dropping it back to his side. "It's been nice to get some sleep for a change. I have you to thank for that." He turned and headed back to the barn.

"I didn't do anything special."

Luke stopped dead in his tracks before he turned to face me. "Didn't do anything special? Yeah, ya did. Before ya grabbed my hand at the fireworks, I was back over there, in combat. In my head, at least. Ya brought me back before anythin' bad happened. Ya have no idea how much that means to me."

"Well, I do *now*." I smiled. "So, you're welcome."

"Shall we go back inside?" Luke opened his arm so I could loop my hand in his elbow. He placed his hand over mine and whispered, "I want everyone in this place to know who I belong to. Heart. Mind. And soul."

My heart pitter-pattered in my chest as heat flamed up my neck to my cheeks.

"By the way, have I mentioned how gorgeous you look in that dress?"

"Well, I think earlier you said beautiful, so it's improving." I giggled.

Once we returned to the barn, everyone was dancing, laughing, and having a good time. I could feel the heat like laser beams zapping me from some of the women's eyes. I inched my hand from Luke's arm, but he squeezed my hand between his ribs and elbow, leaned over, and softly said, "Don't you dare."

I slipped my hand back in place, unable to speak.

For the rest of the night, Luke didn't leave my side. It was nice to be out with a man who didn't expect me to be seen and not heard or to have to hide bruises and pain. Luke was the kind of man girls spent their entire lives dreaming about, hoping one day they would meet him in person. I knew I was on my way to losing the fight against my heart being completely lost to the man, but I couldn't risk him getting hurt by Gary. I knew Gary was out there, waiting to pounce when he had the chance. That thought alone terrified me more than anyone would ever know. Not knowing *when* he would come after me was a close second.

"You've been awfully quiet tonight," Luke said as he walked me home with Quinn fast asleep, nestled in his arms.

"Sorry. I didn't mean to be. Just taking the night in. It was a new experience for me. It was nice."

"Everyone loved you."

"Not everyone," I corrected. "There were a few ladies giving me the death stare when we went back into the barn."

"They were jealous."

"Of me? Not hardly." I laughed.

"Don't do that, Em." Luke's voice changed to a somber tone.

"Don't do what?"

"Don't act like you aren't anythin' special."

"I'm not. I'm just me." I opened the door to the cabin. I swung my arm out to usher Luke inside. "After you."

Luke quickly laid Quinn down in her bed and was by my side in a matter of minutes. I wasn't sure what it was, but something had shifted that night.

"Em." Luke turned me so that I had to look at him. With desperation in his voice, he continued, "You're the most special person to me. You have to know that."

"Thank you. I appreciate that." I smiled. "You've become

quite a special person to me, too."

Luke enveloped me in his arms and held me close. It felt like home there. Safe. Secure. Like I could count on him for anything. *No! You can't do that again, Em. Why can't my brain and my heart get on the same page?* Luke was showing me everything that my life could be, but my brain fought it with a vengeance. Every time I took a step toward loving Luke, my brain kicked me in my shin to stop me.

"I'd better get goin'," Luke told me in a hushed tone.

"Okay."

My heart always felt heavier when Luke left. Lonelier. Lost. I was happy, though, that he stood so strong in his convictions. A lot of men would have taken advantage of the situation—being alone behind closed doors.

Luke leaned down. I wanted nothing more than for *him* to kiss *me*. But as his lips lingered above mine, a blood-curdling scream came from Quinn. It jolted us away from each other and back to reality. We scrambled to Quinn's room.

"What's the matter, baby?" I asked as I scooped Quinn into my arms.

"I woke up," Quinn sniffled and wiped her nose with her shirt sleeve, "and saw a man outside my window."

My eyes grew wide as I glanced up at Luke. I knew in my heart of hearts it was Gary. "What did the man look like?"

"Daddy Gary." Quinn rubbed her eyes with her fists.

Before anything else could be said, Luke bolted out the door.

"It's okay. Everything'll be alright." I stroked Quinn's hair. "Do you want to sleep with me tonight?" I needed her to be close to me. To know she was safe.

Quinn nodded.

"Okay. Let's go."

I closed the curtains to Quinn's window and grabbed her jammies as we left her room. She jumped up onto my bed, Horsey in tow, as I closed the rest of the curtains in the cabin. In every room. "Let's get your jammies on, Quinn."

Luke stood in the doorway of my bedroom. "Well, he's gone. I did find some boot prints outside the window, though."

My hand flew to my mouth. My voice cracked. "What am I going to do, Luke? I can't keep living like this."

"We could go to the police." Luke's shoulders lifted in a shrug.

"And tell them what? A man is possibly stalking me? And I don't know where to find him? The police can't do anything until something happens. Been there. Done that."

"It was just a thought." Luke extended his hands out to his sides.

I closed my eyes and sighed. "I know. I'm sorry." I covered my face with my hands.

Luke gathered me in his arms. I didn't ever want to leave them. Especially that night.

"Mommy, where's my jammies?" Quinn asked.

I wiped my eyes of the tears that were threatening to leak down my cheeks. "Right here, sweetheart." I glanced up at Luke. Fear pooled in my eyes.

"Well, I'm not leavin' the cabin. Your couch and I are becomin' best friends." Luke scratched the back of his head.

"You don't have to do that. I'm sure he won't be back. Tonight at least."

"Em, I don't care. I want to make sure you're safe. Tomorrow, we'll talk to Colt and Callie about a safety plan."

I didn't have the strength to argue with him—not tonight. I had to comfort Quinn back to sleep. I sighed heavily. "Okay. Good night, Luke."

"Try and have sweet dreams, ladies." Luke's fingertips lightly caressed my arm. Goosebumps were left in their wake, and a small ember of heat radiated just under the surface.

"You, too." I did my best to plaster a genuine smile on my lips. I really did appreciate Luke staying. I just didn't want it to become a habit that might lead to something more. Who was I kidding? Deep down, I knew I did.

Chapter 32

Emelia

It had been a couple of weeks since the incident after the festival dance. I was relieved that Gary hadn't made his presence known since then. But I felt him. Everywhere. Watching. Waiting. I tried not to let it get under my skin. That was exactly what he wanted—to watch me suffer. It was his greatest joy in life.

The next few days would not be marred by Gary and what he might do. Quinn's fifth birthday was three days away, and I wanted to give her the birthday of a lifetime. "Callie!" I called out from the kitchen.

"Oh, hey, Emelia. How's it going?" Callie peeked her head around the corner from the living room.

"I wanted to talk to you about something." Nerves rattled my stomach.

"Sure. Come on in."

Luke and Colt had fought over who was going to have Quinn help them with chores. It was cute, actually. Two grown men fighting over the affection of a little girl. And she was smitten over them just as much. When I left them at the stable, the boys were playing Rock, Paper, Scissors to determine a winner.

I sat carefully on the couch.

"What's up?" Callie asked from the chair across from me, book in her hand.

"Quinn's fifth birthday is on Saturday. I wanted to see if we could throw her a surprise party." I glanced down at my hands neatly folded in my lap. Heaviness rooted itself on top of my heart. My eyes welled with tears. "She's never had one."

"She hasn't? Then, we must! We absolutely must!" Callie clapped her hands in excitement.

"I have no idea where to start." I scraped my bottom lip with my teeth.

"Let's go to the store and see what we can find. I'll text Colt to let him know we're going out." Callie plucked her phone from her back pocket.

"New phone?" I giggled.

"Why yes. Colt bought it for me for my birthday last month. He said . . ." Callie rolled her eyes, put her hands on her hips, and deepened her voice. "'The flip phone has to go.'"

Laughter burst straight from my belly.

After Callie returned her phone to her pocket, we piled into her Jeep and darted down the road. I wasn't sure when it happened, but I had fallen in love with Edenton, North Carolina and with Redemption Ranch. With the people. I would hold that nugget deep inside until it was safe for it to be on the outside.

Luke was another story altogether, though. I felt myself having feelings for him. Feelings that weren't safe to have. But I wasn't sure my mind would win the battle with my heart. It was only a matter of time.

"Earth to Emelia." Callie waved her hand in front of my face.

I closed my eyes and shook my head from side to side. "Sorry. What?"

"What kind of party are you thinking about having?"

I glanced in Callie's direction and laughed. "Do you *really* need me to answer that?"

"Horse party!" Callie and I shouted at the same time. We burst into a fit of giggles.

"So, anything pink and horse we find?" Callie smiled.

"Exactly. But without spending too much." I sucked my bottom lip into my mouth.

"Let me worry about that." Callie tapped my hand with hers.

With that, we raced inside the store. I couldn't wait to see what we could find. We scoured every party aisle in the store. We grabbed everything with pink and/or horses on it. There was even a piñata.

"We don't really need a piñata, do we?" I scrunched my face in concern about the price.

"You can't have a birthday party without a piñata." Callie laughed.

"Okay. Okay." I held up my hands in surrender. "Well, we'd better get some candy to fill it, then."

"Yes, let's." Callie dragged me to the candy aisle. She swiped almost every kind of candy into the cart. She giggled. "What? You can never have too much candy."

A chuckle escaped my lips. "If you say so."

"Oh, I do. Now, we need to order a cake. We know exactly where to go for that." Callie glanced over at me.

"Courageous Café and Bakery," we chimed in unison.

"Let's pay for this stuff and head over." Callie headed toward the checkout lines.

"Sounds good."

After loading up the back of Callie's Jeep, we made our way to the bakery. I hoped Quinn loved her party and everything we got for her. My hands twisted in my lap until we parked in front of the bakery.

I braced myself for the bells on the door, but when they clacked, I didn't cringe. I didn't cower. *Progress?* I plastered a grin on my face and lifted my chin. *Is life changing for me? Am I finally letting go of the past?* Well, some parts of it, at least? I sure hoped that was a sign of better things to come.

"Hey, Callie. Hey, Emelia. How are ya today?" Marci greeted us as she wiped her hands on a towel folded into her apron.

"Hey, honey, have you seen the—" Chuck walked out from the kitchen covered in flour. "Oh, sorry. I didn't know anyone was here."

"Oh, Chuck." Marci peered at him before covering her giggles with her fingers. "Callie and Emelia were just getting ready to tell me what they are here for."

"Well, we need a cake for Quinn." Callie's lips turned into a mischievous grin as we all sat at a nearby table.

"She's turning five on Saturday," I added. "We're planning a surprise party. Horses and pink."

"Of course, horses and pink. Quinn's two favorite things." Marci went behind the counter to grab paper and a pen.

"How's it been at the café since Caitlyn is off at college?" I asked.

"It's been an adjustment. Here and at home." Marci sighed as Chuck took her hand in his and sat down next to her.

"I bet."

Marci went back to her sketch. She twirled the pad around to us. "How about something like this?"

"Oh, Marci," I gasped. "This is perfect." My fingers lightly caressed the drawing of a horse. The word "pink" was written with an arrow pointing to the tail and mane. "Thank you so much. She's going to love it."

"My pleasure. You can come by and pick it up Friday afternoon."

"Great. Thank you, Marci. Good to see you, Chuck." Callie tapped the table with her fingertips. "See you then." Callie stood and sauntered out of the bakery. I scurried along after her.

"I'm so excited," I said. "We'll have to drop off the invitations at the dance studio. I hope everyone'll come."

"They will. But even if they don't, we'll make it a birthday she'll remember forever."

Tears invaded my eyes. "Thank you so much, Callie. For everything."

"Don't mention it." She tapped her hand on mine.

* * *

On Saturday, my singing filled the air. "Happy birthday to you! Happy birthday to you! Happy birthday, dear Quinn. Happy birthday to you!" I swung open Quinn's bedroom door.

"Mommy, what are you doing?" Quinn rubbed her eyes with the backs of her hands.

"Singing Happy Birthday to the birthday girl, of course." I grinned at her. "You have to get up and get ready to go. I let you sleep in."

"Where are we going?" Quinn sat up and flung her legs out the side of her covers.

"There's a surprise waiting for you down at the stable."

"There is?" Quinn's eyes widened with anticipation. She leaped out of bed and onto the floor. In no time at all, she was dressed and ready to go. Her outfit was complete, down to her pink cowgirl boots. "Wet's go, Mommy." She grabbed my hand and dragged me out the door.

"Okay. Okay. Slow down." I laughed.

As Quinn and I stepped closer to the stable, we were bombarded by people jumping out of their hiding places and yelling, "Surprise!"

Quinn squealed. "This is for *me*?"

"Yes, baby. It's not every day you turn five years old."

Quinn bounced up and down and clapped her hands. Her Excitement built as she glanced around at all of her friends from the dance studio. I breathed a heavy sigh of relief knowing they had all come. My heart overflowed. Then, someone stepped out from behind Colt and Callie.

"Caitwyn?" Quinn asked as she stared. "Caitwyn!" She charged at Caitlyn at full speed before jumping into her arms. "What are you doin' here?"

"You didn't think I'd miss your fifth birthday, did you?" Caitlyn slid Quinn down her body to the ground.

"Oh, Caitlyn. I had no idea you were coming." I enveloped her in a hug.

Caitlyn nodded and smiled. "I know. I asked Mom and Dad not to tell anyone. I wanted it to be a surprise."

"A wonderful surprise, it is. So happy you came."

"Quinn, what would you like to do first?" Colt chimed in. "We have horse rides around the paddock, a piñata, cake, food, and Pin the Tail on the Donkey."

Quinn tapped her lips with her index finger. "Can we eat first? I'm so hungry." She rubbed her hand in circles on her belly.

"Of course. We have hot dogs and hamburgers."

"Yay!" Quinn ran over to Luke and leaped into his arms. "Hi, Wuke."

"Hey! How's my best girl?"

"It's my birthday today!"

"I know." Luke chuckled. "Do you like the surprise?"

"I wuv it!" Quinn raised her arms in the air. Then, she wiggled down out of Luke's arms and ran over to her friends.

"Caitwyn, come sit with us!" Quinn grabbed Caitlyn's hand and dragged her over to the picnic table where Quinn's friends were already sitting. All the girls jumped up and ran to give Caitlyn a hug. I hadn't realized how much the girls missed her until that moment.

There was constant chatter about what to do next as the girls ate their food. My heart warmed as another piece of the wall broke away from my heart. Quinn was truly loved.

"Hey there." Luke bumped my shoulder with his arm. "How's the party so far?"

"Hey." I glanced around. "I think it's going well."

Tinkerbell was in the paddock waiting. Colt had put some pink-colored extensions in her mane and tail. Some were light pink, and some were hot pink. She looked beautiful. Almost magical.

"Come on, Caitwyn! We're going to ride Tink now!"

"Okay! Okay! I'm comin'!" Caitlyn giggled as Quinn grabbed her hand.

After each girl had her turn riding around the paddock, they all skipped back to the stable.

"We wanna do the piñata next, Mommy," Quinn told me breathlessly.

"Okay. Everyone, gather around." I motioned with my arm in a circle. "Quinn will go first since she's the birthday girl. You each get three swings."

I wrapped the blindfold over Quinn's eyes and around her head. I handed her the bat and twirled her around. "One, two, three, four, five!" everyone shouted at the same time.

As soon as Quinn stopped spinning, I hurried out of the

way as she began swatting at the air, trying to hit the piñata. Her first swing missed by a mile. Her second swing, she clipped the tail. The third time, she hit it right in the center. A piece of the crepe paper floated to the ground. Every other girl took a turn, too, but the piñata remained intact.

"Quinn, can I give it a try?" Luke asked, looking like a shy schoolboy.

"Yeah!" Quinn handed Luke the bat.

Luke turned, facing away from me, and crouched down, hanging the blindfold over his shoulder.

"What are you doing?" I asked.

"I'm not a cheater. You have to blindfold me and spin me."

I giggled and grabbed the blindfold from Luke's shoulder. "Okay." I tied the blindfold around his head and pushed him around in circles.

After the girls counted to five, I took two steps back. Luke took his stance next to the piñata like a Major League batter at the plate. Feet shoulder width apart. Knees bent. Elbows out. The bat swirled behind his head.

"Hit it! Hit it!" all the girls chanted with arms moving up and down in the air above their heads.

Thwack! The bat connected with the colorful horse. There was a hole at the point of contact, but no candy fell out. Luke tore off the blindfold. He stood like a batter in the batter's box once more. *Thwack!* The horse tore open, and candy spilled to the ground. The girls cheered and ran to the pile of candy.

"Ah, Luke, the hero." I swooned as he approached me.

Luke's cheeks grew pink as he planted the top of the bat on the ground and leaned into it. I bit my cheek to stifle a laugh. I wanted to comment so much about how adorable he looked when he blushed, but I kept that little tidbit to myself.

"We have one more surprise for you, Quinn," Colt spoke

up when all of the commotion of the candy-gathering died down.

Quinn popped her head up from her pile of candy. "What is it?"

"Well, come and stand over here." Colt pointed to the ground at his side.

Quinn jumped up from her crouched position and scurried to Colt. Callie and I handed everyone small bags to put their candy in to take home with them.

"Callie, Jon, Luke, and I have all agreed that we want to make you, Quinnie, the official owner of Tinkerbell." Luke's grin grew as he finished.

"Reawwy?" Quinn's eyes widened with surprise.

"Oh, I'm not sure—" I started. But my voice was cut off by the loud cheers.

That was such a bad idea. If we had to leave right away, leaving the horse behind would devastate Quinn, not to mention Tinkerbell. I know because I was forced to leave Apollo. I thought about him often, and it ripped my heart out more and more every time. I couldn't imagine how it would be for Quinn.

"It'll be okay, Em." Luke wrapped his arm around my shoulder.

"No, it won't." I wiggled free from Luke's arm and moved away from the party, covering my face with my hands. I willed the tears not to fall.

Luke's boots scuffed behind me. "Em, what's wrong? It'll be fine. Quinn loves taking care of Tinkerbell."

"And what happens when we have to leave, Luke?" I turned to face him and smacked my hands against my thighs. "What then?"

"Just . . . don't ever leave?" Luke softly responded.

I closed my eyes and sighed. "You know it's not that easy." I twirled away from him and wrapped myself in a hug.

"I know." Luke sighed and laid his hands on my shoulders. "I wish there was something I could do to help make it easier for you."

I closed my eyes again. "You're doing it already. It's just . . . he's still out there. Somewhere. Looking for me. Or waiting, rather. And I don't know when he's going to make an appearance. I'm terrified, and I don't know if I'm terrified because I don't know *when* he'll appear or just because I know it's going to happen. Some day."

"When that day comes, I'll be here. I promise," Luke reassured me.

"Thank you. We should get back to the party." I swiped my fingers under my eyes to dry them. The cold covered me after Luke removed his hands from my shoulders.

"Mommy, did you hear? Cowt and Wuke and everybody gave me Tinkerbeww! I'm so happy." Quinn giggled as she bounced up and down.

How can I resist? How can I tell that little girl she can't have the horse because we'd probably be leaving? I accepted defeat.

"Oh, Quinn. That's wonderful." I picked her up and wrapped her in my arms. "I love you so much."

"I wuv you, too, Mommy." Quinn squeezed my neck.

"Happy birthday, baby. I hope you've had the best day."

"I did. I had so much fun. Thank you for the party."

"You're most welcome."

209

Chapter 33

Luke

It had been about two weeks since Quinnie's party. Gary still hadn't made an appearance, and there hadn't been any more incidents. I was on guard twenty-four/seven, though. I knew he was watchin'. Waitin'. I knew what I wanted to do if I ever came face-to-face with him. But I couldn't do that to Em and Quinn. They didn't need to know what I was capable of doin'. They had already been victim enough to too much violence.

I had wanted to call the police. I should have insisted. But I shook my head to switch off that part of me and focused on the work at hand. It was the kickoff to fair week. I couldn't wait to ask Em and Quinn to go with me after my chores were done.

"Wuke! Wuke! Are you here?" Quinn bellowed from inside the stable.

I strode into the stable from the back door after letting Tinkerbell out into the corral so she could run off some steam. I plucked my handkerchief from my pocket and ran it across both of my hands. I stuffed it back into my pocket in just enough time to catch Quinn as she catapulted into my arms. Em lingered behind, rocking on her heels. "Hey, Quinnie. What are you and your mom up to?"

"We've been wooking for you." Quinn poked her index finger into my chest. "Do you wanna go to the fair with Mommy and me? Pwease?"

I glanced over at Em. "Are you sure?" Things between Em and I hadn't been completely awkward since our conversation at the birthday party, but there had definitely been a shift. We hadn't had a chance to talk about it.

Em's cheeks turned a pretty shade of pink. She glanced down at the ground. "Only if you want to."

"I'd love to." I grinned. "I was actually goin' ta ask you both the same thing."

I tickled Quinn, which sent her into a fit of laughter. "Okay. Let me get my chores done. Richard usually takes fair week off as most of us go to the fair for the food. Quinn, do you want to help with Tinkerbell? She's your horse now, so it's your job to take care of her." I set Quinn down on her feet and tapped her on the tip of her nose.

Quinn put her hands on her hips, jutted her chin, and in a sassy voice said, "I know. I promised to take care of her at my party."

I grabbed the pitchforks and handed one to Quinn. We mucked the stall out together. We replaced the dirty hay with fresh hay before returnin' the mare to her stall.

Em leaned against the doorjamb of the entry to the stable with her arms crossed over her chest, watching. Her eyes burned into my soul. The pitchfork fell from my grasp. I fumbled to catch it before it clattered to the ground. Em giggled. It was a sweet sound. I felt the heat rise from my neck to my cheeks.

Quinn grabbed Tinkerbell's feed bucket. I lifted her up to scoop some feed from the barrel. Her tongue stuck out of the side of her mouth as she leaned forward and dipped the scoop into the feed. When the scoop was full, I set her down, and she dumped it into the bucket.

"One more scoop?" Quinn peered up at me. I lifted her to repeat. She poured the feed into the bucket and lifted the handle up to her chest. The bucket was almost as big as she was.

"Here, let me help ya." I chuckled and wrapped my fingers around the handle.

Before I knew it, all the chores were finished, and we were at the fair, immersed in the lights of the rides and games. The scent of Italian sausage, elephant ears, and funnel cakes permeated the air all at once. Laughter rang in the air, and from every direction came the screams of kids havin' fun with their friends on every ride from the Scrambler to the Tilt-a-Whirl to the Gravitron.

I was on high alert. The hairs on the back of my neck were standin' on end. I wasn't sure if somethin' was about to happen or if my PTSD was goin' to rear its ugly head. Perhaps both. I preferred neither.

Em looked around us as we stood in line for Quinn to go down the slide. "Do you think we'll be safe here?"

"I think so. There are a lot of people. Gary'd be stupid to do anything here." I kept the part about feeling on edge to myself.

"Wuke, I'm thirsty," Quinn whined.

I glanced around. I saw the lemon shake-up stand. *Perfect.* I leaned over to Em. "I'll be right back."

"O-oh, okay."

I placed my hand on her arm. "I'm just goin' right over there. I don't want Quinn to lose her place in line."

Em nodded as I turned to walk to the drink stand. The line was long, as it seemed everyone had the same idea at exactly the same time. I sighed. I ran my hand through my hair. I hadn't wanted to leave them for too long. I glanced back to where Quinn and Em were waiting for Quinn's turn on the slide. Nothing seemed out of the ordinary, so I turned back around, noticing the line had moved in front of me.

"Mommy! No!" Quinn screamed at the top of her lungs. It was a different scream than when she was ridin' the rides. Bone-chilling. Pure terror.

I twirled around at whiplash speed. I zeroed in on where I had left them. I gasped and froze in horror as Quinn's body flew through the air and smashed into an oak tree. Fear punched me in the gut, and vomit threatened to erupt. I zeroed in on Quinn's body, a tiny heap at the foot of the tree. She appeared lifeless.

A man, who I could only assume was Gary, had Em by the hair. Em's hands clawed his, tryin' to pry them away. Darkness overcame me. As my vision returned, everythin' around me was out of focus—everythin' except the enemy. It was as if I was lookin' through the scope of my M240B machine gun. I barreled toward them.

"Someone help her!" I shouted as I pointed toward Quinn. Blurred figures ran to her side.

Before the man knew I was behind him, my arms wrapped around his neck, squeezing. It took all the strength I possessed not to kill him right there. I placed my mouth close to his ear so he could hear every word. "Let. Her. Go."

"No! She's mine! I'm taking her home." The man's muffled voice came out scratchy, determined, and reeking of beer. Saliva spewed from Gary's mouth.

"I don't think you understood me. I'm a trained Marine. I could snap your neck right here, right now. But I'm givin' you the chance to walk away and live." I squeezed his neck a little more to make sure he understood.

"Okay. Okay," Gary rasped, slappin' his hand against my arm as he untwisted his fingers from Em's hair. Em dropped to the ground and curled up in a ball. I threw Gary to the side, and he scrambled away like a scared rat.

"Can someone call the cops?" I bellowed. I kneeled to Em and offered her my hand.

"Where's Quinn?" Panic filled Em's voice as she twirled in every direction until she froze in place.

I swiveled to where I last saw Quinn. Colt and Callie were crouched next to her. She hadn't moved. I bolted toward her.

"Cops and an ambulance are comin'," Colt said as I kneeled down next to Quinn.

"We have to keep her neck and spine stable," I barked. "We can't move her until they get here."

"What happened to her?" Em cried out from behind me. "I didn't see anything." She covered her face with her hands. Callie did her best to comfort Em, but it didn't work. "This is all my fault. I should have never left." Em sobbed.

When the paramedics finally arrived, I raced to them. "You have to help her!"

"What happened?"

"She was slammed into the tree, and she's been unconscious ever since."

The paramedics placed a cervical collar around Quinn's neck and slid her onto a backboard. "Let's go," one of them said to the other as they belted Quinn onto the gurney.

"Em, you ride with them. I'll meet ya at the hospital." Em didn't say a single word. She just climbed into the ambulance. I sprinted to my truck as I fumbled for my keys. "UGH!" I yelled out as I frantically swiped my keys from the ground and climbed inside the truck.

I raced to the hospital, barely stoppin' at stop signs or red lights. The sound of my hazard lights, while usually unnoticed, echoed in the silence of my truck. Tears pricked my eyes. My heart was beatin' a mile-a-minute. I wasn't sure if it was breakin' or goin' to pound right out of my rib cage.

I skidded to a stop in a parking space close to the entrance to the emergency room. Jumping from my truck, I sprinted to the entrance and barreled through the door. "What room is Quinn Taylor in?" I breathlessly asked the nurse. "She was just brought in by ambulance." I drummed my fingers on the counter, waiting for her to answer.

"Are you family?"

"No!" I shouted.

"Luke, we're over here." Em stood in the doorway of a room a few feet from where I stood. I shuffled into the room. As Quinn laid on the bed with her eyes shut, tears brimmed to the surface once more. *I shouldn't have left their side at the fair. This is all my fault!*

It wasn't long before a doctor rushed into the room. "Hi. I'm Dr. Carter. The paramedics filled me in, but what exactly happened?" He stood on the opposite side of the bed, ready to examine Quinn.

I waited a second for Em to answer. But she sat catatonically in the chair. "She was thrown into a tree," I answered for her. "She must have hit her head really hard. She hasn't been awake since." I ran my hand down my face.

After examinin' Quinn, Dr. Carter raised from his crouched position. "We need to do an MRI and CT Scan. We will use the lowest amount of radiation to lower the risks."

"Okay," Em replied, her entire body trembling. I sat and wrapped my arm around her.

As the nurses wheeled Quinn from the room, Em nestled her face into my chest. I didn't know what to say. I didn't want to tell her everythin' was goin' to be okay because I didn't know. I just squeezed her close and held her. Maybe that was better than any empty words I could give her.

I took in a deep breath as my heart ached in my chest. *I broke my promise to Em. I was supposed to protect them from Gary. I promised her I'd be there if and when Gary decided to appear.*

Quinn's lifeless body floated through my mind. Guilt sucker-punched me. I thought they would have been safe in an open area like the fair with so many people around. I completely underestimated the man. Em had warned me. I should have listened. Gary had been drinking, so he probably didn't care where they were. His only mission was to get Em. And I almost allowed it to happen. My fist clenched at my side.

How is Em ever goin' to trust me to keep a promise again? I doubt she ever will. I'll just have to do my best to be here for her movin' forward. I ran my hand down my face.

When the hospital staff rolled Quinn back into the room, Em's body relaxed in a sigh. I ran my hand up and down her back. The nurse started hooking Quinn up to machines. "This is a heart monitor," the nurse explained as she placed stickers on Quinn's chest before connecting the lines to the machine."

Dr. Carter entered the room. Another doctor followed. "I've asked Dr. Safford to join me," Dr. Carter explained. "He is a pediatric neurosurgeon."

"I'm so sorry we have to meet under these circumstances," Dr. Safford said. "I've asked radiology to expedite the results. As soon as we know anything, we'll be back to see you." Dr. Safford placed his hand on Em's arm. "We'll do everything we can. I'm going to go ahead and put in the paperwork to get her admitted into the ICU."

Em nodded. "Okay. Thank you." She never looked up from her hands layin' in her lap.

A nurse entered the room again shortly after the doctors

left. "We'll need you to wait in the waiting area while we get Quinn prepared for the ICU. Also, a Detective Reed is waiting for you out there."

When Em and I entered the waiting room, a lanky man about my height stood from where he had been sitting. "Emelia Taylor?" He held out his hand to her.

"Ye-yes."

"My name is Detective Brian Reed. I realize this'll be difficult for you, but if we can get the details of what happened sooner rather than later, it'll be extremely helpful."

"Okay."

We all took a seat. Em and I sat across from Detective Reed.

"I'm not sure where to begin. A few years ago, my boyfriend, Gary Mason, started abusing me. I'm not sure how or when he found me here in Edenton. He lurks and waits. What am I going to do, Luke?"

"What do you mean he lurks and waits?" Detective Reed grabbed his notebook and pen from his pocket.

"He drowned a rat in my bathtub, and he looked in the window of my daughter's room and scared her." Emelia ran her hands up her folded arms.

"How do you know it was him?" The detective continued to scribble in his notebook.

"He told me once that if I ever tried to leave him, he'd drown me like a rat. And Quinn told me it was him outside her window."

"Where did you arrive here from?"

"Norristown, Pennsylvania."

"Okay. And what happened tonight?"

I patted Em's arm and answered the question for her. "We were at the fair. We were standing in line for the big slide when

217

Quinn said she was thirsty. I went to get us something to drink while Quinn and Em remained in line. The next thing I knew, someone, a man, had his hand buried in Em's hair at the back of her head. I heard Quinn scream. The man, Gary, flung Quinn so hard she literally left the ground and smashed head-first into the tree." My voice cracked.

Tears made a path down Em's cheeks. I wrapped my arm around her shoulders and gave her a gentle squeeze.

"I heard Gary talking to someone," Em explained. "I tend to go elsewhere in my mind when Gary is abusing me. I think it was Luke he was talking to. Gary let go of my hair, and I fell to the ground in a ball. I wasn't sure if he was going to hit me, kick me, or whatever. But he never did. The next thing I knew, Luke was helping me up. I was a little disoriented and couldn't find Quinn. Callie and Colt were beside Quinn when we finally found her." She laid her face in her hands.

"I made sure no one moved her until the paramedics arrived," I jumped back in. "I'm sure there was a crowd, but I was hyper-focused on getting Gary off Em. I called out to someone to stay with Quinn, but I didn't know it was Callie and Colt until afterward while we were waiting for the paramedics to come."

"We have officers at the fair questioning any and all witnesses, and the crime scene unit is there as well. Do you know where Gary ran off to?"

"I'm not sure if he'll stick around or not," Em answered. "He might be on his way back to Norristown."

"Can you tell me his address? I'll get Norristown PD on it."

"1364 Markley Street."

After jotting the address down, Detective Reed flipped his notebook closed. "Here's my card. If you think of anything else, or he comes back around, give me a call."

"Thank you," Emelia said. But she made no move to take the card.

"Thank you, Detective." I grabbed the card from his hand.

It wasn't long after the detective left that Dr. Safford entered the room. He sat on the edge of the chair that Detective Reed had vacated. "We've studied the images. What we found is a subarachnoid hemorrhage. This means there is bleeding between the two innermost membranes that cover the brain. The fact she still hasn't regained consciousness means it is severe, but the fact she is still alive gives us hope."

"Oh, God, no!" Em covered her mouth with her fingertips as tears flooded down her cheeks.

My gut wrenched with the doctor's words. *This is all my fault.* "So, what happens now?"

"Well, we'll need to do surgery to place a small clip on the blood vessel to stop the blood from leaking into her brain. Then, we will monitor her to ensure there isn't a re-bleed, swelling of the brain, or hydrocephalus, which is extra fluid on the brain."

All of the medical terms made my head swirl.

"When will you do the surgery?" Em softly asked.

"We'll do it right away. They are prepping the OR right now. She'll be in the ICU after so that we can keep a close eye on her condition."

"Can I see her before surgery?" Em pleaded, more with her eyes than her words.

"Yes. That will be alright."

Dr. Safford escorted us down the hall to Quinn's room in the ER. Em went to the side of the bed and laid her forehead on top of Quinn's. "I'm so sorry, baby." Em's tears sprinkled Quinn's face. "This is all my fault. I never meant for you to get hurt."

219

Em's body shook with sobs. I laid my hand on her back. I spoke no words as I knew they would be empty and hold no promise. *Like she needed any more broken promises from me.*

"It's time to take her to surgery now," the nurse from before said. "I'll take you to the OR waiting area."

Em didn't budge.

"Em, honey, they have to get her to surgery." I gently tugged on her shoulders.

Em raised her head and gently laid Quinn's hand on the bed.

As we sat in the wooden chairs with red cushions in the waitin' room, I grabbed Em's hand and prayed silently. *Lord, please be with Quinn. Give the surgeon steady hands. Heal her brain. In Your Holy name. Amen.*

"What's goin' on?" Colt asked as he and Callie bolted into the room.

I stood to meet them in the middle. I jammed my fists in my pockets. "She's in surgery right now. After that, she'll be in the ICU so they can monitor her brain."

"Oh no!" Callie gathered Em in her arms and ran her hand down Em's back. "Can we get you anything?"

"Horsey! Can you bring Horsey?" Em's eyes grew wide. "She didn't want to bring him to the fair. She was too afraid of losing him. She felt bad about it, though. She wanted him to have fun, too." Tears slid down Em's face once more.

"Yes. Anything I can get for you, Luke?"

"No. I'm okay. Thank you." But then I whispered to Colt, "Do ya think ya could bring each of us a change of clothes? I'm not goin' anywhere."

"Yeah. I'll make sure of it."

"Thanks, Colt. Do you think you could also bring a picture of Tinkerbell? I know when Quinn wakes up, she'll want to see her." My voice broke. I covered a cough with my fist.

"No problem. Don't worry about anythin' at the ranch. We've got it covered."

"Thanks. Just need a lot of prayers. I know she's not mine, but that little girl . . ." My lip quivered.

Colt placed his hand on my shoulder. "I know, Luke. She might as well be all of ours. We all love her so much. I'll make sure to pray as hard and as often as I can."

"We'll be back shortly, okay?" Callie reassured Em.

Em only nodded in response, never taking her eyes off her hands folded in her lap.

Chapter 34

Emelia

I paced the floor of the waiting room. It seemed like an eternity that Quinn was in surgery. I ran my fingers through my hair. What was happening? *This is all my fault.* If I hadn't left Gary, Quinn would be fine. *Why did I have to go and do that? Why?* My mind raced to the worst places. I was so stupid to allow such an awful person into our lives. But he wasn't that way in the beginning. *No!* There was no use looking back. I just had to look forward and hope that my baby would be okay.

The door opened, and Dr. Safford strode over to Luke and me as he removed the cap from his head. "Quinn's in recovery. Surgery went well. The next twenty-four to forty-eight hours will be critical. The hemorrhage was slightly worse than anticipated, but the clip should do its job. We won't know the extent of damage, if there is any, until she wakes up. It's just a wait-and-see thing right now. Once she's comfortable in her room, I'll have a nurse come and get you."

"Okay. Thank you." My breath caught in my throat. What if she didn't ever wake up? Dread bubbled up in the pit of my stomach. Blood rushed to my head. I flopped down in the nearest chair and leaned over, grabbing my hair with my fists. *This is all my fault.* I rocked back and forth. The sobs couldn't be contained inside my body. They flowed rapidly and loudly.

Strong arms wrapped around me. *Oh, Luke.* I melted into him.

About an hour later, a nurse escorted us to Quinn's room. I sat by Quinn's bed and held her tiny hand in mine. I ran my hand up her smooth skin. Gauze wrapped her head from her eyes up. Tubes stuck out from every direction. There was a heart monitor and an IV drip. A couple of tubes stuck out from the gauze at the top of her head. She looked so peaceful—like a little sleeping angel.

My lip trembled. The doctor's voice echoed in my head: *It's just a wait-and-see thing right now.* I laid my head on my arm. Before I knew it, my eyelids closed.

* * *

"**E**m, you need to wake up, sweetheart." Luke ran his hand softly up and down my back.

"What? How long was I asleep?" I raised my head and squinted my eyes against the bright overhead lights.

"It's been a few hours."

"What? How could you let me sleep that long?" I snapped, panic rising in my throat, choking me. "Has she opened her eyes? Anything?"

"No. I'm sorry," Luke said, his voice barely audible.

I glanced at Quinn. "I thought Callie and Colt were going to bring Horsey. She needs him." Tears formed in the corners of my eyes.

"They called. They didn't make it back in time before visiting hours were over. They are comin' first thing in the mornin'."

I hung my head. "Alright." I tried not to glance at Luke. Constant worry reflected in his eyes each time he looked at me.

"I need to stretch my legs for a bit. I'm gonna take a walk. Is that okay?" Luke asked before rising from his seat.

"Yes."

"I won't be long. I pro . . ." Luke's voice trailed off.

"Okay."

As I sat in the room alone with only the whirring of the machines to keep me company, my mind searched for some sort of peace in all of the insanity that was happening around me. My eyes darted around the room.

Pray.

You don't want to hear from me. Why would You listen to my prayers? I deserted You a long time ago.

Just pray.

Maybe He would listen since my prayers were for Quinn? I kneeled beside her bed, taking her small hand in mine.

"God, please heal my little girl. I know I don't deserve it. I know I have done so many things wrong. I know this is all my fault, but please don't punish my daughter for it." Tears ran hot down my cheeks like they never had before as I pleaded with the One called Savior to save my little girl.

I had never begged or even asked God for anything in my life, even when Gary was slamming his fists into my face—until that very moment. I stayed silent, squeezed my eyes shut, and prayed silently with everything that was inside me. My body rocked back and forth because I wasn't sure what to do with the nervous energy.

I didn't know how long I sat there with God, but it felt like hours. I wiped my eyes with the backs of my hands and smeared my nose across my shirt sleeve. When I felt I had regained most of my composure, I slid back into the seat.

Shortly after, Luke returned to the room. His eyes were red and swollen. He didn't say a word. He slid into the chair next to me and ran his hand along my back. I didn't trust my voice to say anything.

"Why don't you take my truck and go back to the cabin and take a shower? It might make you feel a little better. I'll call you if there is any change."

"I can't leave her, Luke." A tear fell onto my pant leg. "I just can't."

"Okay." Luke pulled me into him. I was getting used to that. He had done it so many times over the last few months. More so in the last twenty-four hours.

Quinn's little body seized and shook violently. The machines beeped at high decibels.

"What's happening?" I shrieked. "Oh, God! Please! Help her!"

Luke bolted for the door. "Nurse! We need a nurse in here!"

Two nurses and Dr. Safford raced to Quinn's bedside, pushing us out of the way. "Please wait in the hallway," one of the nurses requested, corralling us to the door.

The convulsions didn't last long, but the vision of Quinn's body thrashing about would be emblazoned into my memory forever. "What's happening, Luke?" I stood on my tiptoes to try and see what the nurses and doctor were doing. My hand flew to my heart. It felt as if it was going to burst through my chest.

"Give her some Lorazepam," Dr. Safford ordered the nurse next to him.

The nurse filled a syringe with liquid before inserting the needle into the IV line and pushing the stopper down until the medicine ran through the line and into Quinn's now motionless body.

"Please, someone tell me what is happening!" I pleaded through sobs, my heart still racing.

Dr. Safford motioned Luke and me completely out into the

hallway as the nurses finished up with Quinn. "It appears she has had a grand mal seizure," the doctor explained. "But to be certain and to see exactly what is happening inside her brain, I want to do another MRI. Nurse Jenkins, will you get that on the schedule right away?"

"Yes, doctor." Nurse Jenkins scurried off to the nurse's station.

"What could be wrong?" I asked through fresh tears. I was surprised my body could produce them as I had cried so much.

"There are too many possibilities. Let's get the MRI done, and we'll go from there. Okay?" Dr. Safford flashed a comforting smile as he patted my shoulder before moving down the hall.

Luke and I stepped back into the room. The room was deafeningly silent.

"Luke." My bottom lip quivered. "What am I going to do without her?" New tears brimmed my eyes.

"We can't think like that, Em. We have to stay positive." Luke's voice cracked as he pulled me into his embrace. I couldn't see his face, but I knew he was trying his best not to let his emotions win. His body shook against me.

It wasn't long before they came in and wheeled Quinn off for the MRI. "She'll be back in about thirty to sixty minutes," Nurse Jenkins informed us. "Oh. Someone dropped this off for Quinn." She held Horsey out to me.

I grabbed and squeezed Horsey close. Quinn's scent covered him. I closed my eyes and breathed it in.

Luke and I sat in a painful silence as we waited for Quinn to return. I had no idea what the results would be. I tried to hold onto hope, but there was no hope to be found. I stared at the clock on the wall. I could hear the tick of the second hand making its way around the circle.

Luke squeezed my hand. *He has been so wonderful, hasn't he? He's always been here.* No matter what the circumstances. No matter what he was doing. He was there.

Forty-five minutes later, they wheeled Quinn back into the room. The nurse hooked her back up to all the machines. Quinn looked just the same—lifeless. *God, please don't take her. Please!* I stood over her and took hold of her hand. I swiped a curl from her cheek and ran my index finger down the side of her sweet face.

A light knock came at the door, and Dr. Safford entered the room. I wasn't sure how long it had been since they brought Quinn back into the room. Everything seemed to be moving in slow motion. Nothing seemed real.

"I have the results of the MRI." Dr. Safford straddled the stool on the opposite side of the bed.

"Okay." I gripped Luke's hand and squeezed. My breath hitched in my throat.

"She did have a grand mal seizure as a result of a re-bleed. We put her on a machine to breathe for her until we spoke with you." Dr. Safford cleared his throat and glanced away for a moment before continuing, his tone softer, empathetic even. "Unfortunately, her brain function is now at zero."

"What? What does that mean?" I clenched my hands into fists. I wanted to throw something and scream at the top of my lungs.

"I'm afraid no amount of time is going to make it better. At this point, it's our recommendation to take Quinn off life support." The doctor paused. "I'm so very sorry. I wish I had better news."

I shook my head from side to side. *No! This can't be real!* "No! No! No!" I screamed. My entire body was enraged. My heart stopped beating. Quinn was the heartbeat inside of me.

My vision blurred, and my ears went deafeningly silent. My lungs filled with air that I couldn't seem to expel from my body. I slumped down in the chair. Luke's arms wrapped around me.

"I'll leave you two to discuss what you want to do," Dr. Safford softly said before leaving the room.

"Em?" Luke's voice sounded as if he was calling me from above water, and I was drowning below the surface. "Em?" His hand cradled my cheek. Warmth radiated from his skin into my face and spread through my body.

When I could hear clearly again, I glanced in Luke's direction. One tear fell from each of his eyes and trailed down his cheeks. My lip trembled as tears rained down my own. "What am I going to do, Luke? She's my everything. What am I going to do without her?"

The sobs overtook me, and my body shook with grief and sadness—more than I had ever felt in my entire life. Luke stayed silent, but I felt his body shake as he enveloped me in his arms. He just held me.

How does he always know exactly what I need when I need it?

Because I sent him.

I ignored the voice. How could I believe anything He said to me when He didn't answer my prayers? Finally, my body was numb, and my tear ducts had run dry. I lifted my head and peered up at Luke. His eyes were red, but there it was in the midst of them, compassion—empathy, even. He truly cared about not just Quinn but *me*.

I inhaled deeply. "What do I do, Luke? How can I make the choice to take her off life support?"

Luke took hold of my hand. "That's a choice only you can make. But Quinn wouldn't want things this way. She wouldn't want to be layin' in this bed for the rest of her life. Not bein' able to play and ride Tinkerbell. Not bein' able to dance. Not even breathin' on her own. But just know that no matter what, I'll always be here for you. Whatever you need. Whenever you need it." He ran his thumb down my cheek and whispered, "I pinky promise."

"Thank you. You don't know how much that means to me." I swiped my eyes with my hands as I stood.

With a whimper, I placed Quinn's hand in mine. My legs buckled as I leaned down and kissed her cheek. "I'm so sorry, baby. I never meant for this to happen." A tear fell from my eye onto her cheek. "I hope you know how much you are loved and how much you will be missed." I raised my head and glanced at Luke. "Will you get the doctor, please?"

"I'll be right back." Luke rushed out the door.

I cradled Quinn in my arms, bathing her with my tears. The machines that were keeping her breathing rang in my ears. Footsteps sounded behind me. I twisted to see the doctor and Luke return.

"Luke said you've made a decision?" Dr. Safford asked, stepping next to the bed.

"Yes. Take her off life support. And please, donate what you can." I bit my bottom lip to keep it from quivering and to keep me from changing my mind. I knew I was doing what was best for Quinn, but it didn't mean it wasn't killing me inside.

"I'm so very sorry, Emelia. Since you want to donate her organs and tissue, we'll leave the machines running long enough to prepare the OR. As soon as they are ready, we'll be back to get her."

Once we were alone again, Luke stepped close to Quinn's side. "It's okay. I'll take care of ya mom. I pinky promise," he whispered as he linked his pinky with hers. "Go fly high with the angels and Jesus. I love you, Quinnie. You'll always be my best girl." He kissed her lightly on the forehead and stood from leaning over her. He coughed and wiped his eyes with his hand.

It seemed like only a matter of minutes before the doctor returned. It didn't matter the time frame. A lifetime wouldn't have been long enough. I wasn't ready for it. I didn't want to accept it.

"Okay. We're ready. Would you like to walk with us?" Nurse Jenkins asked.

The words stuck in my parched mouth. I felt my head move up and down, but I wasn't sure if it actually had or if it was a figment of my imagination.

As we stepped into the hallway, a line of nurses and doctors streamed all the way down the hall. Nurse Jenkins leaned into me. "They call this an honor walk. It's to honor the patient donating organs to others."

My hand flew to my lips as tears streamed down my face once again. The team of nurses and doctors who had worked with Quinn pushed her bed slowly down the hall. It was eerily quiet. I would've been able to hear a pin drop. Every footstep of that painstaking, five-minute walk vibrated through my ears and ping-ponged in my head. They were so loud inside of me, I thought I might have gone crazy.

As soon as the doors closed and my baby disappeared from sight, I fell to my knees. Quinn's heart would never beat inside her body again. Her soul was no longer on earth. In that moment, I wanted nothing more than to die right along with her.

Chapter 35

Luke

I was at a loss for what to do for Em. I was at a loss for what to do for myself. My heart was ripped from my chest. The deep ache, the intense pressure, wasn't goin' to go away anytime soon.

"Come on, baby." I placed my hand on Em's back. "We need to go." We had stayed at the hospital long after Quinn disappeared into the operatin' room. At least Quinn's last great deed was goin' to change people's lives—much like she did in her short time on Earth.

Em stood from the seat she had occupied for the last few hours. She ran her hands over her eyes. Her chest heaved with a sigh. "Okay."

I took hold of Em's hand as we walked down the long, narrow hallway toward the exit. Never in a million years would I have thought we would have left the hospital without Quinn. My life already seemed incomplete without Quinn runnin' around, grabbin' my hand to hold, and callin' me Wuke. My life was forever changed. I breathed deeply in and out.

I held Em's hand as she stepped up into my truck. It was a quiet ride back to the ranch.

"Do ya wanna stop by the house and get some leftovers to take to your cabin?"

Em shook her head. Her cheeks were stained from her tears.

"Baby, ya gotta eat somethin'."

Em turned her head and stared out the window. My heart ached for her. It was a twisted pretzel of emotions. I had to be strong for Em. She needed to be able to lean on me. If I fell apart, she wouldn't have anyone. If she ever wanted to lean on me, that is. But I would be there beside her every step of the way.

We stopped in front of Em's cabin. I held her hand once again as she descended from the truck cab. She gripped Horsey tightly to her chest. "Will you stay with me?" she mumbled so softly I almost didn't hear her. "At least until I fall asleep?" She glanced up at me.

How could I resist those eyes? "Of course. I'll sleep on the couch. You can holler if ya need anythin'."

"Thank you." Em laid her hand on my arm.

An electric charge tickled my arm. I opened the door and rested my hand on the small of Em's back as I led her inside. That was one of the few times I didn't give a thought or care to the appearance of bein' improper. She needed me to stay. And just like the other times, I would stay. We would know the truth about what was happenin' behind closed doors, and so would God. I didn't really care about anyone else. I never really gave it much thought to begin with where Em was concerned . . . until Austin.

"Whatever you need, Em. I'm here. I always will be." I ran my fingers down her arms. Little prickles of electricity were left in their wake. She nodded before turnin' toward her room and slinkin' away.

I took my boots off at the door before slumpin' down on the couch. Suddenly, I was exhausted. It was as if I'd plowed a field or somethin'. I laid down and dangled my legs over the armrest at the other end of the couch. My arm covered my eyes.

When I was conscious again, I heard cryin' comin' from somewhere in the cabin. *Oh, Em, I have no idea how to help you. God, give me Your wisdom in what to do for her.*

I started down the hall. Em wasn't in her room. A sniffle came from Quinn's room. A tear threatened my cheek.

"Em, honey." I kneeled beside the bed. She was curled up with Horsey nestled in her arms where Quinn usually slept.

"I just don't know what to do, Luke. I miss her so much already. How am I going to get through a lifetime without her?" Tears rained down her cheeks like a waterfall.

I climbed over Em and sat on the other side of the bed and cradled her in my arms. "We just have to ask God to help us and guide us."

"I did ask Him for help!" she lashed out. "I asked Him not to take Quinn, but He did anyway. How could I possibly love Him after that? How could I ask Him for anything, knowing that the *one* thing I needed Him to do, He didn't?" She left the bed and stormed out of the room.

My chest raised and lowered in a deep breath. Every. Single. Step. Of the way. I couldn't stay in Quinn's room. I couldn't catch my breath. It was like a plastic bag was wrapped around my head and being pulled tight.

I bolted outside and gulped in air, tryin' to fill my lungs. I did the only thin' I knew to do. I sat down on the rockin' chair and had a silent conversation with God.

God, I don't know why You had to take her. You are the all-knowin' God. Guide me and use me to help Em. To help her see that she needs You. Help me to have the wisdom to stand beside her and love her through this. I know You use all things for Your glory. Help me to continue to glorify You. I love You,

Lord. I hope one day, You'll show me why this had to happen. Amen.

I opened my eyes and found Colt leanin' against a beam, thumbs in his pockets, at the entrance of the porch. "Thought I might find ya here," he said. He headed to the chair on the other side of the table. "How's she doin'?" He planted his elbows on his knees and interlaced his fingers.

"About as well as anyone can expect." I sighed. "She's beside herself. She's angry at God. It's goin' ta be a long road, but I made a pinky promise to Quinn that I'd be by Em's side every step of the way."

"We'll all be. Whatever she needs, we'll all step up and do what needs to be done."

"Why do I feel like I've lost my own kid?" I placed my head in my hands.

"Because she became all of ours. We're all heartbroken. That little girl made her way into the hearts of all of us in no time at all. She was definitely one of a kind. This ranch won't be the same without her. We just have to trust that God has a plan." Colt sighed. "Have ya heard anythin' about what's goin' ta happen to her ex?"

"I'm not sure. Em gave a detective—Detective Reed—his address in Norristown. We both assume Gary went back home. The detective said he'd be in touch."

"Reed is a good guy. I've known him a long while. He'll do what needs to be done. Just make sure you're here if and when he gets in touch. She's goin' ta need ya."

"I don't plan on bein' anywhere else for a while."

"Don't worry about the ranch right now, either. We'll all pitch in a little extra."

"Thanks, Colt." I glanced over at him and did my best to smile.

"It's the least I can do. Y'all pitched in a lot for me when Callie got bit by that Copperhead. It's what we do around here."

We both stood at the same time. We wrapped our arms around each other and gave one another a pat on the back.

"I'll have Callie bring breakfast by in the mornin'."

"Thanks again, Colt."

"No problem. Try to get some sleep."

"Yeah." I ran my fingers through my hair and retreated into the cabin.

* * *

The next mornin', my eyes opened to a thumpin' of a hand on the front door. I scrubbed my face with my hands. I felt like I hadn't slept a wink. The fist continued to rap on the door. "I'm comin'. I'm comin'," I barked at the person on the other side of the door. I threw it open and shielded my eyes from the glare of the mornin' sun. "Yeah?"

"Hey, Luke," Detective Reed greeted me.

"Oh, hey, detective." I opened the door a little wider and ushered him inside.

"Is Emelia available?"

"I think she's still sleepin'. Let me go get her."

"I'm sorry to have to do this now, but there really isn't a good time."

"I know." I sighed. "I'll be right back."

I disappeared down the hall to Em's bedroom. I knocked gently on the closed door. "Em?" I asked, slowly creepin' the door open. "Em? Detective Reed is here. He needs to talk to ya."

Em turned over in bed, her eyes swollen and red, no doubt from spendin' the night in a pool of tears. A sharp pang shot through my chest. I'd have done just about anythin' to take the pain from her. I wished I could. I took her hand and pulled her up from the bed. She fell into my arms and wrapped hers tightly around my waist. "Thank you," she said, her voice muffled by my chest.

"For what, sweetheart?" I ran my fingers down her back.

"For staying. Just knowing you were here was enough."

My heart fluttered. I left my arm around Em's shoulder and guided her out to the livin' room. My chest puffed out a little because my presence was enough for her. I had never had a woman say that to me before. Em made me want to be a better man. For God. For her. And for me. And especially right now, for Quinnie.

"Hi, Emelia. I'm so sorry for intrudin' on your mornin'. Can we have a seat?" Detective Reed motioned toward the couch.

Em and I flopped down on the couch, and Detective Reed carefully sat on the chair.

"I've read all of the medical reports. They all state Quinn passed away from her injuries suffered at the fair as a result of Gary's actions. I've already made a call to the Norristown PD. They will be servin' the arrest warrant today. He's goin' to be extradited to North Carolina and will be charged with endangerin' the welfare of a minor in the first degree, resultin' in death, which is a Class B felony. He could be sentenced from 144 months to life without parole. As soon as he's in our custody, I'll let ya know. Do you have any questions for me?"

Em shook her head.

"If you think of anythin' or need anythin', just give me a call. You have my number."

"Thanks, detective." I shook his hand.

"I'll see myself out."

236

Once the door was shut, Em and I sat on the couch, enveloped in each other's arms, just bein'. We sat that way for what seemed like an eternity. There was no place I would've rather been than there in that moment. With her.

Chapter 36

Gary

"**G**ary Mason! Norristown PD! Open the door!"

I was startled awake by the sound of banging on my front door, my arms and legs flailing in every direction.

"Gary, we know you're in there! Open the door, or we'll bust it down!" the cop bellowed again from the front porch.

Panic bubbled up from my stomach. A bead of sweat trickled down my forehead. I glanced around the room. *How do I get out of here?*

"We have your house surrounded, Gary. We're coming in!"

The sound of the door being busted in was no comparison to the sound of my heart pounding in my ears. *What is going on? Why are they even here? Did Emelia call the cops for the incident at the fair?* The man, Luke, I think was his name, floated through my mind. *I should file charges against him. He assaulted me.*

The door flew open, and a sea of cops flooded my house.

"Down on the ground! Get down on the ground!"

The cops pointed their guns directly at my head. Sweat ran down my face and trickled down my spine. I sprawled out on the ground with my arms spread out from my body and my legs spread apart.

"What's going on?"

"We have a warrant for your arrest," one of the cops stated. A knee impaled my back. The cold, hard metal of handcuffs encircled my wrists. *Click. Click.* "Let's get you up."

One cop on each side of me slid their hands into my armpits and hoisted me from the floor to my feet. They sat me down on my couch.

"What. Is. Going on?" I huffed again.

"Well," the cop, whose nameplate read *Miles*, started, "like I said before, we have a warrant for your arrest from Edenton, North Carolina. Know anything about that?"

I swallowed hard. All I did was pull her hair. I'd done much worse to her before. Why would she call the cops after just a little hair tug? My eyes grew wide. The cowboy. *He* must have called the cops. Anger churned in my stomach.

"No, I don't know anything about that," I lied. *I didn't do anything wrong.*

"Apparently, there was a little girl who died as a result of you assaulting her."

My mouth went dry. "What?" *Quinn? That couldn't have happened. I didn't even push her that hard.* I shook my head. *This can't be happening.*

"Let's go. There will be a couple of officers from Edenton coming to pick you up tomorrow. Tonight, you'll be a guest in our lockup." The cops pulled me up and escorted me out to the car.

Flashing red and blue lights surrounded me. My neighbors were standing around, no doubt gossiping about what they had heard. Cops were lined up with their hands in their bulletproof vests. Glaring. At me.

"Watch your head." Miles put his hand on top of my head and guided me into the back seat of his cruiser.

I glanced over my shoulder as my house disappeared behind me. *Will I ever see it again?* I lowered my head. I closed my eyes. *This has to be a dream. Wake up, Gary! Wake up!*

The car stopped, and the cop slid from the driver's seat. He sauntered around the car, then opened my door. After unbuckling my seat belt, he hefted me out of the car. I planted my feet on the ground, and two officers escorted me inside.

"Step to your left. We need to book you." The cop started typing into a computer. "Come over here. We need to take your mugshot."

I stood as still as a statue as the flash blinded me.

"Turn to your left."

Snap!

"Turn to your right."

Snap!

"Empty your pockets."

They turned my pockets inside out, seeing what I had in them.

"Perfect. Let's get your fingerprints in the system. Since you'll be in a holding cell overnight, you can remain in your own clothes, but I'll need your belt and your shoelaces."

I unlooped my belt and handed it over. I sat and unlaced my shoes.

"Welcome to your home for the night."

I stepped inside the metal bars. The clinking sound they made as they closed rattled my ears. I sat on the bench and rested my head in my hands. *How did I get here?*

You didn't abide in Me.

What? I looked all around. Where had that voice come from? My breath hitched in my throat. "Who's there?"

No answer.

Am I going crazy now? I spread out on the cold, hard cot,

the springs digging into every part of my body. It was going to be a long night. The fair flooded my brain. I had been in a drunken rage, so I didn't remember much. Flashes of Quinn soaring through the air swam through my mind. My eyes widened. *What did I do? What did I do?*

Chapter 37

Emelia

I sat in the funeral home, frozen in place. I had to bury my daughter. How am I going to get through this day? I glanced across the room. Luke was there. Just like he'd been since Quinn and I first arrived at Redemption Ranch. Really, since the bus station in New York City. Always making sure I was okay. Always knowing exactly what I needed when I needed it. I wanted so much to love him, but I wasn't sure how. I wasn't sure I could. My heart was shattered, and I had no idea if it would ever be whole again.

I took Horsey out of my bag and rose from my seat, and as if on cue, Luke was right by my side. I stood next to my baby's casket and laid Horsey in Quinn's arms, right where he should be. The little body inside the casket couldn't have been my little Quinn. It just couldn't. Tears flowed down my cheeks. She was going to come running through that door any minute and tell me something that Luke or Colt said. Wasn't she?

The casket Callie and Colt picked out was stunning. It was a pale pink. If I hadn't stared at it, I would have thought it was white. The pink silk inside was just a slightly darker shade. Someone had placed a little blonde Precious Moments angel inside.

"I'm so sorry for your loss. She was such a wonderful

242

girl." Marci wrapped me in a hug. Her warmth was genuine and warmed me.

When Marci retreated, a shiver ran down my back. Chuck nodded as he placed his arm around Marci and walked by.

"You okay?" Luke's hand landed on the small of my back. I nodded slightly.

The line of people seemed never-ending. *How had Quinn made such an impact on all of these people in such a short time?* That was my Quinn.

Callie made her way to the front of the line. I fell into her arms and sobbed uncontrollably. She ran her hand up and down my back. "We're all here for you," she whispered in my ear.

"Thank you. And thank you for picking out such a beautiful casket." I held Callie's hands for just a moment.

"Anything for our Quinn." Callie shook my hands before letting them go.

Colt was next. "I'm so sorry, Emelia." He wrapped his arms around me. "She was a wonderful girl. She'll be missed and never forgotten."

"Thank you, Colt. I can never thank you enough for the love you showed her." A lonely tear trickled down my cheek.

"It was truly my pleasure." Colt's lips grew to one side as his eyes glassed over.

All of Quinn's new friends showed up, eyes filled with tears and bearing hugs for me. They were all so sweet.

"Caitlyn, what are you doing here? You should be at school," I remarked.

Caitlyn melted into me. Her body shook with sobs. "I'm so sorry I wasn't here. I should've been here." Her voice was muffled into my shoulder.

"It's not your fault, sweetie. There wasn't anything anyone could've done to stop it from happening."

243

Caitlyn raised back to standing. I tucked her hair behind her ear.

Everyone took their seats for the service to begin. I heard the pastor speaking, but I couldn't make out what he was saying. My entire being was numb. I twisted a tissue in my hand. My eyes locked on the tiny casket.

"If anyone would like to say a few words about Quinn, please feel free to come up."

Colt stood and walked to the podium. He cleared his throat. "None of us have known Quinn and Emelia very long, but Quinn changed the entire ranch in her few short months with us. She brought so much light and energy . . ." Colt's lip quivered as a tear fell from his eye. "She brought so much love and excitement. She wanted to learn everythin' about horses. She'll be greatly missed. Emelia," he said, focusing on me with his hand over his heart, "we're all here for you. Whatever you need." He nodded before taking his seat next to Callie.

Luke rose from his seat next to me. He placed his hands on either side of the podium and leaned into it. He lowered his head as his body shook. He raised himself to stand. "What can I say about Quinnie? She was my best girl. She stole my heart from the first time I saw her. It's my fault she's gone." His voice cracked, and the tears streamed down his face. "I'm so sorry, Em. I didn't protect you like I promised."

Colt appeared next to Luke. He wrapped his arm around Luke's shoulder and guided him away.

After the service, I stood at the casket. I stared, willing Quinn to wake up, to open her eyes. No amount of anything was going to make her do that, though. It was wishful thinking. I moved Horsey so that he was in the crook of her arm. I leaned over and gently kissed her forehead. It was cold. *This can't be my Quinn.* I couldn't bring myself to stand. Tears fell from my eyes and onto her face.

"Sweetheart, it's time to go," Luke whispered.

I shook my head, over and over. "I can't," I whispered back.

"We have to," Luke pleaded.

I glanced up at him. "Please? Just a few more minutes?"

"I'll see if that's okay."

Luke's absence from my side left me feeling lonely and weary. With everything that was in me, I lifted my body up from the casket. I swiped my nose with the fresh tissue that had somehow appeared in my hand. I pressed my palms into my eyes to dry them. I stared at Quinn's body as I knew as soon as the lid was shut, I would never see her again.

When I turned around, I almost collided with Luke's chest. I splayed my hands on his shirt. "Oh. I'm sorry. I didn't realize you came back."

Too close. Not the right time.

"I told you I'd be here every step of the way." Luke breathed into the top of my head.

"Thank you." I finally exhaled for what I felt was the first time all day. I latched on to Luke.

"You ready to head to the cemetery?"

No. But I nodded into his chest. He never let go. We left the funeral home arm-in-arm.

* * *

After the burial service at the cemetery, everyone went to the main house at the ranch. When we arrived, Detective Reed was waiting for us. "Hey, Emelia. Hey, Luke. I know this isn't the best time. I keep sayin' that. I'm sorry."

"It's okay. Thank you for stopping by." I flashed him a small smile.

"I just wanted to let you know Gary's in custody, and two officers should be arriving with him tomorrow."

My breath left my body, and I wondered if it would ever return. My knees buckled under me. Rage surged through me. I wanted to kill Gary. I probably would've if I'd ever been alone with him in a room somewhere. I wasn't ready for him to be in the same town as me again.

When I finally mustered the courage to speak, I said, "Thank you for letting me know." I held my hand out to the detective.

"Of course." Detective Reed took hold of my hand and covered it with his other one. "I'll keep you posted about anythin' else." He dropped my hand and returned to his car.

"I'm gonna go inside. You comin'?" Luke asked.

"I think I'm going to sit out here for a little bit if that's okay." I glanced up at him.

"Of course, sweetheart." Luke disappeared inside.

I sat down on the top step, elbows on my knees. I had felt suffocated in the funeral home and didn't want to feel the same inside the house. Too many people. Too much emotion. I was depleted. I couldn't seem to feel anything.

I missed Quinn so much. Her giggles. The way she said the letter "L." Her sweet green eyes. But I missed her hugs the most. I needed one—oh, so badly.

"Hey, Emelia. Care if I join ya?" Caitlyn asked before sitting down next to me.

I shook my head. "Thanks for coming, Caitlyn. You didn't have to come all the way back here."

"Yes, I did. I love Quinn." Caitlyn wrapped her arm around my shoulders.

"I know. She loved you, too. She talked about you a lot."

Caitlyn's eyes brightened along with her smile. "She was a

sweet and lovable little girl. I guess you saw that from the line at the funeral home."

I nodded and smiled.

"My life won't be the same without her. But it's definitely going to change." I wasn't sure what Caitlyn meant by that.

"It's my fault." I burst into a raging sob. "It's all my fault she's dead. I'm the one who brought Gary into our lives. I'm the one who stayed long after I should've left. Is God punishing me? Does He hate me?" I glanced over at Caitlyn. All I saw reflected in her eyes was compassion.

"Oh, Emelia. God doesn't hate you, and He certainly isn't punishing you."

"But I asked him not to take her. I asked him to heal her body, and he didn't. Not the way I wanted him to, anyway." I twisted my hands in my lap.

"Emelia, God doesn't always answer our prayers the way we want Him to. He doesn't work that way. He does offer us grace, mercy, compassion, love, and forgiveness. Most importantly, He offers us His redemption."

That word, "redemption," brought to my mind the quote on the wall of the barn.

"God gave His ultimate sacrifice so we could find that redemption. In Him. You can't earn it, and it's not about what you have or haven't done. You just have to ask Him for it. He just wants *you* to love *Him* as much as *He* loves *you*."

Tears formed in my eyes. *How is it possible I have any tears left?* "Do you think Quinn is in heaven?" My eyes caught Caitlyn's once more.

"Why do you think she wouldn't be?" Caitlyn's brows furrowed.

"Because when I was pregnant, my mom and dad told me we were both going to hell because I wasn't married when I got pregnant." My face contorted in pain. The thought of Quinn in hell was almost more than I could bear.

"I can tell you for a fact she is, indeed, in heaven."

"How can you be so sure?"

"Well, not long ago, Quinn accepted Christ as her personal Lord and Savior. I know that because I helped her."

"Really?" A little ping of hope sprung into my heart.

Caitlyn nodded.

The ache in my heart was still present, but it didn't feel so heavy. A smile formed on my lips as the tears changed from tears of great grief to tears of gratitude. Quinn was in the arms of God. The window of hope began to blossom.

"Thank you, Caitlyn." I wrapped my arms around her neck.

Caitlyn and I stood from the stoop and walked into the house. My eyes scanned the room for Luke. He was across the room, talking with Colt and Callie. The man had been there for Quinn and me before we even set foot in Edenton. Before I even knew his name. That seemed like a century ago. So much had happened. So much had changed. Luke said he loved me once. I wondered if he still did. I wondered if he always would. He had shown me, not just with his words but with his actions, how he felt about me. I wanted to fall completely in love with him.

I closed my eyes and did the last thing I ever thought I would do again. I had nowhere else to turn. If Quinn loved God and put Him in the center of her heart, maybe I could start to do that, too. So, I prayed.

Lord, I want to start to live for You again. I'm sorry I got so lost along the way. I know I've done so many things that didn't bring You glory. Some of those things should've resulted in my death. Please forgive me! Come live in my heart. I don't know why You had to take Quinn. I hope one day, You will show me. Please bless lives with what she was able to donate. There has to be a bigger picture—a bigger plan. Show me the way, Lord. Show me what You want for my life. Help me to get through this time. Help me to open my heart to Luke. I need You. God, I can't do this myself.

A sense of peace washed over me. I knew it was going to be a long road to muddle through the grief and to fully commit my life to Christ again, but as long as I had Luke to help me, I knew I could do it. I knew I would get through to the other side.

"Hey there." Luke touched my arm. "Are you okay?"

"Yeah." I smiled up at him as I opened my eyes. "I just had a talk with Caitlyn. Quinn is in heaven. Did you know Caitlyn helped Quinn get saved? I wonder why they didn't tell me." My brows furrowed in confusion. "But it lifted my heart a little, out of the pit of despair." I flashed Luke a lopsided grin.

"Yeah? That's so good to hear. I didn't know that." Luke wrapped his arm around my shoulders and squeezed me close.

"It truly was so good to hear." I sighed.

"Em, can we talk outside?" Luke's voice filled with concern.

"Su-sure."

Luke and I stepped out onto the porch, and I sat down on the rocking chair. Luke kneeled in front of me. *What is he doing?*

"Em, I feel like all of this is my fault. I made you a promise, and I failed." Luke's head lowered. His warm tears rained onto my legs. "If I had just made you and Quinn come with me to get something to drink, she'd still be here. I'm so sorry. I hope you'll be able to forgive me one day."

"Luke." I placed my hands on each of his cheeks and lifted his head so that our eyes met. "There is nothing to forgive. You couldn't have known what would happen any more than I could. If it's anyone's fault, it's my own. I brought that man into our lives. I put up with the abuse. I ran. But if all of that hadn't happened, we wouldn't have come here. We wouldn't have met you."

"I love you so much, Em. I know I said I'd wait until you took all the time you need, but I just needed to say that to you. I needed you to know that, especially today," Luke softly confessed.

"You do?" A hot tear rolled down my cheek. I wasn't sure I'd ever get used to hearing those words from Luke's lips, but I hoped he'd never stop saying them.

"I do. You stole my heart so easily and quickly. You've made me want to be a better me." Luke's lip quivered. "I never thought in a million years I'd ever feel this way about someone."

I cradled Luke's cheek in my hand. My heart cracked open, and warmth flooded in. *Is this what real worldly love feels like? I want more.* In that instant, I wanted everything He had to offer. I wanted everything *God* had to offer.

Even though the loss of my daughter was the most tragic thing to ever happen to me, finding Redemption Ranch saved me. They took Quinn and me in when we had nowhere else to go. God taught me, through his people on that ranch and in that town, about His everlasting love. His faithfulness. His forgiveness. His Redemption. Especially in the midst of despair. They taught me that not all Christians were like my parents.

And Luke taught me what true love was really supposed to be like. Gentle. Kind. Warm. Unlike anything I'd ever experienced. I flung myself into the safe haven of his arms. "Oh, Luke. I love you, too. More than you could possibly know."

Luke placed his hands on either side of my face and drew it to his lips. His lips touched mine in the tenderest kiss. I had kissed him at the dance, but this kiss was everything and more.

I hoped I could continue to love and kiss this man for the rest of my life.

Epilogue

Luke

I couldn't believe it had already been six months since Em told me she loved me. That day was bittersweet. It was the worst day of my life burying Quinn, my best girl. But for Em to say she loved me made it the best day at the same time. Em had even started attending church with Colt, Callie, and me.

"I think I'm going to go see Gary this afternoon," Em informed me as we sat on the couch in her livin' room. She played with the hem of her shirt.

"Do you want me to go with you?" I glanced in her direction.

"No. This is something I have to do by myself." Em sucked her bottom lip between her teeth.

"Are you sure?" My brows furrowed in concern.

"No." Her hands twisted like a pretzel in her lap. "But that's how I know it's something I need to do alone. Can I borrow your truck?"

"Okay. Yeah. Sure." I sighed.

"Will you be here when I get back?" Em peered up at me.

I locked eyes with her. "Em, you already know I will be. Always."

Em's lips turned upward. "Thank you. I love you." She pecked my lips with hers.

"I love you, too." I beamed. I'd never get tired of hearin' her say that.

Em smacked her hands on her knees. "Guess I'd better get going, then."

"Okay. You're sure you don't want me to go with you?"

"Yes. I'm sure." Her eyes rolled up into her head as a giggle escaped her lips. She stood from the couch, grabbed the keys to my truck, and sauntered out the door.

Ever since Em appeared in my life, my demons seemed to disappear little by little. Sure, they still reared their ugly heads, but they were so few and far between. Em brought me peace. She brought me hope. She brought me love. I hoped it would never end.

I took the little black velvet box out of my pocket. I flipped open the lid and watched as the diamond in the center of the antique silver ring danced in the sunlight shining through the window. The stone wasn't big, but I knew it would make Em smile. The diamond was in the shape of a heart. I had already given her my whole heart. But I wanted her to wear it as a symbol on her finger.

I inhaled and exhaled deeply. *I'm such a dork. Maybe I should get a different ring.* I shook the thought from my head. No, this was the one. I knew it the minute I saw it. I just hadn't been able to find the right time to ask her. The past six months had been extremely hard on both of us, but especially her. She needed to grieve the loss of her daughter. But when was the right time for somethin' new to be born?

In My time, son.

Yes, Lord. In Your time. I grinned up at the sky. *Forever and always, Quinn. I will keep my promise to you.* I stuffed the box back into my pocket. I knew when God felt the time was right, He would make a way for me to ask her. Until then, I would be there for Em. Every step of the way. As promised.

* * *

Emelia

It had been six months since Quinn's funeral. Six long months without the presence of my daughter. The one man responsible was sitting in a jail cell in town.

Luke and I had been attending church together, and I was learning more and more about the relationship I could have with God, through sermons and fellowship, but also through Him. God was teaching me about forgiveness, for myself and for others.

God had been working on me to go see Gary. I couldn't bring myself to do it, but it had been eating away at me. Every time I thought about going there, bile rose to my throat and threatened to spew out of my mouth.

As I stood in front of the Chowan County Jail, my heart pounded. My palms were clammy. *What am I doing here? Am I really ready to see him?*

I knew I needed to see Gary in order to put that part of my life behind me. Not the part where I was grieving Quinn's death—I wasn't ready to let her go just yet. No, I needed to let go of the torturous years with Gary in order to live out my life the way God wanted me to, especially if that life included Luke. I knew I couldn't fully open my heart to Luke, not the way he deserved anyway, without putting Gary in my rearview mirror.

I inhaled and exhaled deeply before putting my hand on the door and swinging it open. I moved slowly to the front desk, willing myself forward instead of turning and running back to the safety of Luke's arms. "I'm here to see Gary Mason," I timidly told the officer.

"Sign your name here. I need to see your ID, please." The officer didn't look up until I pushed my ID forward on the desk. "Thank you. Have a seat in the chairs along the wall. Someone will come to take you back in just a few minutes."

"Thanks." I slid my ID back into my pocket.

My leg jiggled as I waited in the plastic orange chair. *Stay here, Em. You have to face him sometime. It might as well be now. Get it done and over with so you can be done with him. Luke deserves that much.* I closed my eyes and took in a deep breath. I held it. Then, I exhaled just as deeply.

"Emelia Taylor?" a uniformed officer asked from just outside the door he had walked through.

"Yes. That's me." I stood from the chair. I wiped my clammy hands down my pants.

"Come with me, please."

I followed. My breath wouldn't move past my throat. We walked down a hallway before coming to a stop where there were chairs in front of windows with chairs on the other side of the glass.

"Have a seat. He'll be brought out shortly."

"Thank you."

I glanced around the small space. The gray cinder-block walls were as cold as the air circulating around me. A shiver spread throughout my body. I ran my hands up my arms.

Gary appeared with an officer from behind a wall. "Have a seat," the officer ordered him.

When Gary glanced up at who had come to see him, his eyes widened with surprise. He motioned for me to pick up the phone hanging on the partition to my left. I lifted the receiver and put it to my ear. My words were frozen to my tongue.

"Emelia, what are you doing here?" Gary swallowed hard.

"I'm not sure," I softly admitted.

"I have some things I'd like to say if that's okay."

Who is this guy? The Gary I know would never ask if it was okay for him to say anything, especially to me.

"Su-sure." I leaned forward with my elbows on the ledge in front of me.

"I wanted to say I'm so so sorry for what happened to Quinn. I never meant for that to happen." Tears flooded his eyes. "I know sorry isn't good enough to make up for what I've done." Gary's head lowered as his shoulders shook. He coughed. "I also wanted to say I'm sorry for all of the things I've done to you. I'm not sure why I was so angry. I hope that one day you can forgive me."

Forgive him? How am I supposed to forgive him? Anger boiled just beneath the surface. I couldn't listen to Gary anymore. I slammed the receiver down and stood to leave.

I have forgiven him just as I have forgiven you.

The words knocked me back down to the chair. As the tears threatened the corners of my eyes, I placed the phone back to my ear. I closed my eyes. *Lord, give me Your eyes to see him.*

When I opened my eyes, everything was a blur—until I looked at Gary's face. His facial features were the same, but he didn't look like the same man. There was a faint glow, perhaps from the fluorescent light above him. My brows furrowed. It was as if I were seeing him for the first time. Not as he had been but who he could become.

Thank you, Jesus.

"There's a Bible study here every week," Gary informed me. "I've been going and reading the Bible every day. I've asked God into my heart. He has forgiven me, Em." He sighed. His voice was just a whisper. "That's what the pastor said, anyway."

"I forgive you, too," I stated, barely audible to anyone but me. *What? That's not what I opened my mouth to say.*

A sense of peace flooded my entire being, just as it had the day I asked God into my own life six months before. In that moment, I knew I had done what God had asked me to do. I had forgiven Gary. And I'd meant it.

"You do?" Surprise filled Gary's voice.

I nodded.

"Thank you," Gary whispered.

"I know they are offering you a deal. You should take it." I bit the inside of my cheek.

"You think I should?"

"Yes. Unless you want the chance of spending the rest of your life in jail."

"Isn't that where I belong?" Gary drew circles with his index finger on the ledge in front of him.

"Not if you've really changed. God gives second chances to those who accept Him. If you've truly changed and are living for Him, that includes you." I knew these were God's words and not my own. "Take care of yourself, Gary." I hung the receiver back on the hook, rose from my seat, and strode out the door, never looking back.

* * *

Gary

The visit with Emelia left me dumbfounded. Once I was back in my cell, I dropped to my knees. I covered my face with my hands as the uncontrollable sobs shook my entire body. She forgave me. I couldn't believe she actually forgave me.

Lord, thank You so much for the blessings I don't deserve. I know it could only have been You.

257

God had been doing a work in me ever since the first time He spoke to me that first night in the jail cell in Norristown. I had been meeting with the pastor who came every week to teach us about God. I was learning so much about myself, my past, and what God could do in my life, even in prison.

My anger stemmed from my father and how he had treated my mother. God was helping me with forgiving them. I was struggling to forgive myself for what I had put Emelia and Quinn through. And for what happened to Quinn.

As I stood from the cold concrete floor, I grabbed my Bible along with a piece of paper and a pencil. I was going to take Emelia's advice and take the plea deal offered.

Dear Mr. Hosea,

I'm writing to you to accept the plea deal of involuntary manslaughter in my case. Please let the prosecutor know. I'll accept whatever time the judge decides to give if he doesn't agree with the terms of the deal. Emelia has expressed to me today that I should take it. I think that eleven years is acceptable. It's not what I deserve. I deserve to die in prison, but I'm thankful and grateful for this opportunity. I won't waste my second chance at life.

Thank you for everything you have done for me in this case.

In Christ's Redeeming Love,

Gary Mason

I folded the piece of paper and slid it into the envelope. Peace engulfed me. I closed my eyes and savored the moment. I had never felt that in my entire life. It felt wonderful. I finally was starting to feel whole. I wished it hadn't taken a prison sentence to get me there, but I would embrace it anyway.

I placed a stamp on the outside of the envelope and wrote my attorney's name and address. I sent a silent prayer up as I dropped the envelope into the mail slot. Even though I would be spending time in prison, the Lord had broken the chains that bound me. I had been redeemed. I would do everything in my power not to waste it.

Available Soon . . .

GOD BLESS CAITLYN
(*Edenton Bay Romance* Series, Book 3)

BY ELIZABETH WOODROW

Dear reader:

Thank you for your interest in and purchase of *Finding Redemption Ranch (Edenton Bay Romance Series, Book 2)*. If you enjoyed this book, please be sure to obtain a copy of Caitlyn and Wyatt's story, *God Bless Caitlyn (Edenton Bay Romance Series, Book 3)*, available soon at major book retailers.

Sincerely,

Van Rye Publishing, LLC

From the Publisher

Thank You from the Publisher

Van Rye Publishing, LLC ("VRP") sincerely thanks you for your interest in and purchase of this book.

VRP hopes you will please consider taking a moment to help other readers like you by leaving a rating or review of this book at your favorite online book retailer. You can do so by visiting the book's product page and locating the button for leaving a rating or review.

Thank you!

Resources from the Publisher

Van Rye Publishing, LLC ("VRP") offers the following resources to readers and to writers.

For *readers* who enjoyed this book or found it useful, please consider receiving updates from VRP about new and discounted books like this one. You can do so by following VRP on Facebook (at www.facebook.com/vanryepub), Twitter (at www.twitter.com/vanryepub), or Instagram (at www.instagram.com/vanryepub).

From the Publisher

For *writers* who enjoyed this book or found it useful, please consider having VRP edit, format, or fully publish your book manuscript. You can find out more and submit your manuscript at VRP's website (at www.vanryepublishing.com).

Thank you again!

Acknowledgments

God: Thank you for giving me another story to tell. I hope it brings You all the Glory.

Ania Ray: For creating a space called Quill & Cup. It has blessed me beyond measure in so many ways!

Mandi Grace: Your amazing help on this novel has been invaluable! Love you so much, Hedgie Sister!

Rebecca Carpenter: Thank you, once again, for being my editor! This book wouldn't be the same—and *I* wouldn't be the same—without your tutelage. Hope we can work together for years to come!

Van Rye Publishing: Thank you, once again, for taking a chance on me to help me get this story out into the world. I am eternally grateful.

The Logan Family: Thank you for allowing me to continue the story using your beautiful family and your gorgeous girl in this story.

About the Author

ELIZABETH WOODROW was raised in a small town in eastern Indiana called Connersville. Faith and family are considered most important to Elizabeth and are reflected in her writing. Elizabeth holds a Bachelor of Science degree in Criminal Justice and a Master of Public Administration degree, both from Indiana Wesleyan University. She currently resides in Whiteland, Indiana with her Chihuahua/Dachshund dog, Payslee, and her Tortoiseshell Calico cat, Princess. Elizabeth is also the author of *Mending Broken Roads*, Book 1 in the *Edenton Bay Romance* Series. For updates about Elizabeth and her books, please be sure to follow her on Facebook (www.facebook.com/ElizabcthWWrites), Instagram (www.instagram.com/elizabethw_writes), Twitter (www.twitter.com/writerellie1), or TikTok (www.tiktok.com/@elizabethw_writes).